"Get Down Off Your Horse, Roxana. We Are Going to Have a Talk, Here and Now."

Sebastian's voice brooked no denial. "Just what did you think you would accomplish? You cannot run from me. You should know that.

"'Tis time you learned that your dreams are not real. We live not in an age of knights. We are living here and now in Ireland."

His hands stroked her hair, soothing her. He drew her head forward, gently, tenderly. Tears were streaming down her cheeks now.

"Why can't I have my dreams?" she cried. "Miracles do happen."

"Aye!" his voice was tender now. "Miracles do happen, but they don't always happen in the way you think."

Dear Reader,

We, the editors of Tapestry Romances, are committed to bringing you two outstanding original romantic historical novels each and every month.

From Kentucky in the 1850s to the court of Louis XIII, from the deck of a pirate ship within sight of Gibraltar to a mining camp high in the Sierra Nevadas, our heroines experience life and love, romance and adventure.

Our aim is to give you the kind of historical romances that you want to read. We would enjoy hearing your thoughts about this book and all future Tapestry Romances. Please write to us at the address below.

The Editors
Tapestry Romances
POCKET BOOKS
1230 Avenue of the Americas
Box TAP
New York, N.Y. 10020

Tame the Wild Heart

Serita Stevens

A TAPESTRY BOOK
PUBLISHED BY POCKET BOOKS NEW YORK

An *Original* publication of TAPESTRY BOOKS

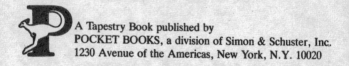

A Tapestry Book published by
POCKET BOOKS, a division of Simon & Schuster, Inc.
1230 Avenue of the Americas, New York, N.Y. 10020

ISBN: 0-671-49398-1

First Tapestry Books printing October, 1983

10 9 8 7 6 5 4 3 2 1

POCKET and colophon are registered trademarks
of Simon & Schuster, Inc.

TAPESTRY is a trademark of Simon & Schuster, Inc.

Printed in the U.S.A.

To Frances Rosenberg Mendelson,
my late mother,
and to Claire, Dan, and Albert
for their help and support

Tame the Wild Heart

Chapter One

IT HAD BEEN A SOFT DAY, BUT NOW THE THICK mist coming off the river Liffey shrouded Dublin in a gray mantle. Despite her fur-lined cloak, Roxana Alden shivered. The mist seemed to chill her to the very bone.

Desperate for warmth, she pulled her cloak closer about her. Blast Gilpatrick! She wished he would hurry. She wished, too, that she had not been forced to come tonight dressed ready for the ball. For this assignation she should have been wearing her buckled breeches instead of her green satin gown—but her Uncle Patrick Sarsfield insisted on promptness for all the court balls, especially when King James was to be present, and there would be no moment to change. She hoped only that Gilpatrick would not notice the dress. He shouldn't, if she kept the cloak closed and stayed well into the shadows. She also hoped that no one from the court would recognize her standing here on the bridge. Why had Gilpatrick insisted on meeting here, of all places?

Music coming from the castle made Roxana's stomach knot in hatred and disgust. James II was no king. He could not rule the Irish; nor could he rule the Scots, nor the English. He could not even rule himself.

A hand of ice seemed to form about Roxana's heart, squeezing it every time she thought of His Majesty and how he—as duke of York—had seduced and abused her mother. He had led her on, and then, when he had done with her, had wed her to his loutish friend, the duke of Ruxford. Roxana held no affection for her father, and thought even less of the king. Yet she could still recall the way her mother's eyes had lit up at York's presence, the way her mother had forgotten her Irish pride and had groveled to live near the fringes of the English court, wanting to be near the man who had ruined her, who had lured her from Ireland and the wonderful house at Lucan.

James was not to be trusted! Had he not promised to make her uncle earl of Lucan? Even now, for all her uncle's loyal support, the king had done nothing to reward him. Nay, James lived only for his own pleasures.

Swept by a sudden wave of dizziness, Roxana grasped the cold stone of the bridge for support. She had been feeling feverish, and the long, cold wait was taking its toll. Where *was* Gilpatrick? If she had not had news for him to pass on to William's forces, she would not even have left home this night. But cold as it was, and miserable though she felt, Roxana had vowed that she would do all in her power to defeat James—even if it meant spying, and even if it meant abusing the trust placed in her by Uncle Patrick.

Roxana's full lips came together in a thin line. She tucked the loose strands of her dark, glossy hair into the depths of her hood so that Gilpatrick would not notice them.

It was true that she loved her uncle dearly. He had taken her in at the tender age of ten, had raised her at Lucan, and had given her the love and guidance that her mother had been too preoccupied to give. Yet, despite her affection for her uncle, Roxana could not agree with his philosophy or his support of James II. The king was a Bourbon puppet, a pawn in the hand of Louis XIV.

Didn't Uncle Patrick and the others see what would happen? If James prevailed, then France also would win—and if France won, it was more than likely that Ireland would be deeded over to the French as a reward. Ireland's lovely hills and valleys would be forgotten by the wretched English—used and discarded, just as her mother had been. Nausea rose in her as her heart hammered fiercely. With all her soul, with every ounce of her power, she had to see James defeated.

Roxana sighed deeply. William had personally promised her that Uncle Patrick and Sebastian Steele would not be injured, but she had already seen too many good men die these past few months.

3

She shivered again, not so much from cold but at the mere thought of Sebastian Steele. How could her uncle have such regard for that man? True, Uncle Patrick was misguided about James, but then uncle did believe in the divine right of kings. Why had he chosen Sebastian Steele—an Englishman—as his right hand?

Roxana's head was aching now. If Gilpatrick did not show soon, she would have to go to the ball and return the next evening. She hated the idea of coming yet again to this lonely bridge.

Glancing back toward Dublin Castle, she noted the grim signs of the fire—the jagged, gaping holes, the blackened walls—which now seemed ominous in the misty night. It was no wonder that James hated this castle and called it the worst in all Christendom. But, then, his regard for the Irish matched his regard for the castle.

How could the man expect the Irish people to lay down their lives for him when he entertained in lavish style and forced his own soldiers to subsist on dried crusts of bread? The man was not a king, he was a fool.

Roxana glanced about the enveloping fog uneasily, feeling as if someone were watching her. No, that could not be. She was careful. She had always been careful.

Suddenly she heard a burst of raucous laughter from the castle, and for a moment her thoughts turned to this night's ball. She had heard that Sebastian Steele would be escorting Lady Conway. How many conquests did that now make? The man was worse than his king! She tasted the sourness in her mouth. Sebastian Steele was despicable. Had she not loved her Uncle Patrick as she did, she would not have included Steele's life in her bargain with William. For her own part, she would have let the man rot. She wished she had been courageous enough to ask for his death—but that would have devastated her uncle.

Roxana fought another wave of fever and pushed her damp, dark hair again under her hood. Oh, to be in bed this instant, to be home in Lucan! Well, at least they would be returning to the manor this night, and for a short time she would be free from those all-knowing slate gray eyes of Sebastian Steele. It was almost as if the man had some supernatural power—or was purposely trying to unnerve her. Did he know what she was about? No, she was sure not. He was not the type to tolerate such a scheme. If he knew, he would have long ago turned her in.

The old clock struck seven. It seemed as if Gilpatrick would not come this night. That was a nuisance, but Roxana knew that there were times when it was impossible to get away.

Turning back toward the castle, she stepped out of the shadows of the bridge and clutched her cloak, shivering again. No, she would not be ill. She could not afford to be.

Blinking, she wondered if her eyes deceived

her. Out of the blanketing fog approached a ghostly figure. Her breath tight in her chest, Roxana waited for the greeting.

"Ho, Alexander!" the man said, stepping up to her.

"Gilpatrick," Roxana replied gruffly, trying to muffle her voice with the cloak and turning away so that the man would not see her feminine features beneath the hood. "You're late."

"For that I ask forgiveness. His Majesty kept me a moment more than needed. D'ye have news?"

Roxana nodded and handed him her report. She would not trust herself to speak it; her voice was too difficult to disguise, and only the few chosen by William should know her true identity.

No doubt it had been foolish on her part to choose the name of Alexander for her contact. People would surely connect the two names—Roxana and Alexander. But hadn't she been named for Princess Roxana—and hadn't Alexander the Great swept the princess off into his arms? Her mother had told her the romantic story when Roxana was a child, and she had always fancied the name Alexander. Someday she'd find her own Alexander—but not in the midst of this war.

Gilpatrick finished reading the report and cleared his throat. "This is excellent, Alexander. The king will be pleased with you."

Roxana nodded and pulled her cloak close around her shoulders for warmth.

"You had best take care in this cold," the

man said kindly. "His Majesty would hate to lose such a valued servant."

Again Roxana nodded. It was true, and she knew it. There were others at James's feet who played Janus, but Roxana doubted anyone else was privy to the information she gleaned from her Uncle Patrick, as well as from Sebastian Steele and Lord Tyrconnel.

Just thinking of Steele made her stomach tighten and her heart pound with anger. What right did he have to command the loyal Irish forces? Her Uncle Patrick, a true Irish subject, she could understand; d'Arcy, a Frenchman whom she hated, she could rationalize; but the Englishman Steele? No, she could not accept it. The only answer, of course, was that James favored him.

Roxana's head pounded as she realized that Gilpatrick was talking to her again.

"Shall it be one week hence? Ormond Quay?"

Roxana grimaced—that place was not much better than this—then nodded. Yes, she would meet him. She would be meeting Gilpatrick until James no longer called himself "king of Ireland."

Chapter Two

FROM WHERE ROXANA STOOD, IT WOULD HAVE been an easy walk to the castle grounds, but also difficult to explain. No, as Sarsfield's niece she had no choice but to arrive by coach.

Despite the chill, she waited until Gilpatrick disappeared into the fog. Struggling against lightheadedness, she took a deep breath. Once she was within the warmth of the castle, in St. Patrick's Hall, she would feel better. She must. The duc de Lauzun had recently arrived from France. There would surely be news and gossip this night—news that might be valuable to Gilpatrick and friends.

Roxana walked to the end of the bridge, where her coach was waiting. Her loyal coachman held the door open for her, and she climbed inside. She could hear the gay shouts of greeting as the nobility began to arrive for the queen's birthday ball. Did these English have no feelings? Hadn't they seen the sorrowing, hungry Irish? Why did James flaunt this luxury when the people had nothing?

She thought of William—a true king. William ate only what his soldiers ate, slept only where his soldiers slept.

She paused to examine her instructions, then frowned. They could not be serious! Her stomach tightened. Her orders were to befriend Lord Bristol—Sebastian Steele.

Worried at Roxana's silence, the coachman asked, "To the castle, m'lady?"

"Yes, Dory," Roxana answered, feeling her heart pounding with uncertainty. "And we'd best hurry, or my uncle will be furious. It would not do for me to arrive after James." She could not bear to call him king.

"Aye, m'lady," Dory said, his brown eyes meeting her green ones as he shut the door.

Momentary panic rose in her. "Dory! Do not lock the door, please! You—you know I cannot abide being locked in."

The coachman opened the door for a moment. "Aye, m'lady," he said respectfully. "I do know of yer fears."

Roxana breathed more easily as her panic subsided. "Dory, they want me to befriend Lord Bristol."

The coachman shook his head. "Well, we are both small fish helping a bigger one," he said, "but take care, d'ye hear? I'd not trust that Lord Bristol if I were you. Those eyes of his are too knowing. They give me the chills!"

Dory closed the door softly, then mounted

the coach and clucked his tongue as the horses moved forward. Roxana knew Dory wanted to reprimand her for being out on a night such as this, and knew he wanted to take her back to Lucan now and see her safely put abed with a poultice; but she also knew that Dory was as devoted to the cause as she.

Roxana let a sigh escape her lips, and shuddered at Gilpatrick's instructions in her hands. How in the world was she to befriend a man like Steele? He could no more be a friend to her than could a cat to a dog, or a fox to a sheep. They were natural enemies. Tearing the note to pieces, she let the fragments flutter out the window and sank back into the velvet seat.

Lost in thought, she was jarred awake by the opening of the iron gate. Looking outside, she noticed that theirs was not the only carriage pulling into the courtyard at this belated hour. As they drew up to the steps that led to the long gallery and St. Patrick's Hall, Roxana felt foreboding prickle her skin. A shiver ran through her as she recognized Steele's equipage ahead of her own.

Did she have to see the man so soon? Her heart hammered rapidly as she tried to calm her thoughts. Maybe he would not notice her. Maybe he would go ahead with Lady Conway—then Roxana would not have to see him until much later in the evening, when she had decided how best to "befriend" him.

Her throat dry, she tried to wait patiently in the coach. Dory knew her feelings—he would open the door for her only when Steele and his lady for the evening had gone ahead.

"M'lady," Dory called, "shall I put down the stairs?"

"If he is gone," Roxana replied, her hand on the inside knob.

"M'lady, I—." Dory's words were lost as the door swung open. Sebastian Steele stood framed in the entrance.

"Might I have the honor of assisting you, Lady Roxana Alden?" His mellow voice seemed to vibrate in the air about her. How dare he use her Christian name?

Roxana stared at him and then glanced at Dory, who stood behind. The coachman gave a helpless shrug. Her eyes returned to Steele. In the misty moonlight she could see the gleam of his dark curls—no false wigs for him. Steele's eyes darkened now as he watched her and waited.

"If you don't mind, I'd rather do it myself."

A smile tugged at the corners of Steele's generous mouth and curved his neatly trimmed mustache. He shrugged his broad shoulders.

"As you wish, Lady Roxana." He stepped aside, making a small bow, which infuriated her more.

"You are late," she said, quick to find fault with him.

"I am," he responded placidly, watching as she balanced on the portable steps.

She had wanted to unnerve the man as he unnerved her, but all she seemed to do was amuse him—the lout!

11

Steele's smile now reached those slate gray eyes that seemed to pierce her very being.

"So, might I add, are you," he noted. "Come, let me escort you in."

She glared at him. "Do you not have another to escort?"

He raised a brow and looked about. "Do you see another?"

The laughter in his voice was making her irritable. She held herself in admirable control while feeling the blood seethe inside her. "I understood you were to escort Lady Conway." Roxana's tone betrayed her estimation of Lady Conway. Truly, she thought, the woman was only a French maid who had elevated her station by marrying one of James's favorites. Her husband had since been killed—and Roxana knew the grieving widow had made her adjustments promptly.

Steele pressed his lips into a thin line, watching her for a moment. "Your information was correct—to a certain extent—but because of my tardiness, Ardella went ahead."

Roxana felt herself stiffen at his familiar use of the lady's name. "I did not realize that you were on intimate terms with Lady Conway."

The smile again came to his eyes, and touched his lips. "Indeed? For someone who enjoys gossip as much as you appear to, I felt certain you would know. Most of the court knows—and in fact keeps a running tab of the ladies with whom I am supposedly intimate at the moment."

"What do you mean, *supposedly?*" She felt

her heart skip a beat, feeling that this was a subject she did not want to broach with him.

He offered her his arm again. "I mean that things might not always be as they seem, and that even you might not have the complete truth." He paused. "Will you take my arm or not, Lady Roxana?"

Furious with him for being there at all, she nonetheless accepted his offer. Placing her arm directly upon his—ever so gingerly—she averted her face. She did not want to meet those intense eyes of his. Touching him like this was punishment enough.

They did not move. Instead, he bent to whisper in her ear so that she could feel his hot breath on her lobe. "It will be most difficult to escort you if I cannot have a proper hold on you."

Roxana shivered. "I—." She turned away as a wave of fever caused her body to tremble with aching pains. Steele held her patiently, giving her the gentle support that her momentarily weakened body needed.

"You should be home abed," he said softly. "Have you such a burning reason for being out this night?"

She turned and glared at him. "My reason is none of your concern, Lord Bristol. As to my health, give me leave to know my own capacity. I am quite well—'tis a passing indisposition. I am sure that if you would stop arguing with me, we could enter the castle, where it will be much warmer."

"So I am arguing now, am I?" There was a mixture of laughter and concern in his gray

13

eyes. "Very well, Lady Roxana, we will go in now." Without another word, he took her arm and escorted her up the castle steps. "We had best hurry. We should not arrive after the king."

Roxana almost curled her lip in disdain. "Nay," she said, "it would not do to arrive after the king." She had not meant to sound bitter, but as she saw his brow rise slightly, she knew she had made an error. She began to doubt the wisdom of whoever had decided she must befriend Lord Bristol. Did they know what they asked?

Music, loud laughter and false gaiety surrounded them as they passed through the castle entrance. Richly dressed ladies, their faces powdered and rouged, some framed by curled wigs, some behind lace fans, whirled past them. Roxana had to admit that, compared with the grayness outside, the company here was colorful indeed. Silks, satins, brocades and muslins abounded, all in the latest Paris fashions. The partygoers were all butterflies, willing to alight on any surface that would give them some momentary pleasure or help them to ignore the misery just beyond these walls.

Roxana glanced up at the paintings covering the walls. This long gallery and St. Patrick's Hall, plus the north wing, were among the few remains from the original Norman castle. What had stood before had been mostly destroyed by fire five years before. How ironic it was, Roxana thought, that it had been

Cromwell's son who had rehabilitated the castle that James now occupied.

"May I take your cloak, Lady Roxana?"

She turned abruptly. For just a moment, she had forgotten Steele's presence. Her heart hammered with the suddenness of remembrance. She was appalled at her distraction. She could not afford to slip, even for a minute. For him to catch her off guard might easily mean her death—or worse. No, she must be always alert when Steele was near her.

"May I take your cloak?" he repeated, looking at her curiously.

"No," she responded curtly, taking off the cloak herself. "In case you haven't noticed, my lord, I am not one of those simpering females who fall all over you just because of your good looks."

His laughter seemed to come from deep within his chest. He grinned now, and his eyes twinkled with the myriad lights that gleamed in the golden chandeliers. "Indeed, Lady Roxana, I would be a fool not to have noticed it," he said, taking off his plumed hat and great fur-lined cape and handing them to a footman. He was as well-dressed as ever, wearing a deep blue brocaded waistcoat and beribboned breeches.

"However," he continued affably, "you must concede that men do like to help with that sort of thing. You are doing a disservice to us by not allowing us that pleasure."

Roxana, feeling the blood flood her face, snapped, "Of course it is a pleasure—

especially when the woman in question is the niece of the man's superior officer."

Steele raised a brow and stared at her, making her feel very exposed now in her low-cut green satin gown. She wished that she had thought to cover herself with a modest folded kerchief. Gently he took her cloak from her.

"You do me a great injustice, Lady Roxana, if you believe my compliments to you are based solely upon my affection for your uncle. I do not think Patrick has anything to do with the delicacy of your white skin, nor the way your green eyes sparkle like the Irish hills, nor the glossy beauty of your hair," he said, reaching up to push a stray curl behind her left ear and sending a shiver through her with his touch.

"I—." She glanced up at him, suddenly finding herself speechless. He was a fox trying to trap her. He was lying. He had to be. There were women in the next room who had ten times her beauty and sophistication—women who were far more suited to his charms than she. He was toying with her, and she hated him for it.

"I had best go seek my uncle," she said stiffly, turning to go.

"Ho, now; wait just a moment, m'lady."

Hearing a warning tone in his voice, she turned back and saw her mud-spattered cloak in his hand.

"It would seem that your uncle does not take care of you as well as one would wish. How is it that you have mud on your hem?"

Scarlet flamed her cheeks. "I—I often walk in the evenings," she said simply.

"Is that a fact?" He raised a dark brow, watching her. "D'ye know you should take care? There are men about who would easily take advantage of a girl of your beauty and innocence."

She felt the heat rise again and the prickly sensation under her skin. Her head ached. Oh, why did this have to happen tonight? Steadying herself with a deep breath, she met his eyes as coolly as she dared. "My lord, I am quite able to take care of myself. My uncle"—her voice trembled; even she could hear it quaver—"my uncle does not need to watch over me as if I were a child." She cursed herself for not having better command of her senses. She had to be pleasant to this man. Swallowing her pride, Roxana replied, "But I thank you for the warning." She lifted her eyes to meet his. "If you'll now excuse me—." She turned then, spreading her fan, and left him. She would seek a safe corner of the room from which to watch the events of the ball. Almost despairing, she began to wonder how she would ever manage this difficult assignment; but her thoughts were interrupted by the blare of trumpets, announcing the arrival of the king.

Roxana turned to see the man whom her mother had loved to distraction and whom her uncle now worshiped.

James wore a tall plumed hat and silk ribbons in his hair. His elaborate Venetian-lace collar fell over an embroidered jerkin of blue, gold and silver. His knee-length coat was of gold brocade and embroidered with little diamonds. He even wore red hose to match the ornamental bows on his shoes. In every way the man was a copy of Louis XIV, his patron—and in every way Roxana thought him a fool.

Feeling Steele's gaze on her from across the room, she turned and looked at him. He graced her with a smile. She gritted her teeth. She must be pleasant to him! To get this fop off the throne of Ireland, she would be pleasant to the devil himself.

Chapter Three

WITH THE BLARING OF THE TRUMPETS, THE music had stopped; and now all eyes turned toward James, who smiled—in her direction!

Roxana felt her stomach churn as bile rose in her throat. Was it not enough that he had ruined her mother's life? Did he have to plague hers as well?

Roxana looked at the man she detested. She knew that it was not proper to meet a king's gaze directly—it was far too bold, even for a lady of her station. However, Roxana did not consider James a king. Certainly he was not *her* king. William was that.

As James came forth, the crowd parted like the Red Sea, so that she was exposed to him. Too late Roxana realized that he had taken her boldness as a sign of welcome. It would never occur to James that a woman might reject him. As His Majesty drew closer, his obnoxious smile became a leer. What had she done? She had not even been presented to him!

Pressing her lips together in fearful anticipation, Roxana was aware of the pounding of her heart and the flush of her face. Dizzy, she leaned against the post behind her, thankful for its presence. One slip, one wrong word, could easily ruin her—and her beloved uncle. Roxana frantically looked about. Surely Patrick would. . . .

The high-pitched voice of James intruded on her thoughts. "M'lady, you are both beautiful and familiar. You haunt my memory; and for the life of me, I cannot place you."

Roxana closed her eyes for the briefest moment as she tried to steady herself and regain her composure. Forcing herself to smile, Roxana allowed the king to take one of her slender white hands and lift it to his lips. A shiver went through her at his clammy touch. Her stomach tightened. She had to keep control of herself. Taking a deep breath, Roxana again focused her green eyes on the blue gaze that had so captivated her poor mother.

"'Tis for good reason that my features haunt you, Your Majesty," Roxana said as sweetly as she could. "I am said to look much like my late mother, the Lady Mary Elizabeth Sarsfield Alden."

"Ah, yes." A nostalgic gleam came into the king's eyes, and for a moment he seemed transported into the past. "My little Mary Elizabeth." His eyes focused again on Roxana's features. "She wed my dear friend, Stuart Alden."

Like a caldron seething but not yet boiling

over, Roxana felt the anger stir inside her. His dear friend and her "dear" father had, on more than one occasion, abused his wife in front of the young Roxana, causing Roxana to cower so that she had vowed she would never again be frightened of any man. Stuart Alden had ridiculed his wife for her love of James, her love of Ireland and the love of their daughter. It had been a blessing to all when he had died in a gaming duel—even though it had put mother and daughter on the mercy of the court.

Roxana restrained herself with great effort. "Yes, Your Majesty." She curtsied low, touching his ring as she had been taught. "Thanks to your graciousness."

"And after the sad event which killed the lad, what then?"

Roxana stared at the odious creature in front of her. Her knuckles were white on her fan. Only the disgust that foamed furiously inside her kept her from fainting. As if from shyness she turned her head, and in that moment she saw that all the court was watching her interaction with the king. Lord Bristol in particular seemed to be watching her with a peculiar intensity. Lord Bristol, Sebastian Steele! Her stomach tightened.

Gathering her thoughts, Roxana swiftly returned her attention to the soft face before her. Once more she curtsied, her voice restrained both from the memory of her mother and from the desire that this man before her not know how she truly hated him. "I—I believe, Your Highness, that she never truly forgot you. We did continue to live for a time at St. James under the mercy of Lady Winchester." The lump in Roxana's throat made swallowing difficult, and tears stung her eyes.

"Is that a fact?" The king raised one thick red brow. "How strange. Things go on beneath my very nose of which I know nothing. Had I but known. . . ."

Roxana glanced up quickly, feeling the anger once again pierce her self-control. How could he not have known? Her mother had been in attendance at court daily, watching and waiting and hoping for some sign, some word from this man who had cast her off.

A man beside them now cleared his throat. "Pardon my interruption, Your Grace," he murmured, "but perhaps you would care to start the music"—he glanced at Roxana—"and continue this—uh—conversation at a later time?"

Roxana straightened to her full height—all five feet, three inches—as she turned to Richard Talbot, Lord Tyrconnel, who was dressed in a crimson coat almost as gaudy as the king's. A favorite of James, he was by no means a favorite of the people.

James frowned at the interruption and looked at Tyrconnel.

"Sire, I respectfully request. . . ." Tyrconnel halted under the glare of his sovereign and turned his attention to Roxana, raking her with his gaze as if wondering what value she might have to him. Deciding he would not be upstaged by her, he again addressed the king.

"Sire, it would be much appreciated if you would start the music."

Was that buzz in her head or in the room about her? It was in the room. Quickly, Roxana averted her gaze from the king and allowed herself the luxury of a true smile. It seemed that people were betting on who would now win the king's attention—she or the masterful viceroy. Fools, she thought. They had little hope of a decent government if Lord Tyrconnel could not distract the king from a simple matter such as herself.

Roxana cleared her throat delicately and the two men again directed their attention to her. "Your Majesty," she began, forcing herself to give a pleasant smile, "much as I hate to relinquish your charming company, I must nonetheless agree with his Lordship." She glanced about, smiling over the top of her fan. "Can you not see how anxious all the others are for your attention?" Once more she forced a smile. It was strange how you could desperately hate someone and yet enjoy making a fool of him—especially when he did not know what a fool he was!

"It would be indeed selfish," she continued, "if I were to dominate your time, Your Majesty." She paused to hide her expression behind her fan. "Perhaps we should continue this conversation later."

Roxana did not like the gleam that appeared in those blue eyes. Another shiver went through her. Perhaps she had gone too far!

Taking a deep breath, she smiled sweetly at Tyrconnel as he escorted his king to the throne at the center of the room. Within moments, the music had begun again. Roxana closed her eyes and leaned for a moment against the pillar. Around her she heard the call for the first dance and the buzz of conversation. She tried to force her dulled senses to absorb phrases and snatches of words that might be of use to her and the mission.

She knew she could not stay here all night like this. She was ill, and she certainly did not want to resume her conversation with James. Opening her eyes, she fanned herself briefly, trying to cool the flush off her face. She would go home soon.

Several court ladies seemed to be staring at her in unison. All were more resplendent than Roxana, in gold thread or silver gown, but they seemed bewildered. What would a king want with a mere chit like her? Indeed, Roxana asked herself, what would he want?

Upset by their scrutiny, Roxana turned away. Almost immediately, she was assaulted by another wave of dizziness. She closed her eyes, just for a second, and bumped directly into the broad shoulders of Sebastian Steele.

"Are you so blinded by love that you cannot see where you are going?" He put his arms about her shoulders to steady her.

Blinking for a moment, she stared up at him. Then, comprehending his question through a haze of feverishness, she felt her anger rising. Her eyes widened. "Blinded by love?" Her voice was hoarse with surprise. "Surely you jest, my lord."

Sebastian took her hand gently in his. There seemed to be both kindness and a warning in his tone. "If you do not intend to play the game, my dear, then you had better not enter the contest. Losers are often quite badly hurt."

Roxana felt her heart hammering. She looked away and pulled her hand rapidly from his, as if burned by his touch. His hand then went to her chin as he forced her eyes to meet his.

Boldly, Roxana returned his stare. He was not going to frighten her! "I play no games that I cannot win," she stated simply, hoping that her trembling voice did not betray the quivering sensation she was feeling.

"Indeed?"

He released her chin, but before she could protest he had bent his curly head and brushed his lips against her fingers, making her painfully aware of her pounding blood and the aliveness of her senses.

Why was it that *he*, of all people, excited these strange feelings in her? Why was it that he could infuriate her so? He was like . . . a needle that crept under her skin. If she could get him out, she would be highly relieved. Or would she?

The rush of blood caused her to feel faint again.

"You should be home abed," Lord Bristol continued, "and not out wandering."

"Who is wandering?" Patrick Sarsfield asked, joining the couple and handing his niece a silver cup of punch. Roxana felt the cold of the metal send a shiver through her slender body as she stared at Sebastian, wishing that her anger could strike him dead this very instant.

Sebastian smiled at Roxana, and his gray eyes never ceased searching her face as he spoke. "Your niece, sire, was telling me some tales of . . . a wandering ghost who cries."

Patrick guffawed and turned to Roxana. "Don't tell me, Roxy, that you're telling Sebastian here stories of our banshee. Why, I used to scare you with those stories when you were young and sat on my knee."

"She is still young," Sebastian said, responding with a slight smile that lifted the tips of his mustache. "Only now it would be more appropriate for her to sit elsewhere than on your knee."

Roxana grimaced, feeling her heart give a jerk.

"Aye," the commander responded, pushing back an unruly red curl. Like Sebastian, he refrained from wigs. "She does need a knee other than mine now. What about yours, lad? You've got two good ones!"

Steele laughed out loud, causing several passersby to look their way. Roxana's eyes darted her anger toward them both as she gripped the silver cup tightly in her hand. She would not be made a laughingstock—certainly not by the likes of this Englishman!

Her voice could not hide the anger she was feeling. "Uncle Patrick, I do not—."

"Hush," Patrick Sarsfield said, smiling. "We mean no harm. 'Tis just a man's way of passing time. But won't you greet your old uncle with a kiss, lass?"

Roxana made an angry face, as if deciding what to do. Her uncle did push Sebastian into her way too often for her own taste, but she loved him anyway. Self-consciously she leaned over and kissed his rough cheek.

"Come now, lass. Why so prim?"

Roxana glanced about. "Uncle, you know how much I love you; but I'd rather show my devotion to you in other ways than by making a public spectacle of myself."

"Is that so?" He raised a bushy red brow. "Ye did not seem to think much on that when ye were talking with His Majesty. Oh, Roxy." Patrick looked sober. "I fear that your time at court embittered and hardened you. Lass, 'tis not natural for a young girl to be as stiff and prim as ye are, nor is it natural for ye to hate as ye do."

Roxana flushed. Was she all that obvious?

"Lass. . . ." Patrick took her hands in his. "You are my own true blood; and God knows I love you, just as I loved your sweet mother."

The words choked in Roxana's throat. "I love you, too, uncle." She could feel the tears sting her eyes; she could feel Steele watching her. Damn the man! Damn him for seeing her so weak. The lump in her throat was painful. "Uncle, I—you're right, uncle. The past is behind us." She tried to gain control again. "Uncle Patrick, you are so good to me; and I don't know what I would do, were it not for you. I know that you have my best interests at heart, only—"

"That I do!" Patrick interrupted. "So why do ye go into a pout when I brag about ye to my men? I cannot help but be proud of so accomplished a girl."

Roxana swallowed hard. Thank goodness they were in a corner of the hall where not many others were seeing them. She took her uncle's hand. "You may talk as you like, uncle; but I'll not be sold off to—to the first passing man, as my mother was."

"Aye," Patrick agreed, winking at Sebastian. "I will let you do as you wish." He smiled and lifted Roxana's hand to his lips. Her anger melted as it always did when she was with her sweet uncle. Impulsively, with one quick glance to see that no one was watching them, she put her arms about her uncle and hugged him. How dearly she loved this man, despite all his foolishness. Oh, if only she could convince him that William was the true and proper king!

"Now, that's my Irish lass. That's a true Sarsfield—made for loving and hugging, not for war and misery." Patrick turned to see Lady Honora de Burgh, his current amour. "You'll excuse me, my little love. I have other business to attend to. Should you require anything this night"—Patrick looked toward his aide-de-camp—"ask Steele. He'll assist you."

Roxana grimaced as she turned briefly to Steele, who was impassively leaning against one of the old marble pillars nearby. At least he'd had the courtesy to step back while she and her uncle talked. Nevertheless, he would be the *last* person she would approach if she needed anything.

"Uncle, I—."

"Now, don't worry, love. Sebastian is trustworthy." He patted Roxana's hand.

"But uncle, I. . . ." How could she tell her uncle that she despised that man almost as much as she despised James? Well, no, not quite as much; but. . . . Roxana sighed. It was no use. Uncle Patrick would not hear of her feelings against James, nor of her uneasiness with Steele. She shivered violently as her fever brought goose bumps to her white skin.

Patrick's eyes narrowed. "Ye don't look well, Roxy. You will stay but one hour— enough to show your presence, and no more. I will give Sebastian instructions."

"Yes, uncle." Roxana sighed again, realizing that he was right. She should return home. In many ways, Uncle Patrick did know best. After all, he had raised her to be independent, to think and speak for herself; but he had also raised her with a healthy respect for the knowledge of others. It was only when it came to Steele and the idea of taking orders from him—an Englishman, to boot—that her upbringing grated against her. Obeying him was like rubbing salt in a wound.

"Will you be home tonight, uncle?"

Patrick smiled as his eyes shifted toward Lady Honora. "'Tis highly unlikely, lass." He leaned over and gave her a kiss on the cheek. "You're warm, my pet. An hour, no more."

Roxana smiled at him. "I'm fine, but I promise I will take care of myself."

"Good lass," he said, touching her arm briefly before he hurried to join his love.

Roxana waited a moment, watching him, then glanced about the room, shivering again as she tried to locate Tyrconnel and Lauzun. She needed to find out how many new troops had come—and what had arrived with them. But as she turned again, she once more collided with Steele.

"This seems to be a night fated for our meetings," he said wryly.

She glared at him.

"Are you searching for someone special?"

Roxana hissed, "I am searching for a way to get away from you!"

Sebastian grinned. "It seems that your indisposition has not softened your temper. Well, m'lady, you'll not be that easily rid of me. Your uncle has entrusted me with your care."

Feeling the tightness in her stomach, she responded harshly, "But I need no one to care for me. Who do you think managed our food and lodgings from the time I was seven until my lovesick mother died? She was so devoted to being around *him* that she was of no use to us." Her head was pounding, and she realized that she had said far too much. It was the illness affecting her, but nevertheless, she had to learn to watch her tongue. She carried no bitterness toward her dear mother—only toward her mother's seducer. Roxana took a deep breath. "Forgive me." She glanced up briefly. His gray eyes were inscrutable. "When I am ready to leave," she said, her voice more controlled than before, "Dory will take me."

A smile broke across Sebastian's face, lighting his eyes as he studied her. "To think that Patrick is always telling me what a good little lass you are. If he only knew that you are not the good, sweet angel he thinks."

Roxana felt herself cringe inside. "After nearly eight years with me, I believe my uncle knows that I am not an angel. In fact, I believe he would have found raising me quite boring if I had always obeyed him."

Again Sebastian laughed. "No doubt he would have. Very well, Roxana. If you are sure you can care for yourself, then I am more than pleased to be relieved of the assignment."

"You are?" The shock made her voice momentarily hoarse. Then she noticed his eyes were no longer on her but on Lady Conway, now smiling at him from across the room. "Oh, yes." Roxana stiffened as myriad sensations washed over her and anger took center place. "Of course. Well, go then. You can be sure my uncle will know how well you performed your duty." She turned and started toward the punch bowl to quench her thirst, praying that she would hear some gossip tonight that would make this misery worth her while.

Sebastian's fingers tightened on her shoulder. The fire of his touch made her shiver as she turned to face his slate gray eyes, now narrowed in an angry glare. His voice was low, yet the threat was enough to make her quake within. "My little Roxana, soon you will have to learn that you can play only one game at a time. Now," he said with the patience of one instructing a naughty child, "do you wish me to accompany you home as your uncle requested, or do you wish to be on your own?" His eyes traveled her face, as if trying to guess her thoughts. "You can choose only one. I, of course, will abide by your desire."

"I. . . ." Roxana swallowed as she felt her heartbeat quicken and the blood rush to her face. It was the fever—that's why she couldn't think. That's what was making her feel so numb and paralyzing her mind.

"Well? I do not have all evening to chat with you if you do not want me. Other pleasures call me."

She willed the tears to stay back as she swallowed the pain in her throat. The man was so obnoxious he would think the tears were for him! She glanced quickly back at Lady Conway and again felt the icy hand close over her heart. Turning, she looked directly into his eyes. Her voice was barely a whisper. "You may go to your other pleasures, Lord Bristol. Far be it from me to keep you where you do not wish to be." She stared boldly up at him.

His eyes met hers and he dropped his hand from her shoulder. "Very well, Roxana. Just recall: you have made the choice, not I. When you tell your uncle of my desertion, be sure you tell him that, as well." He spun on his heel.

"Wait! I—."

"Yes?" Sebastian paused and turned slightly, his brow cocked. "Are you undecided again?"

Roxana gritted her teeth, wishing she could take a bayonet to this patronizing creature, wishing that looks could kill. "No," she said firmly, "I am very much decided." Her voice strengthened. "I . . . only wanted to thank you."

"For?"

"For not telling Uncle Patrick about my walk earlier. He would have been worried. But he needn't be, you see. I am careful."

Sebastian's eyes narrowed momentarily. "Yes, I do see. And you're welcome. I did it not for you, however—Lord only knows that Patrick should have given you a good spanking long ago. I did it for my love of him. Your uncle has enough worries on his mind now without having to be concerned about an impulsive little chit such as you." He paused a moment, then took her hand, kissing it so that his lips and mustache tickled her tender skin. She inhaled sharply.

"Good night to you, Lady Roxana."

Spinning on his heel, he left her staring after him.

Chapter Four

ROXANA HAD ALREADY LINGERED AT THE BALL for longer than her prescribed hour, but she did not yet want to leave. No, that wasn't quite true. Shivering with chills and tired from all the dancing, she would have loved to go; but there was still much too much information to be gathered—and she had not seen her uncle since after the first minuet. No doubt he had gone off somewhere with Lady de Burgh.

Roxana had to smile. Her uncle was in need of a good companion. She so wanted him to be happy. If only he would decide on a woman to marry—but his answer was always the same: he would not wed until all was safe and well with his beloved Ireland. As if all could possibly be well and safe with James here! Getting rid of that oaf who believed himself to be king would not only help all Ireland; it would help her uncle, as well.

Yes, of course, she was doing this for her mother, too; but surely her uncle would want the ghost of his sister put to rest.

Roxana felt the pounding of her heart. She knew that in fact Mary Elizabeth would have done anything to keep James on the throne, just as now her daughter would do anything to get him off. Mary Elizabeth might have felt misery from James's treatment of her, but Roxana had felt the pain and anger, as well—without the love. Someone had to pay James back for his cruelty. Someone had to see that justice was done.

The music for another stately minuet started up. As with all the other dances, Roxana found herself besieged with partners—something she considered strange. With all the other ladies in the room, she found it difficult to understand why so many sought her hand. Of course, most of them were lovesick pups, like Berwick; and some were simply trying to win points with her uncle. Others were old men who had nothing better to do with their time. Still, she'd been more than busy, and most of her partners had been pleasant enough.

Searching the room intently, she focused on Steele's broad shoulders absentmindedly until her attention was caught by an approaching gentleman. She accepted the Lord Grandard for the next dance.

Still irritated by Steele, Roxana clutched her fan and clenched her teeth as she tried to be polite to her partner. Steele had said not a word to her all evening since that moment he had turned heel on her. Anger and indignation continued to boil inside of her.

The minuet ended. She favored Grandard a smile and then hid her face with the fan as she offered her hand to him again.

Only as a chill went through her spine did she glance up to see that Steele's gray eyes were on her from across the room. Her heart skipped a beat as she turned to meet his gaze—and for that moment, time stood still. What was he thinking? Why was he frowning so? She wondered if he suspected something —but no, he couldn't have. She was careful.

Quickly Roxana turned away, allowing her partner to lead her into the next dance. Why did Steele always have to spoil even her smallest pleasures? He might have at least asked her to dance. He could have made an effort to be pleasant with her.

Then, as she and Grandard took their positions, she recalled the command she would happily have forgotten in her feverish state. She was to befriend Lord Bristol—a man who was nearly her mortal enemy! She wished for a moment that she had never started this spying—never even heard of James or William.

Her fever was now burning. She forced herself to glance his way again. Yes, Lady Conway was on his arm, but Lady Melfort wasn't far behind. Well, she sighed, if he did not approach her in another dance or two . . . she would just have to approach him. Perhaps that would jog his memory a bit. But surely her superiors did not expect her to break all the rules and ask him to dance with her! He would certainly suspect her motives.

The music stopped a moment. Partners changed. She scarcely noticed Grandard's departure as she accepted yet again the moist hand of James Fitzjames, the duke of Berwick. Not much older than she, Berwick had already made quite a name for himself in the war. He was a favorite with the ladies—despite his hefty frame—as well as with James. He was related to James, of course. She wondered that he did not feel bitter about being James's illegitimate son—but, then, his mother had continued to remain in favor even while James dallied with others.

Twirling about in Berwick's deft hands, Roxana wondered if Sebastian Steele felt so confident of his position that he believed he could easily afford to ignore her. All she need do was tell her uncle and. . . .

So that was it! If she told Patrick on him, then Steele would tell her uncle about her.

But he knew nothing. Or did he? Automatically, she fell into step with her partner.

Berwick broke into her thoughts. "My Lady Roxana, you are not much with me this night."

"Oh!" She blushed, realizing now that she had taken a wrong step. She had to pay attention. Curse that Steele for taking up her thoughts! She had to be pleasant to her partner—Berwick of all people would surely have some worthwhile information. But would not Steele have information, too?

Dragging her attention back to the dance, Roxana fixed a smile on her face and forced her eyes to wander over the form of her partner. The blond wig, gold- and blue-threaded jacket and richly beribboned breeches were as overdone as his father's clothes. Distastefully, she eyed the powdered face that had been whitened to an almost ghostly hue.

"Forgive me, my lord," Roxana said politely. "My mind wanders. If I am silent, 'tis because I am so worried about the Orange forces. I mean"—she fluttered her lashes, attempting to portray a feeling of helplessness—"they are so close by. They say that William will land in a day or two. Can we possibly protect our own?"

Berwick smiled. His reddened lips curled. "For shame on you, m'lady. You should have faith in His Majesty and in your uncle's magnificent command."

Her heart hammered. Had she said it the wrong way? Pins and needles of fever seemed to run rampant through her body as she tried to think of a proper response.

"I have more than enough faith in my uncle —and in your good command also, my lord." She dipped slightly as the dance required, and kept her eyes on Berwick. "But 'tis natural for me to wonder. I am, after all, Patrick Sarsfield's niece, and I am, therefore, more aware than most of the situation."

Berwick smiled again. His eyes wandered over her curves and lingered on the creamy skin of her smooth white breasts, accentuated as they were by the green silk gown and the tight laces. "I am glad you are so aware, Lady Roxana. 'Tis much more pleasant to converse with a companion such as you." He paused. His arm went about her narrow waist, ready to lead her to the next part of the dance. Roxana wanted to cringe, but she dared not. "I would have no fear, Lady Roxana," he whispered into her ear, so that she could feel his hot breath repulsing her. She turned her wide eyes toward him with a questioning look.

"It is true that the duc de Lauzun is here now," Berwick continued, "but he will be leaving for France soon. He will be returning with a goodly number of new men—and arms. Besides," he said, grinning, "our sources have assured us that His Majesty's errant son-in-law William is now in dire suffering from the flux. Is that not poetic justice?" Berwick's grin widened. Roxana felt her stomach turn. William was ill—and Berwick was happy with his suffering! She wondered what Steele's reaction would be. No, she dared not look back at him. Probably it would be the same. "If he attempts to land at all," Berwick continued, "it will not be before midsummer, and then the Irish will all have united under my royal father."

"All the Irish?" Roxana asked, breathless from the quickness of the dance, her own illness and the audacity of James. "Surely you jest. If we are that close to victory—I am impressed. But Lord Berwick, do not several cities in the north still proclaim for William?"

Berwick whirled her and gave her a mysterious look. "For one so beautiful and so young, I say you are indeed knowledgeable about stately affairs. I assume you are equally knowledgeable in other matters, as well."

"My lord," she responded, forcing herself to smile sweetly even as she felt the trembling inside her. Like father, like son! "I am knowledgeable in all the matters which concern me."

The twinkle in Berwick's blue eyes was not to be mistaken. She had seen the same in his father's eyes earlier. Her stomach tightened in disgust. Did these men think of nothing else? She thought of her own father, her uncle, Steele. . . . Nay, they probably did not. Women and gaming were all that had occupied her father. She supposed Steele was no better. She was tempted to look toward him, but felt that if she did her disgust would show through.

Berwick led Roxana off the floor. "What you say is true. The northern counties do yet need a bit of persuasion, but His Majesty will be riding up in a few days' time. No doubt once they view his magnificent presence and see his nobility, they will quickly succumb."

Roxana could scarcely hide her disbelief. Did he really believe in the divine right of James? A king should be a king for the people. A king should be like William.

Roxana did not hear Berwick's reply as she tapped her fan on her fingertips. Her attention was once again centered on Sebastian Steele. This time he had danced with Lady d'Arcy. The man was nothing more than a social climber, and that was not going to work in her favor if she was to befriend him. After all, her uncle—wonderful though he might be—had not even been made earl yet!

However were she and Steele going to stay on friendly terms—for the purpose of the assignment, of course—when she could scarcely keep her temper with the man?

Roxana bit her lower lip. Gratefully she accepted the cup of punch that Berwick now offered her. Sipping it relieved the pain of her parched throat. Her head ached, her body hurt, her vision swam. All she wanted to do right now was to return to Lucan and sleep.

For a moment she contemplated leaving a message for Gilpatrick. It would be difficult to reach their secret hideaway, but if she did she would not have to worry about meeting him again in a week. The thought evaporated as her head began to pound once more.

"Does something still trouble you, Lady Roxana?"

Roxana glanced up. She had forgotten that Berwick was still at her side—but of course he would be. Was he not one of those who her uncle said were offering for her? She shuddered to think upon it.

She smiled as sweetly as she could. "Nothing troubles me now. I was but observing my uncle's aide-de-camp, Lord Bristol. 'Tis a shame that my uncle need be burdened with such a creature, coward that he is."

"*Coward*, m'lady?" Berwick's brow raised in astonishment. "I have heard many names applied to Bristol, but I confess that is the first time I have heard him called a coward. A braggart and a ladies' man he might be, but I assure you, your uncle's aide is no coward."

"No?" Roxana tapped the fan on her fingers, not wanting to meet Berwick's blue eyes. "I must be mistaken. It only seemed to me that since he seems reluctant to take on certain challenges—where he is not assured of winning—he must be a coward."

Berwick's eyes narrowed. "The only challenge I can deduce you mean, m'lady, is yourself."

"No!" Her reaction came swiftly, and her eyes met Berwick's immediately. She forced herself to quit trembling. "No," she said, more calmly this time. "I do not mean that at all."

Berwick smiled. "Be assured, m'lady, your secret is safe with me. Take care, however, if you plan to tangle with Bristol. He has broken many a heart, both here and in London."

The shiver she felt this time had nothing at all to do with her fever.

"I thank you for your warning, my lord, but I assure you it is not needed. Tangling with Lord Bristol is the last thing on my mind."

Again, Berwick gave her a secret smile. He bent his head to kiss her hand. As the music started, he demurred, "You will excuse me, m'lady. Other duties call me."

Roxana forced herself to smile and then watched as Berwick took the hand of Lady Melfort. Alone, she leaned against a pillar to rest her weakening body. No, Steele was not the man for her. He asked far too many questions. And, besides, how could she ever compete with Lady Conway—she swallowed hard—and the others?

For just a moment, Roxana felt her mind clear as Lord Bristol turned toward her. What was she thinking of? Of course she could compete with Lady Conway, if she wanted to. She had to. But the next time she saw Gilpatrick, she was going to ask to have her orders revoked.

Taking a deep breath, she once more steadied herself against the pillar. For now she would make the best of a bad assignment. She supposed the challenge of dealing with Steele would be good for her. At least her life was not boring, as was—she glanced around her—Lady Conway's, for example.

She put the punch cup down, feeling a horrid sensation well inside her as she tried to swallow back a rising illness. She must leave immediately or suffer a far greater humiliation than that of embracing her uncle. She was sure that her illness wasn't in any way helped by the idea that she had to be nice to Steele.

A wave of faintness attacked her again. Dear Lord, she prayed, let me hold out just a few moments longer. She closed her eyes and felt her body sway dizzily. She would find Dory and have him take her home now—home to her beautiful Lucan. She barely heard the approaching courier.

"Lady Roxana, are you well?"

Roxana's eyes opened wide. Dizzily, she

focused on the blue of the royal uniform. "Of course, I'm well," she snapped. "Would I be here, were I not?"

The courier shrugged and then smiled. "I have been sent by His Majesty to . . . fetch you."

"Fetch me?" Roxana glanced about the room. James, self-assured and smug, sat atop his red velvet throne. His blue eyes seemed to be focused upon her. Acknowledging the man's attention, she nodded briefly, then turned to the messenger. "To dance, you mean?"

The man cleared his throat. Clearly he felt embarrassed at being the bearer of this message. "Nay, m'lady. His Majesty wishes to have a private—uh—talk with you in the gardens. To resume your earlier conversation." He lowered his voice. "The private gardens."

"The private gardens?" Roxana's green eyes were like cat's saucers now. Her voice must have betrayed some of the fear she felt, for the man nodded.

"But I—," Roxana began to protest, feeling another wave of illness sweep over her. She did not know how much longer she could hold out. "I. . . ." The strong arm that went about her supportively startled her. Her heart raced as she tried to keep her poise and looked up into Sebastian Steele's slate gray eyes. The lump in her throat seemed too big for her to speak, as words momentarily left her.

His eyes met hers and he smiled slightly. Was that tenderness she saw there? But why should he feel tender toward her? This man was as hard as the armor that adorned the castle gates. Nay, Sebastian Steele was not a man who could be tender—and certainly not with someone like her.

"You will have to beg the king to excuse Lady Roxana," Steele told the waiting messenger. "She has been promised to me for the rest of the evening."

Roxana found her voice again and began to protest. "But I—." His fingers squeezed her shoulder ever so slightly, silencing her.

The messenger frowned. "'Tis King James himself who requests her presence."

Reflected candlelight glinted in Steele's cold eyes. "I know who requests her," he said, turning toward the king and saluting him with one gloved hand, "but Lady Roxana is with me at this moment. You may make her apologies to His Majesty. If the king wishes to speak to Lady Roxana, he must get through me."

Steele looked thunderously angry. The courier bowed his head slightly. "Yes, Lord Bristol. I shall tell His Majesty." Frowning, he turned on his heel.

Roxana suddenly began to swoon. The fever, the dancing, the stress of the evening—it was all too much. Distantly she was aware that Steele, by her side, was gently supporting her, guiding her to a quiet corner.

"I trust you feel a little better now?"

Numbly she nodded, her eyes closed, aware even through her dazedness that his closeness seemed to be causing unfamiliar sensations in her. Her heart pounded rapidly—but it

45

was from her illness, was it not? As was the fevered sensation that suffused her whole body?

His arm was still about her. Unresisting, she leaned against him in the way he invited. Her eyes were still closed, for she knew that she would be dizzy if she opened them again.

"I believe that you have stayed this evening much longer than your uncle would have desired. You are obviously not well, Roxana; and since you will not care for yourself, I fear that, as your uncle's aide, I must."

Her mind hazy, her brain aching, Roxana's only thought was that she did not want him to do anything because of her uncle. She wanted no one to do things because she was a Sarsfield. She wanted. . . .

Her words wouldn't form. She knew Steele was right, but did he have to treat her like a child? She longed to tell him exactly what she did—just so he would no longer regard her as a silly chit.

She supposed that she should thank him for this, and for his timely interference earlier. Had he not come along, she didn't know what she would have done. After all, one just did not refuse His Majesty offhand. Of the two choices, she supposed that Steele was clearly the better.

She began to speak, but Steele interrupted her at once. "Whether you like it or not, you are going home this instant." To her amazement—and that of all who noticed—Steele swept her up into his powerful arms and carried her off the floor.

"Steele! Put me down!" He was making a public spectacle of her! At all costs she did not want to call any more attention to herself—for a spy, it simply would not do. He was ruining everything for her!

"Please," she pleaded, "put me down."

"Nay, Roxana. I told you. Since you do not care for yourself, I must."

"I can walk myself," she tried to say, as she attempted to struggle free.

"You are making more of a spectacle of yourself by struggling, Roxana. I do not trust you to follow my lead, so I shall take control."

"But—."

She tried again to move, but his arms were holding her far too tightly. She found, too, that in spite of this humiliation, she was grateful for his support and his strength.

Closing her eyes, she realized that she did not have the energy to fight him. She leaned her head against his shoulder. She knew he was one of her enemies, yet she felt strangely safe and warm with him.

"What I want," he said, "is to take you over my knee as Patrick should have done ages ago. I want to teach you some manners."

Opening her eyes, she began to struggle again. "Don't you dare touch me!"

It was clear even to her that Steele was having trouble holding his temper. "Just close your eyes, Roxana, and be still." He paused. "Don't worry, I won't harm you. For a change, just try doing what I say."

Realizing that nothing she said or did was going to make any difference at this moment, she allowed herself again to rest her head against his shoulder, to enjoy the secure comfort that his arms gave her. But why did her rescuer have to be this man?

She was barely aware of the cloak being tucked gently about her, or of the cool lips that touched her fevered brow, or of the light touch that brushed away the damp strands of her hair as they went out into the evening.

Sebastian looked down upon the pixie face of his new charge. What a paradox she was. How angelic she looked asleep, and what a little spitfire she was when awake! How did one cope with someone of her mercurial nature? He never knew when to be pleasant to her or when to treat her like an errant child.

As he held her and watched her steady breathing, his heart warmed more than it ever had in the past. He knew the story of her early years—of Roxana's struggles to stay alive while her mother was besotted with the king, of the merciless treatment she and her mother had received at the hands of Lord Stuart Alden and his family. She needed to learn that not all men were of that nature. Did she not see it in Patrick—in the love he gave her?

It was true, he knew, that Patrick Sarsfield's wish was to see them paired; but this lovely child-woman in his arms would have to grow up a bit, would have to realize what love was—and would have to come to him. He knew he could heal her wounds and ease her pains, but she was not of the nature to be courted and wooed like the other ladies.

He sighed and brushed the hair again from her brow, then gently touched her cheek and felt the burning of the fever. Kissing her again, he laid her gently into the coach. She stirred a moment.

"Alexander . . . ," she murmured.

Alexander? Who was Alexander? Steele felt a prick of jealousy. He knew of no Alexander at court.

"Nay, love," he whispered softly. "'Tis not Alexander. But sleep now." He touched her soft cheek again and felt the fever that was rising within her. His voice was tight with emotion as he leaned out of the carriage window to speak to Dory. "To Lucan, man, but go gently as you can."

Dory touched his cap and nodded as he smiled at Steele. "Aye, my lord. Together, we'll see her safe."

Chapter Five

ROXANA WAS VAGUELY AWARE OF THE GENTLE motion as the coach rocked, of the warmth and security about her. Chilled, she attempted to snuggle deeper into the furs as her head nestled against a comfortable softness.

Opening her eyes for just a moment, she saw—through her feverish haze—the chiseled profile of Sebastian Steele. Roxana was momentarily confused. What had happened? Why was he holding her? Why was he here with her just now?

A vivid flash of memory broke through her mental fog, but her mind still would not focus on the proper words.

"You—you dueled the king for me." Her voice was barely audible.

Sebastian, startled at hearing her, glanced down. His eyes met hers. Remarkable, he thought, how her eyes now shimmered green in the dim light of the carriage. After a moment, he smiled briefly and responded, "I'd hardly say that, Roxana."

"No, really." She struggled to sit up. Finding it too difficult, she fell back into the warm comfort of his protection. "I mean, it wasn't a duel, but it was. You helped me . . . at. . . ." It was terribly difficult to talk, but she had to continue. She swallowed hard. ". . . at great cost to yourself. James—." Dear Lord, what was wrong with her? She could hardly think. She could hardly speak. In fact, all she truly wanted to do at this moment was rest quietly in his arms—but did she dare? Weakly, she persisted with her thoughts. "James will be furious with you."

Sebastian flashed a wicked grin. "Yes, I imagine he will be—but he'll hardly have me drawn and quartered for that."

"No . . . but he'll probably want your commission from you—or something. Your title, or your lands in England, or. . . ."

Sebastian snorted. "I hardly think that. His Majesty is used to women who prefer me to him. It's happened on several occasions."

Anger invigorated Roxana, giving her a momentary surge of energy. Prefer, indeed! She managed to sit up, though chills attacked her as she left the cozy warmth of his arms. The fur blanket slipped off as she deliberately turned away from him, trying to gather her strength.

After a moment, he made an attempt to put the blanket about her.

"Don't you touch me!" she cried, her eyes wide. "I did not *prefer* you. Like all men, you simply imposed your will on me."

"Is that what happened?" Steele raised one eyebrow, looking faintly amused.

"That is what happened," she stated coldly.

Sebastian watched her a moment and then shrugged. "You could have refused me and gone with James. I would not have minded."

"No doubt you would have applauded it," she hissed, as she curled up on the side opposite him and tried to make herself comfortable.

"So why didn't you?"

Roxana glared mutinously at him. "You know why I did not."

"Do I?" He leaned over to put the blanket about her once more, and she moved to escape him.

Too weary to argue, she leaned her head on the side of the carriage. The trouble was that she knew he was right. She *had* preferred him. But, of course, he had merely been the lesser of two evils.

Shivering again, trying to control the trembling in her body, she silently accepted the cover this time as he tucked it about her.

"Why are you smiling?" she demanded sulkily.

"Have I not a right to smile?"

"You're making fun of me, aren't you? You think that I couldn't have handled myself if I had gone with the king. You're thinking—."

"My, my, we are talented. When did you learn to read minds, my little minx?" He gently adjusted her cover. "I suggest you close your eyes again and try to sleep. We're nearly at Lucan."

She would have liked to sleep more than anything in the world, but it seemed that her body, like her mind, wanted to disobey. Try as she could, Roxana could not find a position as comfortable as before.

"Would you like to rest against my shoulder?"

"No!" She darted an angry look at him. Oh, damn him. Yes, she did want to feel him holding her once again; but she would not give him the satisfaction of telling him so. Besides, he might just try to . . . take advantage of her. He was, after all, that kind of man, wasn't he?

"You're sure?" Sebastian persisted. There was a touch of humor in his tone.

"Of course I'm sure," she spat out quickly, before she could change her mind.

Sebastian shrugged as she again tried to find a comfortable spot.

In a moment, he had moved to the side where she now sat. Thinking she should be angry, Roxana said nothing as she felt his strong arm go around her.

The promise of comfort was too great. Soon her aching body had moved back into the snuggling position, and her head nestled comfortably between his chest and shoulder. She fell asleep.

Sebastian looked down upon the dozing girl at his side. "Sleep well, my little minx," he whispered. Bending his head, his lips grazed her fevered brow once more. Noticing the warmth and fire of her body, he crossed himself and uttered a prayer, thankful once again for the years he had spent at his grandmother's side learning herbs. Aye, he would help heal her body—and, with luck, he would heal her mind.

Roxana, deep in her dreams, snuggled next to him and smiled slightly.

Sebastian wondered at her smile. Was it for him? Or for that blasted mystery, Alexander?

Chapter Six

HEARING THE BIRD OUTSIDE HER WINDOW, Roxana opened her eyes. She was back in her bed at Lucan—but how? Closing her eyes again, she tried to recall what had happened last night at the ball.

Smiling to herself, she thought of the wonderful dreams she had had. A man, strong and tall, had come and had carried her away in his arms. How vivid that dream! She even recalled the gentleness of his kiss and the soothing touch of his hands. But, of course, it had all been a dream. She would ask Maggie what it could mean. Dory's wife had the gift, and often she would tell Roxana things that no one else had any way of knowing.

Roxana's brow creased as she again focused, trying to recall the dance. She remembered being with Berwick and, yes, she recalled all that he had told her. In a moment, she would get up and write it down so that she could pass it on to Gilpatrick next week. The trouble was that she recalled precious little else about the evening.

A voice beneath her window made her body go rigid. Wide awake now, she turned her head toward the sound. No, it could not be! What was Sebastian Steele doing here? Had her uncle come home, too, then? Were they perhaps having a conference? But Uncle Patrick had gone off with his lady love.

Wrinkling her nose in disgust, Roxana recalled then that she had become ill at the ball and that Sebastian Steele had taken her to the carriage. Her heart beat furiously. He had taken her home despite her objections, no doubt.

She sat upright abruptly. Beads of perspiration appeared on her brow. And what had happened after he had taken her home?

Frightened, she glanced about the room. No, there was nothing here that would give her away. She blanched. Nevertheless, he had to leave Lucan as quickly as possible. She could not have him roaming the estate at leisure without someone supervising his actions.

In a mild panic, she pulled the red velvet bell cord. She had to know what had happened last night—the whole of it. It occurred to her that if he was here and people learned that her uncle was not, then her reputation was at stake. Heaven forbid that her uncle would consider such a trick, forcing her to marry the man merely because of an illness!

Really, she cared not a hoot for what was proper; but she did have an image to uphold—as the sweet, innocent niece of the famed war hero, Patrick Sarsfield. Frantic for knowledge, she pulled the cord more insistently this time.

Maggie, Dory's wife, appeared almost instantly.

"Praised be the saints and Holy Mary!" Maggie crossed herself. "Ye be awake and alive."

"Of course I'm awake and alive," Roxana responded.

"Well, Miss Roxy, love, we weren't sure ye'd make it, what with that high fever. Six days it's been. The only one that did have faith was *him*."

"Him?" Roxana asked, puzzled, accepting a cup of tea gratefully. Sipping it slowly, she noted with surprise that she was famished.

"Lord Bristol, love."

Roxana's eyes widened. "What?" She nearly upset the tea tray. "Sebastian Steele has been here with me, in this house, for six days?"

"And six nights. Nary a moment did he leave yer side, m'lady." Maggie clucked her tongue approvingly. "'Tis through his good graces—and his herbs and poultices—that ye are here today."

"I was ill for six days?" Roxana repeated, totally befuddled. "And Sebastian Steele took care of me? Why?"

"Aye, Mistress, ye were and he did—though ye did give him some rough moments. I assume, mistress, that he did it from the goodness of his heart. Devoted to yer uncle, he is. Said he promised the master he'd care for ye."

Roxana made a face. Of course, that was it. He had brought her home and had stayed to take care of her merely because he had promised Uncle Patrick. What type of reward did he expect from her uncle?

She closed her eyes as she tried to gain strength. Six days she had been ill? That meant she would have to meet Gilpatrick this night at Ormond Quay! Well, she did not relish the ride, but she had done it on more than one occasion. If she took her horse, Fire, they should be able to do the trip in two hours, no more. Frowning, she decided that she would think about it later. In any case, she could not leave before dark.

Laying her head back on the pillows and closing her eyes, she debated whether to get up and go into the garden or to stay in bed and gain strength for the night. In truth, she was not the type to stay in bed if she did not have to; yet it would not do well for her to collapse on the road this evening.

Having considered all sides of the matter, Roxana opened her eyes. "I should like some water to wash with, and then some assistance in dressing. I still feel a bit weak," she acknowledged to her maid, "but I want to sit awhile in the garden." Truly, she did not. She was sure that all she wanted to do this day was rest, but it would look strange if at dusk she suddenly appeared dressed. Better to put the pretense on now that she was quite recovered.

Maggie's eyes narrowed. "I do not think ye should be up and about yet, mistress. I'll go ask his Lordship."

"Ask his Lordship?" Roxana felt her fury rise. "Ask Lord Bristol if I may get up? I should know my own capacity—and I am your mistress when my uncle is gone. I give the orders at Lucan, not Sebastian Steele."

"Oh, but mistress, he does know about illness and the like. He cured my aching back with a potion—and such hands he has, mistress. Magical hands, they be."

"Witchery," Roxana hissed. She forced herself to sit upright again, not heeding the pounding of her heart or the sweat on her brow. "I'll not have such in my house, and I *will* get up."

Roxana threw back the covers angrily, exposing herself to the chill morning air. Dizzily, she felt her heart race—but that was only natural, wasn't it, after being in bed so long? She stood for a moment unsteadily, trembling as she tried to regain her fast-departing strength. Maggie was frantic.

"Oh, m'lady, please. Don't move farther!"

Roxana's eyes narrowed with the strain. "I . . . am . . . getting . . . dressed. If you won't help . . . me, I can handle it on my own." She took another step forward, clutching the post of her bed for support, concentrating on her movements. She did not hear the opening of the door nor the approach of Steele until the rapid beating of her pulse told her that he was beside her. As she looked up into his gray eyes, her vision swam ever so slightly. But she was well. She had to be well. She had been in bed for six days—that should be enough to get any one back to health.

"Exactly what do you think you are doing, Roxana?" Steele took her by the shoulders, giving her support, yet making her feel all the more unsteady inside for his touch.

She took a deep breath, trying not to betray her vulnerability to this man, trying to prove to him that she had perfect control.

"I am. . . ." She paused, meeting his hard, gray eyes. As they searched her face, they seemed to be searching her soul. "I am getting out of bed and getting . . . dressed." Her head was beginning to ache again. All she really wanted to do was go back to bed, but she recalled that she had already shown Steele enough of her weak side.

"I think not," he said authoritatively. Before Roxana could protest, he swept her into his arms and brought her the few steps back to the bed. "I think you will stay in bed at least one more day," he added, laying her down gently.

"No! I cannot!" Her eyes went wide with anxiety as she struggled to get up. She did not want to leave Gilpatrick waiting. When Roxana Alden gave a promise to be some place, she went. It was part of her integrity, part of her promise. True, events did sometimes hold up Gilpatrick, but not she. She had a reputation for being on time.

Sebastian kept her down with the slightest pressure from one hand. His cool gray eyes narrowed. "Pray, why not? James is out of Dublin and there is nothing pressing in the capital at this moment. At least, nothing that you would want to participate in."

James was out of town? Where was he? If only she had left a message for Gilpatrick! But she had felt so ill that evening.

"Well?"

"I. . . ." Roxana forced herself to meet his eyes. Her mind went blank. "I just cannot." She turned her head, feeling the sweat on her brow. Thinking furiously, she said, "See, the sun is out." She calmed herself as much as she could, realizing that her panic would only betray her. "Wouldn't it be healthful for me to spend time—a few moments perhaps—in the garden? Isn't that what invalids do?"

He relieved the pressure from her chest and frowned, still staring down at her. Lifting a damp, cool rag from a container at her bedside, Sebastian tenderly wiped the sweat from her brow, face and neck. Roxana closed her eyes a moment as the cloth passed over her lids. Maggie was right. He did indeed have magical hands . . . but he was an enemy of hers—she had to remember that.

"That feels better, does it not, Roxana?"

She sighed and focused her eyes again on his rugged features. Truly, she did feel better. Tears came to her eyes. She did not know how to deal with this man—or devil.

"Aye." Her voice choked as she stared at him, subdued.

Sebastian brushed back the dark strands of

61

her hair. "Maggie will comb your hair back so you'll feel refreshed. But I do not think you are ready to go out. Maybe tomorrow."

"But I—." Roxana struggled once more to sit up, trying to think of some other excuse—but just looking at him made her mind go numb. Words would not form in her brain.

"Yes?"

"Oh, never mind." Roxana sank back, frustrated. She would have to think of something later.

"You will stay in bed now?"

There was a bitterness in her mouth. "Of course. I would never think of disobeying you, your Lordship," she said hoarsely.

Sebastian smiled and the tips of his mustache lifted. "Would that it were so." His eyes twinkled with the light coming in from the casement windows. "That's scarcely the Roxy I know." He sat on the bed beside her, causing her heart to catch in her throat. "I do know that it is difficult for you to follow my orders, my little Roxana; but you will see it is all for your own good."

She glared at him. Her voice chilled. "Is it not bad enough that you give me no rights and have no respect for my wishes? Must you call me that as well?" She paused to attempt control in her voice. "The name Roxy is reserved only for my uncle—and those that I love."

"My Lady Roxana!" Maggie cried. "My lady, you shouldn't talk so to his Lordship."

"Nay, Maggie." Sebastian lowered his eyes to hide his momentary hurt. "Lady Roxana is right. I do tend to be too familiar." He looked at Roxana. "I shall not call you that—at least, not until you give permission."

Roxana sank back onto the pillows, feeling drained. She'd been rude—but certainly no ruder than he. "Now what?" she asked, seeing Maggie hand him a cup of liquid.

"It's an herbal brew. It will help you regain your strength."

Her eyes narrowed. "Witch or warlock?"

"Neither. It is a brew my Spanish grandmother taught me."

"How can I be sure it will not harm me?"

Sebastian hid a smile. "Believe me, my lady, there have been many times when I would have liked to put you over my knee; but if I really desired to hurt you, there are other ways I would choose than poison." He handed her the cup. "Now drink."

Roxana, resigned, sipped the drink and tasted the sweetness. "I do not like it."

He moved closer toward her on the bed. What did he plan to do?

"I tell you I won't drink it." She put it down.

"Roxana, stop acting like a child."

Gritting her teeth, she said, "I am not a child. I am a woman."

Her eyes met his, and for a moment there was silence. A flush crept over her body. Quietly he answered, "Aye, in many ways, you are a woman. But also in many ways, you are still a child." He held the cup out to her again. "Drink it."

She took a deep breath. His persistence was irritating her. "Very well."

Lowering her lashes, she felt him watching her over the top of the cup.

Finally, she drained the remainder.

"Good," he said, taking the cup from her. "You should sleep for several more hours now, and you'll feel much better when you wake." He stood and closed the shades. "I'll stop by to see you again later." Touching her cheek tenderly, he said, "Sleep, Roxana."

She wanted to object, to tell him that she had barely woken, but the herbal brew was already beginning its work. He smiled at her. Was it the potion that made him look so handsome?

Helpless, she watched as Sebastian and Maggie left the room. Then her hand went to her cheek where he had just touched her. Yes, Maggie was right. He did have magical hands. Tears came to her eyes. It just was not fair, she thought as she fell asleep.

Chapter Seven

THE SUN WAS LOW IN THE SKY WHEN ROXANA woke again. Hating to admit that Sebastian had been right, she also realized at once that she felt a good deal stronger. But was she strong enough to ride to Dublin and back—without Steele being aware?

Pulling the bell cord, she sat upright in bed. Yes, her dizziness was gone—she hoped permanently. Maybe she should have Dory take her. Could they get away with it? Certainly the carriage would be far more comfortable than horseback.

"Ye be looking better than ye looked this morning, Miss Roxy, that's for certain. There's even some color in yer face." Maggie beamed. "That man's a wonder, is he not?" She seemed as proud as if he'd been her own son.

Though she wanted to deny it, Roxana obviously owed the man a debt of gratitude. Not that she wouldn't have gotten well on her own, but. . . . She glanced at her maid. The man had obviously charmed Maggie as he did most women. But not her. She tasted the bitterness in her mouth.

Roxana had told Maggie nothing of her espionage activities, and now she vowed not to tell the older woman of her resentment toward Steele. She prayed that Dory said as little when in his cups or between the sheets.

Silently, Roxana watched the maid putter about the room and open the shades.

Slipping from her bed, she walked—steadily this time—to the wardrobe. "Maggie, I should like to wash." Her stomach growled. "And something to eat, if you please. Some beef, perhaps?" She bit her lower lip thoughtfully as she tried to decide what to wear. She would need strength for her ride this night, and her mouth began to water as she thought of the thick, steamy beef and the green pea soup that she knew the cook would be preparing.

"Well, Miss Roxy, I don't right know. . . ."

Roxana, now standing in front of her armoire, turned abruptly. "What do you mean you 'don't know?'" She felt a sinking sensation in her stomach, but she persisted in the questions. "Is there no meat? Well, fowl, then. Chicken, duck, goose—whatever."

Maggie shook her head, her brown eyes big and mournful. "Nay, m'lady."

Anger was rising in Roxana. Skillfully, she controlled her temper. "What do you mean 'nay'? Are you telling me that we have no food?" Certain rationing was to be expected, and that was perfectly all right with Roxana—after all, she should not be feasting if her friends in the field were starving. But something else seemed to be the problem now.

She glared at her maid. The older woman was clearly uncomfortable, shifting her heavy feet.

"We do have food, don't we?" Roxana paused for Maggie's answer.

"Aye, Miss Roxy, we do."

"So why may I not have something?"

"Ye can, m'lady. Only...." The older woman paused and glanced at the door.

"Come, Maggie. Only what?" Roxana moved toward her maid. Her nightdress swayed in the gentle breeze from the open window. Impatient, she wanted to get out of her nightgown and put on her riding clothes.

"Well, m'lady," Maggie refused to meet the eyes of her mistress. "His Lordship did say that no matter how hungry ye might be, I should offer ye only gruel, or perhaps some milk toast."

"Gruel? Milk toast?" Roxana's green eyes looked wider against her pale skin. "But I'm famished! I need food. In the last six days I've had but tea and his damned brew. Look at me!" She pinched her waist, secretly pleased with her weight loss. "You've been after me to put on some weight, and now I'm skin and bones."

"Aye, m'lady, but Lord Bristol said that yer body would not be able to handle a heavy meal after being ill for so long."

"His Lordship! His Lordship!" Roxana screamed, unable to hold her temper any longer. "Maggie, who is mistress here? Who gives the orders in place of my uncle?"

"Why. . . ." The maid shuffled her feet. "Ye do, m'lady. Only you've been ill, and Lord Bristol has yer uncle's permission—."

"He had my uncle's permission to take me home. That was that!"

"Nay! Not only that. Why, yer uncle was here for several days. He was quite concerned about ye. 'Tis only because His Majesty wanted the master in Dublin that he left his Lordship here in his place."

Roxana pressed her lips together angrily. "So he gave orders that Sebastian Steele was to be obeyed in his stead." The bile rose to her throat and she swallowed it back. Was everyone against her? How could her uncle do this to her? She clenched her fists and felt tears shimmering in her eyes. Frustrated, Roxana sat down on the bed.

Taking a deep breath, she realized that there was still Dory. Dory understood her and would help her. She would, she decided, go along with Steele's dictates—for now. Let him think that he had her at his command. Wasn't she supposed to befriend him?

Forcing herself to be pleasant, she looked at her maid. "Very well, Maggie. I will bow to Lord Bristol's . . . superior knowledge." She made a face. "You may bring me some . . . gruel."

"Aye, Miss Roxy." Maggie's brown eyes lit

up happily. "I'm glad ye be minding him. I would not want to cross that man."

Roxana felt a shiver go down her spine. Yes, she supposed Steele could be quite cruel. That only meant she had to proceed with even more caution than before.

"I'll bring yer food right away," the maid said, starting to the door.

"I'd like some water to wash with first." It would be silly to ask for a bath. Steele would probably forbid that as well.

Elated that her mistress was not causing problems, Maggie answered, "To be sure. I'll have it for ye in a moment—no more."

As Maggie closed the door, Roxana sank back onto the pillows. That damned Steele. How he plagued her! Her gaze wandered to the top of the canopy. Well, she would get around him—somehow. And she had to do it while being pleasant to him. She clenched her fists again. Aye, she would be pleasant to him—so pleasant that he would not know what had hit him.

Five minutes later Maggie's son, Charley, brought up the first basin of hot water.

"Wait, Charley."

"Yes, m'lady?" The boy turned about expectantly.

"Would you fetch Dory for me?"

"Me father?"

Roxana nodded. "Tell him to come here in two hours' time. You'll do that, won't you?"

"Aye, m'lady."

"And, Charles, when you tell him, make sure that he is alone. 'Tis a secret." She paused. "I will ask Cook to give you a special treat from the kitchen."

"Oh, to be sure!" The boy's eyes lit up. He ran from the room then, forgetting to close her door and returning in a moment to shut it.

Roxana smiled to herself, rather pleased. Glancing toward her wardrobe, she began to wash. Well, two hours should be time enough for Dory. Maybe he could also do something to distract Steele so that she could get away unnoticed.

Closing her eyes for a moment, Roxana realized that she was getting tired again. Even if she was not as well as she would have liked, she had to go tonight.

The gruel was brought in by Erin, Dory's eldest daughter. Roxana stared at the tray in her lap and made a face, then glancing up, realizing that the girl was still there. "Do you need something more, Erin?"

"Nay, m'lady. Only that Lord Bristol said as I was not to leave the room 'til ye had eaten."

"Why does the man have to torture me so?" Roxana exploded.

"Yer not angry with me, are ye, m'lady?"

Roxana sighed and blinked away the fatigue she was feeling. She had to fight it. There were still several hours of riding ahead of her.

"No, Erin, I am not angry with you." She lifted the spoon and took a mouthful of the tasteless porridge. "At least you could have put some milk and sugar in it."

Erin shifted uncomfortably. "Nay, m'lady. His Lordship said that would not serve to heal ye." She paused. "Shall I take it away?"

Roxana stared at the bowl. She had to eat the stuff. She could not afford to have Sebastian Steele tromp in here and find her getting ready to leave—all because she would not eat this . . . mush.

Forcing herself, she took several more spoonfuls, swallowing them quickly with the tea Erin had also brought—being first assured that it was not one of Steele's herbal brews. Then she pushed the bowl away. "Please, Erin. Couldn't you throw the rest away and tell Lord Bristol that I ate it?"

"Well, m'lady, he'll question me," Erin replied unhappily. "I know that he will."

"But I absolutely cannot tolerate this gruel. I'll give you that watered tabby you like so, if only you'll get rid of this . . . vile concoction."

After a moment, Erin nodded. Roxana felt tremendous relief as the girl took the bowl and dumped the rest of the contents out the window. Roxana wished she had thought of it herself—but, nevertheless, she needed Erin's agreement all the same.

"Good," Roxana said. "Now, tell his Lordship that I have gone back to sleep and do not wish to be disturbed again this night."

Erin looked at her. "Will you truly be asleep, m'lady?"

Roxana sucked in her breath. "But of course

71

I will." If she could not fool Erin, how could she fool Steele? "Do you doubt me?"

"Oh, nay!" Erin colored. "'Tis only I wonder if I could have the dress—in exchange, m'lady. Ye see, I am sweet on Rupert Hamilton, and if he saw me in that, he would. . . ."

Roxana felt relief wash over her. So Erin hadn't doubted her. She thought the girl foolish for giving her heart to a man like Rupert, but that was not Roxana's affair. "I would rather wait a day or so, Erin, to see that Lord Bristol does not doubt your story and does not bother me further this night."

Frowning, the girl nodded and, taking the empty bowl, hurried away as Roxana rose from the bed. Steadying herself for a moment by the bedpost, she began quickly to dress. Once ready, she paced before the window.

Startled by a knock, she froze.

"It's Dory, m'lady," came the comforting words.

"Come in—quickly," Roxana responded. "Shut the door behind you."

Dory did as he was told and then turned to look at his mistress. The room was lit by just one well-shaded candle, so that should anyone look up, he would assume her to be asleep.

"M'lady, why are ye up and dressed? Surely ye not be planning to go this night?"

"Of course I am, Dory. I have to. I promised Gilpatrick I would meet him."

"But, Miss Roxy, yer not yet well."

She glared at him. Her teeth were clenched as she spoke. "I am fine, Dory. Truly, I am."

"M'lady. . . ." There was a warning note in Dory's voice.

"Don't tell me that you have gone against me, too?" Roxana's nostrils flared.

"No one is against ye, m'lady. As true as I am Irish, I would never go against ye. It only be that. . . ."

"That what?" she snapped.

"Only that I fear fer yer health. And I do believe that ye sadly misjudge m'Lord Bristol."

Roxana's eyes narrowed. Her body was beginning to ache again. She longed to return to bed—but she couldn't. "And how have I misjudged him? Were you not the one who told me that you did not care for his eyes? That he seemed to know too much?"

"Aye, that I did. And I do still think it. He has got the devil's very eyes, m'lady, and he can stare clear through to yer soul, if he has a mind." Dory crossed himself. "But, m'lady, he does care for ye."

"Oh? You mean because he brought me home? Dory," she pleaded with her servant, "don't you realize? The man just wants whatever reward my uncle will give him. And he beds whatever ladies he thinks can advance his career."

Dory shrugged impassively. "That may be true—and it may not. But he stayed by ye throughout yer illness."

Roxana felt the lump in her throat as she forced herself to swallow her tears. She was glad that the room was dim. "All right," she conceded. "Perhaps in his own way the man does care something for me—as well as for the reward my uncle's gratitude will bring him. But what has that to do with my meeting Gilpatrick tonight?"

Dory planted his feet and took his stand. "Lord Bristol says that it will be several days before yer well. He says yer not to leave your room this day, nor tomorrow. He says—."

Roxana stamped her foot. "I do not care what he says! What I say is that *I am fine*." Already she felt tired, but she dared not admit it. "I am going to meet Gilpatrick tonight, and you are to saddle Fire for me. You may come with me if you are worried, but go I will."

"Nay, m'lady, I will not do it. Lord Bristol had us all swear that we'd take no shenanigans from ye."

"He *what*?" Roxana's eyes went wide. She could feel the tears stinging. "Dory, don't you see?" she pleaded. "He must suspect something. He is trying to prevent me from seeing Gilpatrick."

"I shall go to Gilpatrick, if you wish, m'lady."

"No!" she cried. "Dory, he would recognize you instantly. Besides, I cannot write this message. I must tell him."

"You have written before."

"This is different," Roxana said stubbornly. True, she had noted down the facts that Berwick had given her—the dates of Lauzun's arrival and departure, and his expected reappearance with the new troops—but she had not written out her request that she be relieved of the impossible task of befriending Steele.

Dory turned toward the door. "If ye be well tomorrow, I might consider helping ye; but if ye go this night, 'twill be without my assistance."

"Dory!" Roxana ran after him. "Dory, be reasonable." Tears were streaming down her cheeks now. "Dory." She pulled at his arm. "I must go. I must!"

"Nay," the servant said impassively. "Gilpatrick will wait. He will come again for two nights running if need be. Is that not your way?"

Defeated, Roxana nodded and pulled back. "Aye."

"Then go tomorrow or the next day."

Roxana took a deep breath to steady her nerves. Well, she would go on her own then. Time was of the essence. "All right," she said suddenly, hoping that her servant would be convinced. "All right. Tomorrow then."

Dory nodded, and again started to go.

"Wait a moment."

"Aye?"

"I am famished, Dory. Could you find a piece of meat or two or a pastry in the kitchen for me?"

Dory looked somber. "I donna rightly know, m'lady. I'll have to ask his Lordship."

Roxana turned away in frustration as Dory left, and then opened her mouth, horrified. Steele must not know that Dory had visited her! She raced out the door after him. Dory had already turned the hall corner, and Steele's voice boomed in greeting from beyond.

Cursing, Roxana hurried back to her room and sank down on the dressing chair. What was she to do now?

Weakly, she rested her head against the wall. It seemed that all the wind had suddenly gone out of her. Steele was indeed the devil, for he had bewitched all of her loved ones against her—even Dory, who knew how important her mission was. Full of anger and self-pity, she wiped away her tears. Despair crept over her. She was completely alone.

She *had* to ride this night. If she could no longer trust Dory, whom could she trust?

The door to her room opened. Without looking up, Roxana tensed as she felt Steele's presence. Finally she glanced at him, and felt her heart in her mouth. She felt a strange satisfaction seeing him, even though she knew he meant trouble.

"It seems that being made a peer of the realm has given you airs, Lord Bristol."

"Now why do you say that, m'lady?" His eyes took in everything about the room.

"Because . . . you are turning all the servants against me."

His low laugh caused shivers to go through her. He smiled. "Oh, come now, Roxana. That's a little melodramatic, even for you."

"No, it is not!" She stood, forgetting her clothes.

The pregnant silence between them was as

if the hangman's rope had just tightened about her neck—as if the floor was about to drop from below her.

His voice was soft, but the menace was fully there. "Were you planning to ride, or do you always sleep dressed like that?"

The flush crept up her face. Her eyes met his, but inside she could feel her whole body trembling. Her stomach tightened. There was no sense in lying to him. As Maggie had said, he was not one to cross.

"Yes, I was planning to ride. What of it?"

"At night?" His gray eyes seemed almost black now as he assessed her and then lit another candle.

She shrugged. If she spoke, her voice would betray her trembling.

"I see," he stated evenly, continuing to un-nerve her with his stare.

Again there was silence as her heart pounded.

"Why?"

She shrugged again, swallowing hard, wishing she could sit down, yet not wanting to show him any weakness.

"I . . . wanted to ride. You would not let me out today."

"And what makes you think I will let you tonight?"

"I am not asking your permission." She turned toward the door and opened it.

Instantly his hand was on her shoulder, holding her in a powerful grip. "Lady Roxana, you forget not only that has your uncle entrusted me with your care, but also that I am bigger and stronger than you—especially," he added, "in your weakened state."

Roxana continued to stare ahead out the door. The lump burned her throat and tears stung her eyes, but she would not turn to look at him. Finally, after another moment of silence, she said, "You are hurting me."

His pressure loosened, but he did not drop his hand.

She forced herself to turn. "I feel quite well, and I wish to go for a ride. You may accompany me, if you like." She could lose him, if she had to.

"I do not care to ride this evening. I care about restoring your health, so that I can deliver you back to your uncle."

She glared at him.

"Take off your clothes."

Her mouth dropped. Regaining her composure, she hissed, "I knew you were low—but not that low!"

"Roxana, you will take off your riding clothes and return to bed." His voice had a coldness to it that chilled even her, and his eyes had taken on a silver glint that scared her. He glanced about the room. "You may go behind the screen, if you desire."

Dear Lord, what she wouldn't do for the power to . . . to wring his neck, or something. With a look of hatred, she shook free of his grip and took three long steps across the room. She went behind the screen, and slowly began to take off her clothes.

"I haven't all night."

She heard him moving about the room and wondered what he was doing, but didn't dare look.

"You don't have to stay," she responded curtly.

"Oh, indeed I do."

"Why?"

"Just do as I say, Roxana. You are treading on dangerous waters." He handed her a fresh nightdress around the edge of the screen. "Put your clothes over the top."

Reluctantly, she did as he said.

"I intend to see you firmly tucked into bed."

Grimacing, Roxana dressed.

"You may come out when you are properly attired."

There seemed no point in delaying matters, so she emerged.

"Lovely. Very lovely," Sebastian said admiringly.

"Why do you have my riding clothes in your hands?"

"Because I am taking them to my room. You haven't given me much cause to trust you, Roxana. I wouldn't put it past you to try to ride, despite this . . . incident."

Damn the man! It was almost as if he could read her mind.

"Am I right?" A smile quirked his lips as she glowered at him.

"Yes, my lord," Roxana said sarcastically. "You are right, my lord." She gave a curtsy. "As in all things, my lord, you are perfectly correct."

Despite himself, he laughed. "Well," he

said, his tone softening somewhat, "at least I am now getting honest answers." The silver light gleamed in his eyes. "Would you care to tell me where you planned to ride?"

Her green eyes narrowed. "I told you. I just intended to go out. I . . . like riding in the moonlight."

"Do you now?" He raised a brow. "To my knowledge, only witches ride in the moonlight."

Roxana took a deep breath. "If there is nothing more you'd like to say, I'll go to bed."

Boldly, but trembling inside, she walked past him, her nightdress brushing against him. For a brief moment, she thought he was going to stop her—but he didn't. She slipped into bed.

Sebastian walked to her bed and paused beside her. "I warn you, I'll not take much more of your mischief, Roxana. I am not your darling uncle, whom you obviously have twisted about your little finger. My temper is quite a bit shorter than his, and I'm nearly at the end of my rope with you. If you push me too far, you shall undoubtedly end up over my knees, getting a good paddling."

Roxana dug her nails into her palm to keep her voice calm. "That is for children."

Sebastian brushed a loose curl from her pale brow. She wanted to move away, but didn't—or rather couldn't, as she felt the strange warmth spread through her.

"Aye, Roxana, paddling is for children—but

when you act like a child, you shall be treated as such. Now, would you like some hot milk sent up?"

Unable to speak, she shook her head.

Pulling back, he shrugged. "I am sure whomever you were to meet this night will understand your situation."

Roxana stiffened in alarm. How much did he know?

"Meanwhile," he added, "I have locked your windows and will also lock your door."

"No!" Roxana cried, bolting from the bed. "No! Don't lock me in!"

Sebastian was already at the door. Eyeing her unsympathetically, he turned and closed the door behind him. She heard the click of the metal even as she began her pounding. "Please, don't lock me in!" she cried again, feeling the terror and the panic that had accompanied such moments when she'd been a child.

"Please!" She no longer cared that her fists hurt from pounding or that her throat hurt from crying. "Please, open the door!" she shrieked, hysterical now. Steele's footsteps faded down the hall. Roxana sank to the floor, weeping uncontrollably.

It was Dory, stopping his Lordship in the hall, who informed him of Roxana's fears and of her brutal childhood experiences.

"Good God!" Sebastian cried, angry with both the servant and himself. "Why did I not know of this?"

Quickly he found the key and retraced his

steps. How could he have been so insensitive? It was one thing to prevent the girl from doing harm to herself, but it was quite another to drive her wild with fear. His heart went out to her as he heard her crying on the other side of the door, and with difficulty he pushed it open against her fallen weight.

She was still sobbing. Sebastian bent down and picked her off the floor, holding her head to his chest as he tried to calm her tears. "It's all right, Roxana. I'm sorry, my little minx. I did not mean to frighten you so. Dory only now told me of your fears."

She was still crying. She wanted to stop, but could not. She wanted to show him how strong she was, and yet everything seemed too much for her. Her crying started afresh.

Sebastian carried her slender weight to the bed and sat with her, holding her until her sobs had subsided, until her eyes had closed and she breathed more calmly.

Swallowing the lump in his own throat, Sebastian brushed another stray curl from her forehead. "Where were you headed, my little Roxana? I wish you would tell me. If you do not, my jealous nature will force me to find out on my own."

He stared down at her angelic pale face and long dark lashes, and felt his heart opening once again. She was now dozing in his arms. Bending, he brushed his lips gently against hers. She would have to come to him on her own—he could not force one of her spirit.

Again, he kissed her.

"Kept him waiting . . . ," she murmured.

A frown creased Sebastian's brow. Laying Roxana's head on the pillows, he carefully covered her. He did not, however, secure the door. He had no heart to now.

Chapter Eight

THE STORM CLOUDS ROLLED IN AS IN A DONNY-brook. Roxana pressed her nose to the casement glass, staring out. She was dressed in a quilted red silk housecoat, which well complemented her glossy dark hair and kept off the chill. Behind her, the crackling fire made the room cozy, but since her hair was now dry she saw no reason to sit there idly.

Glancing up at the clouds again, anxiety twisted her stomach. She wondered how long it would be before the storm passed. Perhaps she would be lucky and there would be no storm. She hated riding in the rain, and it would certainly do her health little good—but if it had to be done, then it had to be done. Gilpatrick would return tonight to await her, she knew. Shivering with an internal chill, she thought of the look in Steele's eyes when he had found her last night. What would happen this night? How could she convince him that he should allow her to ride—without telling him anything of where she wanted to go?

Allow, indeed. The idea galled her. That he should have the power to "allow" her anything was absurd. He was not her guardian— and even Uncle Patrick was not as strict with her. Thinking of Steele momentarily made her strangely dizzy. She closed her eyes briefly, and felt her heart hammering as her mind cleared. Nay, he was of no importance to her. She took a deep breath, moving restlessly over to the bedpost.

Presently, she studied the wash water still in the bath. She supposed she should be grateful to him for "allowing" her a bath. Her blood boiled again. Why should she be at his mercy?

Flipping her heavy, dark hair from her shoulders, Roxana glanced in the mirror. She debated putting it up, but decided against it. Later, after Steele had visited, she would dress. Thank heavens she had a second riding outfit.

Her skirt flared as she turned once more toward the window. She regarded the gray clouds uneasily and heard the booming thunder, which reminded her of Steele in his anger. Now pacing back and forth, pounding one fist against the flat of her palm, Roxana knew there had to be some way to win Steele over, to make him trust her, to make him. . . .

Pausing, she felt her heart give a funny jerk. Had he been holding her last night? A chilling sensation went through her. She could not recall the evening clearly. She remembered that he had locked her in, and that she had gone into a panic. Her face flushed just thinking of it. She should have been able to control herself.

Why had she allowed herself to be so helpless? She tried to recall what had happened afterward, but it seemed like a sweet, wonderful dream. Someone strong and gentle had been holding her and soothing her fears.

Blood rushed quickly through her body, heating her face even more than the fire had.

Goodness, but she was becoming silly! It must be from her illness. Perhaps it had been Dory?

She winced again, knowing she deceived herself. But surely Sebastian Steele was not the type of man to hold her and comfort her. All he cared about was the gift her uncle would give him—was that not so? Of course it was! Her heart still jerked irregularly.

She sank into her chair. Within her, Roxana was aware of a sense of longing and a deep sense of loneliness. Tears sparkled in her green eyes. Quickly, she brushed them away. It was true, she admitted to herself, that she would dearly love to have someone—someone who would love her totally, who would take her into his arms—but, she sighed, until this war was over there was little chance of that.

Returning her attention to the fire, she leaned back in the chair and stared at the blue gold flames. Absentmindedly, she picked up a piece of toast, now cold, that had been brought to her earlier. There had to be some way around Steele—some way she could convince him.

Closing her eyes, Roxana felt the fire's warmth on her face. What would Alexander the Great have done in such a situation? She grimaced. Alexander would not have worried over something like this. Alexander was a man, and would not have been hindered so!

Closing her eyes again, she recalled last night's conversation with Steele. Had they not been arguing about her being a woman or a child? Roxana had to admit that, yet again, Steele was right. She *had* been acting like a child. Maybe . . . maybe if she acted more like a woman? . . . Did not Lady Conway— according to rumor—recently receive that gold pendant from him? Well, she wanted something far more precious than jewels. She smiled to herself. She was sure she could do it. She had to do it.

"Pleasant thoughts, I take it."

The deep timbre of his voice startled her. Roxana felt her heart racing as she opened her eyes to find Steele sitting directly across from her. She hadn't even heard him enter! Her heart continued to hammer. How long had he been here?

She stared at him, gathering her thoughts. "It was a pleasant dream. I was. . . ." Roxana searched her mind frantically as a blush crept up her pale skin. "I was thinking of you just now."

"Oh?" He looked at her narrowly. Dory was right. He did seem to see into her very soul.

Uncomfortably, she squirmed slightly. "Don't you believe me?" She met his look and forced herself to smile.

Sebastian gave an impassive shrug. What—didn't he care if she thought of him?

"Well, 'tis true!" She stood, agitated.

Sebastian stood with her and came over to her side. "No need to upset yourself, Roxana." His fingers gently brushed her cheek as he smoothed the hair from her face. She felt the warmth of his touch—it seemed to burn her skin as the strange glow went through her body. Inside she trembled. Her eyes met his and she inhaled sharply.

"I shall believe you," he said evenly, "if that is what you want."

It wasn't the only thing she wanted, but it would have to do for the moment.

His hand brushed her other cheek and then slipped beneath the weight of her hair as he gazed at its dark loveliness. Roxana felt her pulse pound wildly. She had to keep in control of her thoughts and emotions, but how was she to think when he did this to her? Of course, he must realize she was trying to manipulate him. He was doing this on purpose. He was testing her!

Fury rose in her, but Roxana could not speak for the other emotions that were overwhelming her. Her large green eyes were wide as she stared at him. She felt both a desire to be in his arms, and . . . she didn't know what else exactly. She had to take control. Her emotions must not run away with her.

His eyes met hers again and she caught her breath in her throat. Her stomach knotted. His look was . . . well, soft and warm.

"Your hair is lovely like this, with the fire playing on it. It has bluish highlights." His voice was tender and gentle—a tone she had never before heard from him.

"'Tis . . . from my mother," Roxana answered, forcing herself to speak, realizing that she could think very little beyond the heightening senses of her body. What was happening to her? She had to think!

"'Tis a shame that this style is not in fashion." He again brushed her hair back so that every nerve in her seemed taut. "I believe," he continued, smiling gently, "that you would have even more court suitors than you have already. Your uncle would have to chase them away."

Roxana grimaced.

"You do not like having suitors?"

She flushed. "There is no one from the court who—They are all pups or fops."

Both his brows raised. His hands dropped from her hair. "Is that a fact? All?"

Recalling her plan of the moment, she hastily corrected herself. "Well, not all." Her voice was soft as she lowered her eyes effectively.

Sebastian's fingers stroked her chin, causing her blood to course rapidly. Did he detect her tremble? Did he know what he was doing to her mind? She raised her eyes to his. His voice was coaxing and yet hoarse. "Tell me, Roxana, my little imp, who is that one exception." He paused, as if it was difficult for him to speak, too. But surely not. Surely, he had control over himself! "Perhaps I could put in a good word for him with your uncle."

It was difficult to meet his eyes now. She had not planned it this way. She had not planned that her heart would pound so.

"Come. Look at me." His voice was gentle. "Who is he, Roxana? I will keep a secret. Is it this Alexander? I know of no one of that Christian name at court, but then I am not infallible. Or perhaps it is some local fellow."

It was Roxana's turn to be puzzled. She stared at him. "There is no Alexander at court." The flush crept up her face. "Leastwise, not that I know of." She pulled away from him now and walked to the window, wondering how she was going to handle this. What did he know of Alexander? Did he realize it was her code name? Fear joined her torrent of emotions.

"Nay," she paused, stopping to stare at the clouds, wondering how soon the storm would come and how long it would take. Buying time, she repeated, "There is no Alexander at court."

His presence was behind her. She could feel the solid warmth of his body even before his hands touched her shoulders.

"Pray, then, why did you call out his name?"

"I did?" Confused now, she turned to face him. She felt embarrassed. He had caught her in another childhood weakness. Moreover, the situation was dangerous.

"Aye, m'lady, you did." His voice was grave. He seemed to hang on her every syllable.

"Oh." She glanced away toward the window, and then again at him. "Alexander is . . . Alexander the Great."

"What?" There was amusement in his voice. From the look in his eyes, it was clear that he did not believe her.

"To be sure! Have you not heard of Alexander the Great?"

"What military man has not? But pray, Roxana, my little imp, what has he to do with you?"

Roxana flushed. "'Tis clear that, being a man, you know nothing of Alexander's other feelings."

"Oh? What makes you say that?"

"Well." She spread out her hands helplessly. "You question what is obvious. Do you not know the story of Alexander and Roxana?"

His eyes narrowed to slivers of ice. Did he think she was playing him for a fool? "Tell me about it," he said simply.

Flushing, she began, "It was a fantasy of my mother's, I believe."

"Go on."

"There is nothing much to say, except that Alexander, while conquering the kingdom of Bactria, met the dark, lovely Princess Roxana, daughter of Qxyartes. He had captured the fortress stronghold, and proceeded to fall madly in love with her. He"—she flushed again—"carried her off and married her shortly after, and"—her voice quavered as she briefly looked up—"she loved him as well." Memories of her own mother flooded her, and she was forced to pause for a deep breath. "My mother named me Roxana in hopes that I would find. . . ." The lump in her throat was constricting. She swallowed the pain of embarrassment. ". . . my own Alexander to . . . carry me off."

There was a momentary silence while her heartbeat quickened. Suddenly, Sebastian broke out in laughter.

Tears came to Roxana's eyes. "Don't laugh at me!" Her humiliation turned to anger. "I should not have told you. I knew that you would never understand."

Sebastian gained control of himself. "I am sorry, Roxana." His voice was contrite. "I apologize most humbly." He made a sweeping bow. "If only you knew how it affected me."

"I can"—the lump in Roxana's throat was still painful—"see how it affected you."

"Nay." His hand stroked her neck, causing her pulse to quicken. "I do not think you do know. You see, I was. . . ." He paused.

"You were what?" She waited for something of this mysterious man to be revealed to her.

He gave her an odd sort of smile. "Never mind, my little imp. Later, I will tell you. Not now. For the moment, it is good enough for me to know that your Alexander is only a myth."

Roxana's eyes widened as she stared at him. He seemed to absorb her whole attention, for her mind was functioning only on a primitive level; yet she was aware enough to know that there was something here she could make use of—if she wanted. She wasn't sure what it was, however; nor was she even sure that she wanted to use it.

He pulled away. "I believe it is time for me to go. You should rest."

"Nay!" Things were not going as she'd planned, but she could not let him leave. "I am fine, truly. Please, stay a bit longer." She stood next to him. Tears were again in her eyes. "I do so wish you would let me outside today." Her hands, tiny against his chest, touched him pleadingly. She felt her heart pounding wildly as she forced herself to think of what to do next. Looking up into his eyes, she said, "It would be such a beautiful day for a ride."

"Beautiful?" Sebastian glanced out the window. "I would hardly call those storm clouds beautiful."

"Oh, but they are." Her hands were stroking his chest. "It is a perfect time to ride, with the wind in your hair and the smell of the sea in the air. You were perfectly right yesterday, my lord." She lowered her eyes. "But today, I feel as if I can ride. In truth, I feel quite suffocated here in my room."

"Do you, now?"

"I do." Desperate to convince him, she boldly reached her hands up to his neck. "Please, Sebastian." How easily his name came to her lips. "Please, let me ride."

Standing on tiptoe, she raised her lips upward to meet his, and felt his surprise and resistance. Her tender skin touched the bristle of his mustache, and Roxana instinctively pushed forward.

His hesitation lasted but a moment before his arms went about her, supporting her, holding her to him. His darting tongue traced her lips, parting them. She opened herself for his taste, exploring him in the same manner.

Never had she been kissed like this, but her hammering heart told her to follow his lead. Again, she parted her lips for him as her fingers massaged the muscles at his neck. Forgetting everything but his touch, she sank against his chest. Her whole body seemed to tingle with delights as his hands traveled her back.

Sebastian's voice was hoarse as he pulled away. "Pray, my little sweet, what is the meaning of this?"

Left in a void, Roxana felt numb. She did not answer.

"For a maiden, you have a passionate skill, my Roxana; but I need an explanation." His hand touched her cheek ever so gently, and Roxana knew that she wanted that hand to touch her everywhere, to warm her entire being—but no, that could not be! Her mind struggled to make sense of what was happening. That was not in her plans. . . .

"I wait for an answer, my darling Roxana."

She winced, both enjoying that term and yet wishing he meant it more fully.

"The . . . meaning?" Roxana acted puzzled. "Why, my lord"—she lowered her lashes—"I meant only to show you that I am . . . I am not the child you take me for."

He laughed quietly. "No, my pet, you are not a child. At least, at this instant you are not. I do trust, however, that you know what it is you are really doing."

"Of course I know what I am doing! I have told you. I am showing you that I am woman enough to care for myself—and to decide if I should ride or not."

"I see." He dropped his hand from her shoulder, eyeing her coldly. Suddenly she saw the ice in his eyes and felt the chill. What had happened to the warm, wonderful tone his voice had had just moments before?

Roxana could not know how confused she looked. Sebastian relented in spite of himself. "You realize, little minx, that were I not in total control of myself this very moment, you could have started something that might have had disastrous results for us both."

"But I—."

"Roxana, it is time you stopped having your own way over every whim. I do believe that you need a much firmer hand to guide you."

"I can guide myself, thank you." She felt the coldness in her own heart. Did he always have to be so condescending? She glared him now, angry both with him and with herself. She was realizing only now that she would not have minded if their kiss had gone farther— and yet now he was rejecting her.

He ignored her remark. "Since your uncle has put you in my care, I'll not abuse his good offices—but I would dearly love to take a branch to you!" He turned to leave. "You may not ride today, Roxana. Perhaps tomorrow." At the door, he glanced back at her. "In the future, remember: you may not be so lucky with the men you incite. There are other ways of convincing me that you can take care of yourself, my dear."

Flushed, she stared at him. Not knowing what to say, she looked at the fire.

He touched the door handle. "I want you to rest yet another day. I will have Maggie bring up some food."

"Please," she whispered, her voice taut with fear, "don't lock the door."

Sebastian's features softened. "Nay, Roxana, I shall not lock it." He left then, closing the oak door firmly behind him.

Emotions churned within her as her tears began to flow. Picking up a volume of poetry, Roxana flung it after him with all her fury. The book cracked against the door and slid to the floor.

Down the hall, Sebastian shook his head.

Chapter Nine

OUTSIDE, THE RAIN HAD BEGUN TO FALL. So the storm had arrived after all. Roxana felt it in her heart, as well. Over and over she thought of the kiss, of the special way Sebastian had made her feel for that one moment. Yes, she had wanted it to go farther; and much as she tried to tell herself that Steele was her enemy, she knew that she was as taken in by his charms as was every other woman in Ireland, England and France.

She stamped her foot and spun about. Of all the men in Ireland, why must it be he? It seemed that love was a sickness to be dreaded and feared rather than sought!

A lonely chill seemed to seep around her heart. He still thought her a child. Tears again came to her eyes. With all the other women about him, there was little chance that he would ever take her seriously.

She sank down into the feather cushions of the bed, feeling miserably alone. She did not wish to sleep, even though her head ached. Still, she did need the strength for tonight's ride. She had to go. She would have to find a way to leave without Steele's knowing it.

If he knew what she really did—her fist clenched in righteous fury—he would not consider her a child, then. Yet, if he knew, he would probably despise her more than he now did.

Roxana wiped the tears from her eyes with her sleeve. There was precious little chance for him to be her Alexander. The knot in her throat thickened as she tried to swallow. So she would continue as she was, fighting the feelings that she had for him, and hoping that one day they would disappear.

Closing her eyes, she fell asleep with her hand on the cheek where he had this morning touched her.

By evening the storm had blown over. Roxana was thankful for that. The stars were just now coming out and it promised to be a clear, if chilly, night.

Roxana slipped into her plain dark breeches and full black shirt of flannel, eyeing herself in the mirror. She pulled her hair back into a knot and capped it. Men's clothes were so much easier for riding than women's. She wondered if she would be warm enough. Yes, with her cape, she should be.

She paused as she heard movement outside

her door. No! Her heart hammered. He could not catch her again—not a second time. Erin had told her only moments ago that he was dozing by the fire in the library, but that the servants had been alerted to let him know if Roxana stirred. Erin had volunteered this information—but, of course, she was well pleased with the dress.

Holding her breath, Roxana remained motionless.

Footsteps passed her door. A chill went down her spine.

Aware that her head was beginning to ache, she took one of the herbal powders that he had left for her earlier and tried to force the pain out of her consciousness. She was already one day late. Would Dory have Fire saddled? Well, if not, she would do it herself. It wouldn't be the first time.

Slowly, she crossed the room. Her steps were dance-light, yet never had Roxana been so keenly aware of the creaking of the floorboards or of the furious hammering of her own heart. Her palms were sweating. Thank the Lord the library was not directly beneath her—or was it?

She could not recall! Her mind had blanked.

Reaching the window, she unfastened the latch. The noise seemed to echo in the room. Maybe she should try the stairs—but no, there were too many people about, and she could not wait for sleep to claim them all.

The lead casement creaked. Roxana's stomach tightened. Well, if he found her, she'd think of something. She stepped one foot on the ledge, and felt the brisk breeze from the river and noted the smell of the sea still in the air. Mist hung about the shore of the river and reached up to grab at the full moon.

It had been some time since she had been forced to leave in this fashion, but she was sure that the agility was still there. Certainly, her illness hadn't harmed her all that much. Why, then, was she shaking? Why did she feel so unsteady?

With one more glance back at the room—back at the bed, where she had bunched up the pillows and bedclothes under the coverlet—she took a deep breath. Reaching for the nearest limb, she lifted off the ledge.

Heart in her mouth, Roxana swung free. For just a frightening moment she wished she were back in bed, wished she were safe in comforting arms.

No! she scolded herself violently as relief flooded over her with the steadying of her hold. She must not think of that—of him. Sebastian Steele was her enemy and had to remain so. To allow herself to fall in love with the man would only bring heartache.

The stableboy was nowhere in sight. Roxana did not know if that was Dory's doing or not, but she was pleased nonetheless. She was less pleased to find that Fire had not been saddled.

After a moment's hesitation, Roxana mounted him bareback. She much preferred feeling the horse's thick muscles naturally moving beneath her. She enjoyed having total control and total sensation. The cape covering her, she picked up the reins. "Come on, Fire." She stroked his ears as she gently directed him out to the river road. "We're going to Dublin."

Fire snorted in response.

Sebastian awoke with a start. He had been dreaming about that little minx upstairs. Smiling to himself, he picked up the brandy glass. Letting the sweet warmth penetrate his senses, he sipped slowly, rolling the fiery taste on his tongue.

Absentmindedly, he stared into the blue gold, hypnotic flames. The soft light danced upon his face. It was easy to see that he was lost in thought.

Once again he savored the excellent French cognac. Patrick had good taste in brandy, as well as in women, Sebastian thought. It was too bad, however, that he had not dealt a firmer hand with his niece while he was raising her. It might have saved all of them a good deal of trouble now. But then, Sebastian mused, staring into the golden flickering fire, she would not have been the fascinating little imp that she was today.

He smiled broadly, thinking of her. Was she yet asleep? How inconvenient that he had such respect for his superior officer. He had never encountered such passion—and from one yet untaught in the ways of love! Sipping more of the golden liquor, he allowed himself to wonder appreciatively what it would be like once she had been taught the true meaning of love. He grinned.

The idea of making love to her luscious young body, of tumbling in embrace with her, forced Sebastian to quickly down the rest of his drink. He was responsible for her now. He must not think like that. Besides, passionate or not, Roxana was a woman to approach slowly and carefully.

He poured himself another measure. He wanted her first taste of love to be one she would enjoy and remember, not one she would recollect with fear.

Thinking of the girl, he set down his glass at his side. He would bring her some warm milk and go up to say good night.

As much as his heart went out to her, he knew, too, that—little elf that she was—it was hardly likely she would obey him. What would her reaction be when she saw the servant he had placed outside her door as a guard?

Sebastian grinned again as he left his study. She would be furious, no doubt, but he hoped it would teach her that he meant business.

At her door, he paused with the tray of steaming milk.

"There be no peep from her room, sir." Francis, Dory's other son, made a respectful bow.

"Is that a fact?" Sebastian smiled slightly, feeling hopeful. Maybe the girl was coming round sooner than he had expected. "You have not been asleep, have you, Francis, lad?" Cool gray eyes assessed the boy.

"Nay, my lord!"

Sebastian nodded as he opened the door. "Roxana?" He whispered. Noticing how low the fire had gotten, he made a mental note to ask the servants to build it a bit—it would not do for the girl to get another chill.

"Roxana," he called again softly, noticing that no movement had come from the bed. Maybe she was already asleep. If so . . . he placed the tray of milk down beside the bed—and cursed under his breath as he saw the pillows piled high in disguise.

Where the devil was she? Francis had said Roxana hadn't left the room. Of course, he might have fallen asleep and did not want to admit it.

The breeze from the open window attracted Steele's attention. In two strides he had reached the casement. With ice in his eyes, he stared at the road in the moonlight; and, as his lips pressed in anger, he saw the clearly outlined figure of a slightly built, but obviously experienced, rider pounding hard toward the Dublin road. There was no doubt in Sebastian's mind. She was a magnificent rider. Her body seemed to merge with the animal's as if they were one.

Even as he continued to watch, Roxana's cap came loose. With a defiant toss—either from irritation, or maybe just to taunt him— she shook her long, dark curls free in the wind, racing ahead like the wild and untamed spirit she was.

His heart seemed to stop for that moment.

It was obvious that she was riding toward Dublin. Steele had no idea why, but he intended to find out. If she was meeting someone special, then he would put a stop to it. Perhaps she was not as innocent as she appeared to be!

Sebastian stayed at the window, watching until he could no longer see her . . . and yet he continued to stay and stare. That girl was a thorn in his side—yet she was so free, so alive. Did he or any man have a right to try to tame her?

For just a moment, he tasted her kiss again.

His heart felt heavy as he turned on his heel and left the room.

It was nearly dawn by the time Roxana returned to Lucan. Carefully she climbed the tree to her room and entered by the window. Her whole body ached. She longed for one of Maggie's hot, salted baths to soothe her aches, but she dared not ring for her.

Exhausted, she slipped from her clothes and pushed them under the bed. Her mission had been a success. She'd met Gilpatrick and had given him the schedule of French landings. William had not known. He would be proud of "Alexander," Gilpatrick had said, and "Alexander" would be suitably rewarded when it came time for William to be established again at Whitehall.

Roxana, disguising her voice best she could,

had told Gilpatrick that she wanted aught but to be free of her current assignment—that of befriending Lord Bristol.

Gilpatrick had frowned, and had said that he would find out what he could. However, considering Steele's place at court, it was doubtful that the assignment would be rescinded—unless, of course, she simply could not do it.

"Of course I can do it!" Roxana had hissed, furious at the idea that Sebastian could get the better of her. She knew she could get information from him. The trouble was that she wasn't certain she could do it without involving her heart.

Roxana froze as she spied the tray by her bed. Had that been here before she had left? She did not think so.

Her hand went out to it, touching the silver cup of milk. She felt a chill go through her. Sebastian had brought this up to her—she knew that he had. She could feel his very presence in the metal. Did he then know of her departure?

Roxana shrugged. She was too tired to think of that tonight. She picked up the milk and quenched her thirst. She knew she would have to deal with him in the morning.

Aware of every protesting muscle in her body, aware of her head's pounding, she crawled between the smooth silken sheets and felt their chill against her naked body. She had not taken time to put on a nightdress, though sleepily she was aware she should have. What if Sebastian broke into her room? Well, he had no business being in here, anyway. Her eyes closed, her lids heavy as she realized that he had put something in the milk. He was in her thoughts before she slept.

Chapter Ten

Roxana stifled a yawn. She had slept late this morning, but that still had given her only a few hours of rest. The warmth of the sun felt good on her face as she slowly strolled down the river path, pausing every so often to pick a flower or smell a rose, or just to stare at the lush green meadows across the water. She should be glad that the ogre had "allowed" her out of her room. Instead, she felt only a melancholy sadness. Maybe the despair she was feeling was from the remains of her indisposition, or perhaps from her tiredness.

Roxana pulled her shawl closer about her slender shoulders, being careful not to step on the broken twigs—remnants of yesterday's storm.

Pausing again, she looked at the gleaming waters of the river Liffey as they lapped the stone wall before her.

Why in the world did she feel so sad?

Lost in thought, she turned again toward the shade of the wooded glen. Even from here she could smell the hyacinths and other flowers for which her uncle's gardens were famous. She loved Lucan, loved it almost as much as she loved her darling uncle.

Why would he not accept William as king? How could he support a man who had so humiliated his sister?

Brushing aside a low branch, she paused to listen to a songbird—so sweet, so gentle. Tears sparkled in her green eyes. Aye, the house and grounds were lovely and she was lucky to be enjoying them. It was not fair that her countrymen suffered so!

She turned, attempting to dry her eyes as she searched her pockets for a linen. Irritated as she found none, she used her sleeve, sinking down onto a low stone seat away from the water's edge.

As much as she might lie to herself, Roxana knew that her depression was not due just to her fatigue or the state of her country. It was also due in part to . . . that man.

She took a deep breath and inhaled the scent of the spring buds, as she tried to steady the trembling anger within her. He had not come to bid her good day this morning. In fact, she had not seen him at all.

It was true that she had slept far later than usual, but nevertheless she was much disappointed not to have seen him—and then to have learned from Maggie that he had gone to Dublin! He had not taken her, not said goodbye, not even mentioned he was going. . . .

Maybe it was just as well. Maggie said he had been in a foul mood, cursing and yelling at all the servants as she had never yet seen him do before.

Was it because of her? Did he suspect something? She was certain he had noted her absence. What would he do to her? Roxana was vexed to realize that she actually missed the man.

Ruefully, she stared at the perfect rose in her hand and stroked the velvet-smooth petals, wondering what he would say when he returned. At this moment, she felt rather like the flower—plucked from its bed of soft earth and at the mercy of whoever might pass. Tears came again. She sniffled.

"A farthing for your thoughts," a deep voice said. She was handed a linen, and a shadow darkened her lap.

Roxana's heart jumped to her throat. She felt her eyes widen. He had appeared out of nowhere! "I—I thought you were in Dublin. Maggie said—."

His eyes darkened to a coal black, and then lightened to an icy gray. He looked as if he had planned to say something and had then changed his mind. "I was," he stated simply, taking the bench beside her.

His hand touched her knee, and she could feel the warmth and pressure of his touch as her blood coursed rapidly through her body. She could say nothing.

"I am pleased to see you feeling better."

Roxana nodded slowly. Recalling Gilpatrick's insistence that she still remain friends with him—and recalling her own embarrassing reaction to the kiss the night before—she found her voice to respond. "I am." Lowering her thickly lashed lids, she found it difficult to play the grateful recipient of his attention when she was being torn in two ways. Her voice trembled. "And it is to you that I owe my health."

"Is that a fact?" There was a mocking tone in his voice that she did not like.

"But of course," she answered, with what she hoped sounded like sincerity. Her uncle had never doubted her little lies. Why was it that he saw through her so easily? She forced herself to look up and meet his gaze, and felt tears veiling her sight. "If . . . it were not for you, I would not have recovered so quickly."

"*That*," he said dryly, "is a fact. However, I wonder if you truly believe it." He went to stand at the water's edge. His strong back was to her, but his shoulders had rounded slightly, making him appear hurt and vulnerable at this moment.

Roxana suppressed an urge to run to him, to hug him, to tell him that she truly did believe it and truly did thank him.

"But I do." Her voice cracked ever so slightly. "Truly." She took a deep breath, hating the effect he was having on her. "Cannot I do even that without us arguing?"

Feeling her own heart heavy, she rose and went to stand behind him. Her hurt animated her tongue now, and before she could stop herself the words tumbled out. "'Tis true that I think you a braggart, a bore, a callous social climber and an abuser of women; but that does not mean I cannot be properly grateful for the time you spent with me—no matter what your motive might have been."

He turned toward her, seeing the pain in her eyes. "Well,"—his voice was softer—"at least I am getting an honest response for a change. One thing I cannot tolerate is dishonesty."

Roxana winced and hoped that he did not notice.

He smiled slightly as he regarded her. "Your thanks are accepted, though I cannot help but wonder what *your* motive was for that kiss the other day."

She flushed now, deeper than the rose she had been holding. "I . . . I told you. I wanted to show you that I am not a mere child—that I can take care of myself."

"Ah, yes, you did say that."

His eyes searched her face and then seemed directed toward her heart. It was almost as if he could see the pace at which it raced.

"Tell me, did I abuse you when you kissed me?"

Her color heightened once more. She wanted to say yes just to spite him, but she could not respond that way.

Tears sprang to her eyes. She blinked them back and lowered her lids. "No," she choked. "You—you did not."

"Good." His tone was approving. "We have yet another honest answer. Soon, little Roxana, we will have you telling me the truth the whole time."

Lifting her head, she glared at him. "Do you

doubt me often, my lord?" Her hands had gone to her hips and she clutched her skirt, ready to turn and run.

The sunlight danced in his eyes; the skin about them crinkled in delicate lines as his mouth turned up. "Only at times." His mood of the moment was light, but as his hand went to her shoulder, preventing her from departing, she knew there was more to come.

Feeling the warmth of his touch as it penetrated her skin, she felt the glow settling about her heart, despite her anger with him. In confusion she realized just how very handsome he was, with his deep-blue velvet coat and lighter-blue breeches. Blue suited him—so calm and yet so commanding. He was in style, yes; a fop—never.

"Tell me, Roxana, how did you sleep last night?"

She glanced at the hand on her shoulder, which had momentarily tightened, and then looked up at him as she bit her lip, wondering how much he knew. Finally, she responded, "Tolerably well."

This time his smile did not touch his eyes. They were cold as ice, and she shivered inwardly as he said, "I am glad. Why, then, are you squirming?"

"That, Lord Bristol, is because you are holding me too tightly. You do not like dishonesty, and I do not like being bruised."

He dropped his hand. "I am pleased to know you slept so well."

The ice of his eyes seemed to chill her heart. The deceptive softness of his voice made her heart thud. Why could she stand up to the king and not to this man?

"It is strange, however," he continued. "Looking at you—at the rings under your eyes—I would say that you slept none too well. However"—he smiled slightly, his eyes now gleaming with the sun—"there is an infallible test to see if a lady is well rested."

Roxana caught her breath. Anxiety tightened her stomach and fear clutched at her heart. "What is that?"

His all-knowing eyes centered on her lips. His finger traced their slender outline, creating dizzy sensations within her. "If a woman kisses well, then she has slept well."

She stiffened and pulled away. "That is a strange test. Why have I never heard it before?" Her nerves were taut. If he learned the truth—if he turned her in. . . . She thought of how it might affect her poor uncle. "I do not think that such a test exists. I also think that you must be mad."

The smile came again. "You are right. I must be mad. In truth, however, the test does exist." His eyes gleamed. "I, myself, have given it many times."

The green monster stabbed a spear at her heart.

"And it does work."

She took a breath as she tried to steady her emotions. "Are you asking me to kiss you?" Looking at him, her eyes narrowing, she felt the pressure of her throbbing temples as the blood rushed through them. "That—that is blackmail."

He stood but a few inches from her now. "It is." He grinned. "However, if you slept well, you need not worry."

"I need not worry at any account, for I did sleep well and I will not kiss you."

Sebastian shrugged, and glanced up and down the path. They were alone—just the two of them. "Very well, Roxana. I am indeed sorry to hear that you had such a poor night."

"But I didn't. I had a marvelous night."

"Oh?" He waited. The pause between them drove her crazy. In her innocence, she didn't know whether to believe him or not. Was he just taking advantage of her? Or baiting her for information? Conflicting emotions raged in her. If he wanted to kiss her because he wanted her. . . . She felt the lump in her throat. The idea of kissing him did please her. The idea of blackmail did not.

"What do you care whether I slept well or not?"

Sebastian lowered his voice. "Ah, but I do care, little Roxana." He paused. "It does matter. You see, Fire was not in his stable for much of the night."

"What!" She allowed her eyes to widen in astonishment and hoped that her surprised look would fool him. "Are you quite sure?" Her mouth suddenly became dry.

"Quite."

"But I—." She turned and picked up her skirts to flee.

"Where are you going now, m'lady?" The coldness in his voice frightened her. His hand again stopped her.

"To—to the stables. I had thought to speak with the boy there."

"I have done that already. He does not know who rode your horse."

Pretending indignation, she now faced him fully. Could she stare him down?

"Are you accusing me of disobeying you, my lord?" She narrowed her green eyes, forcing her anger to come through.

His gray eyes were like the waters of the river on a stormy day. She shivered with fear but would not look away.

"I said nothing on that matter."

"Oh." She flushed, backing down a bit as her color rose. She had given herself away! Damn the man for his tricks. "Then—then what are you saying?"

"Roxana. . . ." His hand slid up and down her neck, stroking it so that she shivered and trembled inside, so that she longed for his warmth, his touch, his kiss. "I am saying that a kiss from you would"—he grinned slightly— "convince me of your innocence."

"And . . . if I am not?" Her heart was nearly ready to stop. "Or . . . if I refuse?" She felt now like a trapped bird in a cage, fluttering desperately for release.

His eyes stared into hers, which were green pools of fear, as his fingers continued to create those magical sensations on her throat, on her face. His voice had a husky timbre to it that seemed to envelop her. "But you will not refuse, will you?"

Conscious only of his fingers delicately tracing the outline of her lips, conscious only of his eyes upon her and of the hypnotic desire to be in his arms, Roxana closed her eyes without responding, knowing that her silence was in fact an answer.

Smiling, Sebastian lowered his mouth to hers. His lips gently grazed her lips and then traveled down her neck, inflaming her senses, igniting her whole body.

A murmur came from somewhere—surely not from her.

His lips met hers again; his silver-tipped tongue parted her mouth, meeting only momentary resistance. She lifted her slender arms to go about his neck and felt herself succumbing to a wave of desire. As her blood coursed warm, Roxana let her hands stroke his neck. She kneaded the tight muscles there even as her tongue explored him, tasted him, touched him. She wanted and hungered for him with a fervor that made her senses spin.

Impulsively, she pressed closer to his body. She could feel his hard calling of desire through the material of their clothes, and another moan escaped her as she fought to bring him closer to her.

His magical hands were roaming her back, stroking her, caressing her.

Kissing him as deeply as she could, she felt the burning bristles of his mustache, the pain and pleasure as they rubbed her tender skin. Her fingers tightened in the curls of his hair.

What was she doing? This was far beyond her required assignment of befriending the man—but then few in William's employ knew of her true sex. And no one knew of the battles that now raged within her.

One of his traitorous hands slid over the front of her dress, caressing her soft, unbound breasts, stroking them, delighting them, igniting more fire within her.

Wanting yet more, Roxana pressed herself against him, pressed herself toward his hardness. She felt his nature calling out to her as his hand freed her left nipple—tugging at it, playing with it, pleasuring it. The warmth spread between her legs as his mouth left hers and descended to gently suck.

Roxana gave a gasp and moaned with delight as the unexpected onslaught created a warm sensation all over her body.

Quickly, Sebastian raised his head and backed away as he touched the still-throbbing softness back into its enclosure. It was, it seemed, his turn to blush. His mouth formed a thin line, frowning.

"I am sorry, Roxana. I had not meant for that to happen."

"No?" Her voice was weak. She swallowed hard, trying to fight down the impulse to throw her arms about his neck again and beg for more—beg to be freed from this gnawing hunger he had started within her.

With the greatest of effort, she remained calm. "I trust I passed your test." She felt his gaze roam her body. What was behind that dark storm she saw in his eyes?

"Aye," he said curtly. His face showed no emotion. Roxana could not tell if he believed her or not. In fact, she did not think he would ever believe her. Biting her lower lip, she again picked up her skirts, wondering what she should do now.

"If you'll excuse me, then, my lord, I think I will return to the house."

"Before you do, Roxana, you should know that I saw your uncle while I was in the city."

"And?" Her voice caught in her throat. Surely he had not told Uncle Patrick of his suspicions. Fear replaced the warm glow she had experienced moments before. He was coolly regarding her again, absorbing her with those damned gray, stonelike eyes. A shiver went through her as she wondered what unmerciful god had caused her to love a devil like this.

"You are returning to Dublin tomorrow."

This time her astonishment was genuine.

"Your uncle has left for the north to join His Majesty. I shall follow after I have seen you safe."

"But I—why must I go to Dublin, then? Why may I not stay here? I have done so in the past."

"In the past, Roxana, things were different. You are no longer the child you once were. It is not wise for a young woman to be alone at a time like this."

His voice was chilling her now.

"Surely, my lord"—she swallowed hard under his scrutiny, wishing she could read his mind—"considering the state of the city, with the soldiers upset and hungry, I would be far better off here with my servants and. . . ." She lowered her eyes, unable to face his gaze.

Sebastian frowned. "You will not be alone in Dublin."

"I won't?" Her gaze shot up again. Her heart gave an unbidden jump of joy. "But you just said that you were going north."

Was that a smile flickering across his lips? She could feel her own lips still burning. Damn those eyes of his. His smile disappeared before she could realize how she had given her feelings away.

"That is correct. I will be in the north with His Majesty's forces, laying siege to Derry and Enniskillen. You, my little imp, will stay with Ardella."

Deeply hurt, she stared at him wide-eyed, unable to believe what she had just heard. "Ardella?" Her voice cracked now with the pain that seemed to numb her heart.

"Pardon. Lady Conway."

"But I. . . ." She flushed deeply again. The tears came quickly to her eyes as jealousy squeezed her heart. "Was—was that whom you saw in the city this day?"

He regarded her a moment. The silence between them was unbearable. "Aye," he responded, watching her. "She, among others. Lady Conway says she will be happy to watch over you, to guard you and see that you do not get into any mischief while your uncle and I are away."

"Mischief? Me? Pray, my lord, I think that with your passion for playing with women's feelings, it is *you* who had best watch the mischief. From what I hear, the northern women do not take kindly to English Catholics—lapsed though they may be!"

Roxana glared at him, and hissed, "I will not stay with your mistress!"

"Lady Conway, my dear Roxana, is. . . ." He paused. "Ardella's relationship with me is none of your concern. She is expecting you by late afternoon tomorrow. I, personally, will escort you there. It is your uncle's wish."

Helpless and frustrated, Roxana said spitefully, "I hate you! You did this to me on purpose!" Glaring at him, she sobbed, "May the siege destroy you, Lord Bristol!" Turning, she ran through the grove back to the house.

He did not try to stop her. For a moment Sebastian remained still, watching her disappear. What a little puzzle she was. But faith! He had never been kissed with such desire before. If only he could get Roxana to admit her feelings. Smiling to himself, he felt—despite her protests—a good deal closer to his goal.

Chapter Eleven

ROXANA HAD NO CHOICE, IT SEEMED, BUT TO BE a dutiful niece and obey her uncle's request that she stay with Lady Conway while he was up north fighting. Still, she wondered how much influence Sebastian Steele had exercised in the choice of her companion. Why "Ardella," of all people?

As she obediently allowed herself to be presented to the Lady Ardella Conway, Roxana, curtsying sweetly, could not help but think she was an unlikely guardian. This blond vixen with the ice blue eyes and heavy French accent was scarcely someone she would want to ward her child—even for a short time.

Sebastian escorted Roxana from the parlor to the foot of the stairs, where a servant waited to guide her to her rooms. Glancing again at Sebastian, Roxana wondered what he saw in Lady Conway. She herself could think of nothing to recommend the woman.

Smiling at her, Sebastian tightened his hand on Roxana's elbow. She glared at him. Did he think she would run at this point? He did not know her as well as he thought he did!

Even Lady Conway herself had not appeared to be pleased with this situation. What must he have done to make the lady agree? The flush crept up Roxana's skin and made her blood boil as her heart pounded with jealousy. She did not want to think of that.

"Ardella will be sending me reports on you every other day," Sebastian warned. "I trust you will do nothing to embarrass your uncle or me."

Roxana glanced at the hand still on her shoulder and then looked at him through narrowed eyes. "My uncle I care about," she hissed. "You I do not. I would dearly love to have your head right now if I could."

He gave her a brief, but sad, smile. "No doubt. The fact remains that it is safer for you here. Even though you may think otherwise, I would not like to see you hurt. Do try to be reasonably good." He paused. "I shall miss you, little imp."

Before she could give him a suitable retort, he bent and brushed her lips with his.

Roxana's anger faded into nothingness as she felt her blood stirring again. Her voice broke. "Then do not leave me." She grasped his hand, feeling the thickness of his fingers compared with her own. "I will obey you in *all* things if you take me."

He looked down at her and smiled. "Roxana, my precious, I doubt very much if you would obey anyone in *all* matters, even if your life depended on it. But, in any event, there is no place for a young woman at the siege."

"Oh, but there is," she continued to plead, thinking of all the information she could be gathering if she were there—all the vital details she could give to William's forces. "You will need food cooked, clothes washed, messages carried—I do not know. Whatever it is that a woman does up at a camp."

Sebastian could not hide a grin. "You would do all of that for me?" His tone told her that he did not believe her.

"Oh, but I would!" She responded even more fervently. "What can I do to prove it? I want to go with you. I want to be with you, to be away from here."

"Which is it?" His eyes were twinkling now as he confronted her. "To be with me, or to be away from here?"

Roxana's heart did a somersault. Her eyes were as liquid as rivers. She suddenly realized how carried away she had become. Afraid he would guess her emotional turmoil, she responded, "To be with you, of course."

"I see," said Sebastian. He suspected that she thought she was lying, but he detected—or hoped for—a grain of truth in her words. He tapped his fingers together thoughtfully, as if he were actually considering her offer. "Roxana, do you truly realize what you have just said?"

She flushed as red as her silk gown. "I said I . . . would cook and clean for you."

"And?"

"And carry messages, if . . . if necessary." Her voice trembled.

He waited a moment more, but she did not volunteer a second time.

"Dressed as you are?"

"Nay! I have other . . . old clothes of my"—she thought rapidly—"of my uncle's. I could wear those."

"As you did the other night when you rode against my express command?"

So he had seen her. She lowered her eyes. She could feel the tears burning, and hated herself for being so weak with this man. "Please." Her voice was a bare whisper. "Please, take me with you. I shall be good."

"I have no doubt you want to be good, Roxana," he said softly, "but you are best off here for the now. Your uncle and I will return shortly. Despite your protests, I cannot see you cooking for me or washing my clothes." He stroked her cheek, causing her to feel the now familiar warm sensation flooding her. "The king does not expect those beggars to be able to resist for more than another week at the most."

Roxana felt her spine stiffen. Rashly she said, "Lord Bristol, I believe you underestimate the Irish. They have resisted since last December. I doubt His Majesty, King James, will break them now."

Sebastian's eyes narrowed. Roxana felt her heart pounding. Damn the man! He was forever provoking her and then getting the best of her. She grimaced. Her tone had been too proud and too spiteful just now.

Sebastian chose to ignore her outburst. He leaned forward to kiss her. This time his lips and mustache brushed against her brow and lashes, tasting her tears.

"Don't cry, Roxana, my sweet. I will be back for you, and"—he paused with a lightness in his tone that warmed her, as well—"I trust the reports I receive about you will be spotless, for I should not like to be in your place if they are not." His voice turned husky and tender. "*Au revoir*, Roxana." Turning on his heel, he left without looking back.

With a heavy heart, she turned to climb the stairs.

In the two weeks that followed, Roxana did her best to be an exemplary guest; but Lady Conway, with her thick French accent, irritated Roxana to no end. There was scarcely anything they could discuss civilly.

Was it not enough that she was Sebastian's current *amour*? Did he have to torment her with the woman's company, as well? As for Lady Conway, it was clear that she fully expected Lord Bristol to become her next husband.

There were times when Roxana wondered if Sebastian knew of Ardella's plans for him—and then there were times when Roxana wished for all the terrible things that could befall him. Roxana was lonely, and restless, and . . . bored.

In truth, all the excitement was in the north. Even Gilpatrick—who, of course, still believed she was a man—had, on their last assignation, asked her to meet him in the north. She had been forced to decline, requesting to meet again at Ormond Quay. She told him that the news of the French court came first as gossip to the ears of the ladies, and that she needed to stay in the city for that now.

Gilpatrick had reluctantly agreed. However, on the matter of her assignment regarding Steele, he had informed Roxana that His Highness, William, thought it most necessary. Because of Steele's standing at James's court, and his position with Patrick, someone had to watch him. Furthermore, if Roxana refused the assignment, she would do so only in deep disgrace. She would be relieved of any further espionage duties, and would in addition be forced to give up the future court position promised her by William.

Roxana cared little for the court position, but she cared deeply about being thought disloyal—or cowardly. She would have to continue.

That meant, she realized, she would have to find a way up north.

Throughout her stay in Dublin, stories of starving women and children floated down to Roxana from her sources. Derry, it seemed, was the hardest hit of the two cities. Roxana felt her heart going out to the people there. Oh, to be with them—to be fighting James! Even if she died, it would at least be for the cause.

In June, Roxana heard of the Battle of

Windmill Hill. Her heart seemed to stop. Who had been hurt? Had her uncle? Had Sebastian? Terror hit her stomach. Oh, she should not have cursed Sebastian so!

Pacing her room, Roxana wondered what she could do. She was convinced she could be of use up north—but how to get there?

Well, one thing was certain: she would have to perfect her disguise as Alexander. She determined that that was exactly what she would do.

Dressed in men's riding clothes, Roxana quickly walked past Lady Conway's suites, grimacing as she heard the low moans and laughter. And that woman claimed to be in love with Steele! She could not even be faithful to him! Were he mine, Roxana thought bitterly, I would be loyal to him. Her whole body seemed to ache with the memory of him—but he was not hers. He still thought of her as a child in need of protection.

Hearing movements behind Lady Conway's door, Roxana quickly left her a note and hurried down the hall to her meeting with Gilpatrick. She would tell him she was ready to go north. If she could not be of use here, at least she could be of assistance to the brave souls in Derry or Enniskillen. She wondered if she would have the same courage, if it all came to that.

Gilpatrick was pacing the bridge when she arrived on horseback. It was the first time

Gilpatrick had seen her in broad daylight, and Roxana prayed her lad's costume would fool him. It did.

"What news, Alexander?" Gilpatrick asked.

Roxana answered carefully. "I've not learned much since our last meeting. I believe my usefulness here is nearly at an end. I wish to be of more service to the valiant fighters in the north."

Gilpatrick put his gloved fingers together and thought. "Aye, you could be of use there, lad. Their morale is low—nearly as low as their food supply—and the damned shipmaster, Kirke, will not break the blockade. 'Tis foolhardiness!" He glanced at her. "Would you be willing to bring food in your saddlebags, and messages of support?"

"Of course!" Roxana nodded, continuing to disguise her voice. She felt a burden lifted from her. "I shall leave this night and ride through."

Gilpatrick frowned. "The ride is a good day and a half, even two days. Do not damage your steed," he warned, nodding at Fire behind her. "Here's what you will do. . . ."

Why was it that she would take instruction from Gilpatrick, but from Sebastian she would not? Whatever the reason, she was on her way.

Only as she remounted, her saddlebags filled with dried beef and messages of support in the fake heel of her boot, did Roxana think of the danger. What if she met Steele or her uncle? Her heart stopped for a moment, and then she picked up the reins quickly.

Well, dressed as she was, she doubted either would recognize her. She would just have to bluff her way. Besides, they were at Enniskillen, were they not? Her heart hammered again. Did she really want to see Lord Bristol? Nay! Of course she did not! He was a scoundrel and a blackmailing rogue. Nevertheless, her lips still burned from his kiss.

Roxana took a deep breath and nudged Fire forward. She rode quickly through the city, passing the guards without incident. Once outside the city gates, she directed Fire north and gave him his head. Stroking his ears, she whispered, "To the folks at Derry." Squeezing her legs, she felt his smooth movement under her, and knew that he would not disappoint her.

As Gilpatrick had predicted, the ride was a grueling one. She paused only twice in two days, forced by Fire's need for water and grass and her own need to sleep. Her dozes had been fitful and always filled with dreams of Steele.

Though her stomach growled in hunger, she dared not stop at any of the towns along the way, for she did not know who would support her. Neither would she partake of the food in her bags—that was for the proud folk of Derry.

Nearing Newtown-Stewart, Roxana knew she was nearly at her destination, for the magnificent Speer Mountains were to her right. Soon she would be able to rest.

Washing her face in the cold stream water, trying to keep her senses alert, she knew, too, that the next few hours would be the most critical of her trip. Standing, she inhaled the sharp scent of the sea and glanced about her. In the pink dawn, she could still make out the stark outline of the ruins of Atrim Castle. Her heart seemed to stop at the beauty. Aye, there was beauty about her. If only there would be no war.

Closing her eyes for just a moment, she reviewed her trip, and then wondered how exactly she would get past the siege posts.

From her bags, she removed her uncle's scarlet caplet, which she added to her own costume. They would think she was bringing a message to him. She hoped only that he and Steele were truly at Enniskillen, as her sources had told her.

She glanced down the deserted road once more and felt an aching desolation for the once green and proud land. Once William had won the battle and was truly king, it could all return to prosperity.

Bending, she drank some water from the stream and then remounted.

Roxana had passed the mountains and could now see the walls, cathedral and battlements of Derry facing her as she edged Fire slightly northwest. This was the final leg of her journey. The trouble was that she could also see Hamilton's army spread out before her.

Pausing to think, she stood in her saddle. Hamilton's army was encamped in four divisions about the town, commanding all roads of access. There was no way she could avoid them—not even if she tried to use the secret river passage that Gilpatrick had told her of.

Sucking in her lower lip in thought, she recalled that Hamilton had made his headquarters out toward Culmore. She supposed that was where her uncle and Steele would be—so that, she thought, dismounting once more to check her information, was the point she must avoid.

At this spot, both banks of the river were heavily wooded. Would she be able to take advantage of that fact?

Roxana felt her heart pounding as she realized that one wrong move could easily cost her her life. She shivered. Until now, her spying had been a lark, an exciting challenge. Of course, she fully believed in William's right to be king and hated James with a passion, but seeing the armies for the first time made her realize the seriousness of her position.

Why had she been so foolhardy as to volunteer for this? Glancing toward Derry again, she knew why—but for just this moment, she wished she had stayed back in Dublin with that awful woman.

Well, she was here now, and she would make the best of it.

Deciding that her chances would be better

at dusk, and deciding, too, that she was now totally exhausted and would need all of her wits about her later, Roxana once more put the maps in her pocket. Giving Fire his choice of a spot near the stream, she settled under a tree for a short nap. In another hour or so, the sun would be going down.

Pulling her cloak over her, she nestled among the leaves and promptly fell asleep.

Her heart was in her dry mouth as she jerked awake and recalled where she was. Disoriented and confused for the moment, she focused on the river and her horse still grazing by her side.

Carefully, feeling stiff from her long ride, her muscles aching from the awkward position, she rose. Rinsing her face, she wet her eyes and lips, and drank a little.

The voice behind her shook her to her bones.

It could not be! But no, her heart pounded quickly, it was no dream. The deep timbre she was hearing belonged to none other than Sebastian Steele.

Had he seen her? Her heart hammered; her stomach tightened. Did he know she was there? Fear knotted in her as she sucked in her breath, paralyzed for a moment.

She glanced toward her horse. Fire was still munching contentedly on the grass. He snorted then, seeing his mistress's fear. A shiver of apprehension froze her blood. She prayed that Steele had not heard the horse's noise.

Numb with fear, Roxana's body refused to

move. Beads of sweat crept onto her brow as she tried to think. She had two choices: she could remain here, totally silent, and pray that he would not notice her or the horse; or she could make an effort to stand—quietly, of course—and lead Fire to a point where she could mount and escape without being noticed.

Even with those choices in front of her, Roxana found herself unable to act. Finally she decided. Unsteadily, she rose. Each breath seemed harsh and painful. Each pound of her heart seemed to bring the blood rushing through her ears.

She took a step toward Fire. A twig snapped. So, at that moment, did her heart, she was sure.

Whom or what was he talking to?

Curiosity got the better of her. After all, maybe he was planning something that, if she learned of it, would help the poor people at Derry.

Her throat dry, her head aching with the fierce, pounding blood, Roxana pushed aside a few leaves and waited breathlessly as they closed behind her.

Fear clutched at her gut now. He had stopped talking! Had he heard her? She glanced behind her, wondering if she should run for it. Wondering—but no, she could not leave now, not until she found out what he was doing here, and why he was in Derry when her sources had told her Enniskillen.

Pushing away the last branch, Roxana felt her heart go to her throat. What in the world?

He was kneeling over . . . over what looked to be a rough cross and a grave.

Roxana inched forward as close as she dared and saw tears shimmering in his gray eyes. Sebastian Steele was crying! He had a heart. The discovery, simple as it seemed, sent her mind reeling.

Mesmerized by the scene before her, she felt tears come to her own eyes. Whatever this was, she knew that it had little to do with the war. It was obviously a private moment.

Her heart went out to him. She wanted to go into the clearing, to hold him, to comfort him, to—lost in her sympathy for him, she wasn't alert when Sebastian stood up.

Panic set in. She had to get out of here before he saw her!

Turning quickly, she took two long strides before she felt the hand clamp down on her shoulder.

"Ho, boy! Were you spying on me? Whose company are you with?"

"MacCarthy's, sir," Roxana choked out, trying to hide her voice.

"Is that a fact?" He spun her about forcefully. "If you're with MacCarthy, lad, you wouldn't be in these parts."

"But, I—." Roxana's usually quick mind numbed as she faced him. She could not think of any other excuse.

Sebastian's expression changed from rage to suspicion. Before she could say another word, he pulled off her tweed cap. Roxana's glossy ebony curls tumbled down her back.

For a moment, he seemed to be actually

speechless. He frowned. "I might have known it was you. I ought to take you over my knee here and now, you little fool," he hissed. "What are you doing here?" His hand tightened on her upper arm painfully.

"I—." She struggled with her tears. "How did you know it was me?"

His coal gray eyes searched her face and her soul. She felt as if her whole being was exposed to him.

"Did you really think I would not know you had left Dublin? Did you not think that Lady Conway would send me notice of your unexplained absence?"

"But I—I wrote her a note."

"Yes." He grimaced. "Saying you were going to Lucan."

Mutinously she glared at him, and then shrugged.

"In fact, it was only a few moments ago that I gave the guards orders to be on the lookout for you. It's true that I did not expect you to follow the messenger by a scant hour, but I believe I know you—perhaps even better than you suspect."

Silently, she absorbed his words as her heart beat faster. Just how much *did* he know about her? She forced herself to speak. "If you were so worried about my appearance, then why are you here, alone, by this . . . grave."

Sebastian glanced backward at the crude cross. A cloud passed over his rugged features. His voice seemed to constrict with emotion. "I told you, I was not expecting you so quickly." He paused. "I was paying my respects to Jean-Paul, one of my messengers. He was killed yesterday in the firing from the wall. I now shall have to write his mother."

"Oh." Roxana felt her heart squeeze with a chill as she tried not to show the tears or her fear. "I—I am sorry, then, if I interrupted you."

"You didn't."

She glanced up at him. His dark features were unreadable, but his eyes had a misty look to them. Roxana could not guess what that meant; she knew only that her voice quivered as she tried to keep control of her emotions and to keep her heartbeat regular. "What will you do with me?"

There was a momentary silence. "That all depends on what you are doing here."

The blood rushed to her face as she tried to think. He would never fall for her ruse of bringing a message for her uncle. She had to think of something else. "Would you . . . believe that I . . . missed you?" She swallowed hard, feeling the truth of her words hitting her in the stomach. "I missed you and I wanted to see you."

His grin created tiny creases about his eyes, but no humor reached his brooding, gray gaze.

"You missed me and came to see me, did you?" His tone mocked her. It was obvious that he did not believe her, and yet . . . part of her wanted to cry out how true it was.

Her tone was husky as she forced herself to stay calm. "Aye." She would not meet his eyes. "It is true."

His finger touched her chin lightly, directing her face toward him. "Well, if that is true, my sweet, you must show me, I think, exactly how much you have missed me."

Roxana's green eyes widened as she stared at him, her senses spinning. Surely he didn't mean . . . !

His hand on her neck was moving slowly over her skin, burning into her as he caressed the sensitive spot behind her earlobe. Leaning over, he bent and licked her ear with his darting tongue. Pulling her numbed body forward, with the touch of his fingers still on her chin, he let his lips seek her mouth. Roxana felt a heady rush. His mouth now descended upon hers as he parted her lips. Her senses reeled. Her mind cried out for her to make some response but, confused, she could not. With tears in her eyes, she pulled away and swallowed hard.

"Come now, Roxana, my pet. You can hardly expect me to believe you missed me if you do not even want to kiss me in greeting. Didn't you, after all, risk your life for the privilege of being with me?" There was a husky hunger in his tone that raised her pulse.

She flushed deeply now. "Aye, but, I—."

His hand was on her chin again, gently guiding her face upward. She saw his eyes, dark with passion, as once more his mouth possessed hers.

Roxana felt her fears melt in pliant response to his loving demands. Satisfied with her acknowledgment, Sebastian broke away this time.

"Now, tell me, Roxana," he asked, his voice deep. "Why have you come? The truth."

She took a deep breath and decided that she would not lie to him. "'Tis because of the children."

"The children?" Clearly, he was puzzled now.

Her green eyes now blazed with righteous indignation. "No matter what your men do, I'll not let little children starve!"

His eyes darkened almost to black as she felt her gut tighten. What would he do now?

Sebastian's voice was so low that she had to strain to hear it. "Who sent you?"

Dizzily, she met his gaze. "Friends."

Her breath was coming in short, tight gasps. She saw his lips tighten, and his eyes narrowed.

"What are your plans? Have you food?"

Roxana took a deep breath, trying to calm her churning stomach and fast-beating heart. Her limbs were trembling. She nodded slowly.

"Show me."

Stiffly she turned to retrace her steps. He followed closely behind. She could feel his body heat, could feel the stare of his eyes on her back, and a shiver of anticipation went through her.

Fire still grazed by the stream. Approaching the saddlebags, she unlocked them and withdrew a piece of the dried beef.

"Is that all you have?"

Roxana nodded mutely.

"No messages of any kind?"

She stared up at him again, lost in the dark

depths of his eyes. Did he know? Her heart hammered as she shook her head.

"'Tis only food I bring."

"And how did you plan to get in?"

"I—I don't know." She stared down at her muddied boots.

"Roxana, my little fool, do you take me for a dolt? Isn't there some secret passage you've been told to use?"

"I—." Her heart was in her throat, her voice was thick. She stared up at him now, barely seeing him. Suddenly, she knew that no matter how their beliefs might differ, she would have to trust him.

This time she nodded. Her voice was a whisper. "By the river."

Grim-faced, he glanced at her horse and then at her. "Very well. Come with me. I will pass you through the lines."

"You will?" Roxana was astounded. All this while she had been hoping and praying that he would merely look the other way while she left. She never expected him to aid her. Was she wrong about him? Her heart leaped with joy—and then sank with the knowledge that no matter what his personal considerations, Sebastian still fought for James. And, of course, there was always the matter of Lady Conway.

Sebastian was watching her intently. "Though I cannot say the same for you, m'lady, I have not yet lied to you."

She swallowed and tried to speak. "No." She felt the pain stab at her. "No, you have not."

"Then do we go?"

Nodding, she accepted his assistance as she mounted.

"Cover your hair again. It would not do for the men here to know that a female is about." Without looking at her, he took Fire's reins. "If you only knew how you have endangered yourself, you little fool."

She felt hot tears sting her eyes. "I had to. I could not see children suffer."

His tone was dry. "No, I do not suppose that you could." He turned and began to lead the horse along the trail.

They passed two groups of guards. At each, Sebastian paused to chat and give them future orders. Roxana saw the respect in the men's eyes as they saluted him.

Again, she wondered. Had she misjudged the man? If only she could convince him to come to William's side!

Her thoughts were again interrupted as they rode near the bank of the Foyle.

"You should be fine from here." He turned to face her now. "I will let you go only on two conditions: that you return to this spot before nightfall, and that your horse stays here."

"But, I—."

"You can carry your saddlebags on your shoulders."

Roxana nodded silently. It would not do to press her luck. Far from being upset that she had found him, she was now grateful. How could she repay him?

As Sebastian lifted her off the horse, she put her arms about his neck. Sebastian's mustache turned up in a smile; but before she could kiss him, he said, "I do believe you should now show me how happy you are that you've found me. If another man had discovered you, my pet, you most certainly would have been in terrible danger. I believe you should kiss me again."

Upset that he had taken the choice from her, her hands now went to her hips. "That is blackmail!"

"Maybe." Sebastian grinned. "But I can have you sent home under guard this instant, if you so wish."

Roxana glared at him. Her heart pounded in fear and in anticipation. He could send her back, and she knew it. If she kissed him, she rationalized, it would be merely for the sake of her mission.

"Come, Roxana. Let me know if you've missed me as you claim you did." He brushed a loose curl back under her cap.

She took a step forward and felt his lips graze hers. Benumbed, she placed her arms about his neck, opening her mouth, welcoming his silver-tipped tongue as it explored, caressed and tasted her sweetness.

Lost in delight of his taste and touch, Roxana was only vaguely aware of her own roaming hands now touching and holding him, of his groans and hers as their lips locked and their bodies pressed tighter. Her whole being was quivering with delight and hunger as his magical fingers ignited her fires.

His delicious hands smoothed over her round bottom, now tight and hard from days of riding and well shaped by the breeches that she wore. Eager for his touch, she pressed closer. Forgetting the present, Roxana allowed her hands freedom that she had never allowed them before. As she continued to explore him, her hands instinctively brushed his hard desire.

Abruptly, she pulled away.

"Don't stop now," Sebastian murmured, his voice deep and throaty as she came to her senses.

Flushing, she shook her head, realizing that she had touched where she had never planned to touch. What he must think of her! Even through their clothes, she had felt his burning desire. It both delighted and alarmed her.

"I—I am sorry," she stammered, flushing again. She could not meet his eyes. "Forgive me. I did not think."

His teeth gently nipped her ear and touched her lobe, sending delicious shivers through her. The huskiness in his voice excited her. Admirably controlling himself, he kissed her nose.

"Do not let it concern you, little minx," he said with a low laugh. "Though I fear it is right that we must halt this progression here and now—for otherwise my great reputation as a womanizer will be stained. It would not do for my men to see me kissing a lad."

Horrified, she felt rejected yet again. It would serve him right if his men did see—if Lady Conway did get her way and then played him for the fool! "Indeed, my lord," she said stiffly and full of hurt. "That would not do at all."

She reached to take Fire's reins, and his hand closed briefly over hers.

"The horse stays here, Roxana. I will personally return him to you if you return before sunset."

"That doesn't give me much time," she protested.

"You do not need much time."

Their eyes locked a moment as the confusing emotions of love and hate swirled through her. Why him, of all men?

"Very well." She heard her own voice thick with emotion. "Until sundown."

Taking the saddlebags, she hoisted them onto her slender shoulders and turned toward the river—and the cave passage that Gilpatrick had told her would lead to the city.

She glanced once behind her as she reached the bank. Was he still watching her? No, he had already gone. Pausing for a moment, she wondered if he could ever grow to love her the way she now knew she loved him.

Chapter Twelve

GETTING INTO THE CITY WAS NOT AS DIFFI-
cult as she feared it would be. Oh, she had
been challenged all right, but as soon as she
gave the guards Gilpatrick's password they
opened the underground gate. Roxana was
greeted with wild affection by the defenders of
the city. For the first time, she was glad she
had come. She delivered the food and the
messages, and hid a return missive to Gilpatrick in her boot.

Having heard so much about Major Henry
Backer and the Reverend George Walker, the
dual governors of Derry, she was both astonished and pleased to meet them in person. The
Reverend Walker was seventy-two if he was a
day; yet despite the lack of food, the constant
stress and the rigors of command, he was as
fit as any man she knew—except maybe one,
her traitorous heart responded.

With pride, she allowed the Reverend Walker to show her the cathedral and the sorely attained French colors so brazenly taken from James's troops in a quick foray at the beginning of the siege. He was also proud of the two guns mounted on the cathedral roof.

Walking the ramparts with her, the Reverend Walker patted one gun. "This piece of metal is our Meg, lad." He grinned. "Our Roaring Meg, we do call her." He eyed Roxana strangely. "Perhaps ye'll see her in action on the morrow. Those French are a decadent lot. We'll out them, have no fear."

Roxana stared at the gun, then at the view from the battlement. It hit her like a cannonball. Sunset! She spun about. "I must leave now," she cried, climbing down the wall.

"Here, lad." The Reverend Walker put a hand on her shoulder. "Ye canna leave now. Ye just came. D'ye not wish to stay and see the ships break the blockade?" He glanced toward the harbor, where the three ships anchored, awaiting word from their commander. "Any day now it will happen—though 'tis beyond my comprehension that he has not broken through afore now."

Torn between her desire to stay and her promise to Steele, she paused. "I should like to stay . . . ," she began, then glanced down toward the enemy encampment, "but I really must be going." She turned and started down the steps, only to stumble on a loose stone in her hurry.

The good reverend caught her. Sucking in his narrow chest in a wheeze of surprise, he exclaimed, "Well, if I ain't Irish! It's a woman ye be!"

Roxana flushed and nodded.

"Well, girl or lad, ye'll have to stay the night. There is no exception made the rule. That door does not open past twilight."

"But, I—." She glanced again toward the river, toward the place where Sebastian had said he would meet her. Would he be furious with her for not keeping her promise, or would he understand?

It would be fruitless to argue. Suddenly Roxana felt very tired, too exhausted to make that long hike from the secret door up the river and through the forest. She nodded.

"Come then to my place." The Reverend Walker motioned to the street beneath them, where strands of smoke from the evening fires could now be seen. "The mistress will take care of ye."

"If you do not mind," Roxana said slowly, looking around her again, "I would like to walk here a bit." She took in the cathedral, the town of proud people, the wide city wall—wide enough for forty men to stand abreast. "I am tired, true, yet I do not think I could sleep just yet."

The Reverend Walker shrugged. "As ye wish, lass, only do be careful. The French are a mean lot. They be known to shoot at whosoever they see. 'Tis Van Rosen's orders from afore—he believes it will discourage us." The man paused. "'Tis not Christian to wish a man go to his reward, but he is one who all were glad to have seen taken!"

Roxana knew that he spoke of James's former French commander. She had hated the man as well. "I shall be careful," she responded.

The Reverend Walker nodded. At the foot of the stairs, he paused. "Be it a man that troubles ye, lass?"

Again, Roxana blushed. "How did you know?"

"'Tis love and anguish written all over yer face."

Roxana was horrified, even as her heart pounded. She looked at him miserably.

"He is one of them, then?"

Tears welled up, burning her eyes, veiling her sight. She could not answer for the lump in her throat.

"Ah, well, 'tis not often that there is a true love found. Follow yer heart, lass. The war is bigger than either ye or me."

Roxana stared at the minister-governor and bit her lower lip. Her voice trembled. "He . . . loves another."

The man paused, his brow raised. "Perhaps ye be mistaken, lass. But if yer love be true, he'll be longing for ye as ye long for him. Well, walk if ye like—but it will not move the way. Our future's in the Lord's hands, lass."

Roxana wiped her eyes as the Reverend Walker left her. With a heavy heart, she stayed up on the ramparts, walking, her eyes focusing often on the spot where Sebastian should be standing. Even as she looked, thinking she might see him, she willed that he would love her as she did him. The stars were now out.

Roxana inhaled the sea air and felt the chill. She prayed, asking that the war would soon be over—and wondering what would happen then.

Roxana had thought that she would sleep poorly, but—exhausted from her long ride and her worry—she slept like a child.

With the first approach of daylight, she drank a bit of the milk and brandy that the Reverend Walker pressed upon her, kissed the old man on his wrinkled cheek and made her way to the underground gate.

Would Sebastian be there, she wondered? Would Fire be with him? What would he do now? Would he turn her in? She prayed not, and yet the idea filled her with dread.

Her heart was heavy as she left Derry. *I really ought to be here with them, fighting, showing my support*, she thought. Well, if Sebastian were not waiting, maybe she would return to the city. She knew the Reverend Walker would welcome her.

The sunlight blinded her for a moment as she stepped out of the cave passage. Blinking, she realized that indeed Sebastian was there —his arms folded across his chest as he await- ed her. He looked handsome in his brilliant scarlet coat—and angry. For a moment her heart leaped with the joy of seeing him, until she realized just how furious he was and how stonily his face was set. She looked at his eyes. They were of ice.

Roxana's heart pounded. She looked behind her down the secret passage. She could simply return. They would protect her. The blood rushing through her ears was all she could hear. She met his eyes again. Nay, he would think her a coward. No matter what else he thought of her, she was not a coward. Pressing her lips tightly together, she approached slowly, her heart pounding louder with each step.

He continued to stand there, staring at her with his stone gray eyes, quietly watching her approach.

Trembling, her head high, she stopped two feet from him and matched his gaze. The heat of anxiety crept up her. Would he not say anything? Was he not even glad to see her—as she was to see him?

Her eyes, bold and green, did not waver. She would not reveal her fear. But if he had any feelings for her at all, they did not show now. She wondered again what he planned to do with her.

Her throat ached with the pain. She wanted to look away, but she dared not. If he planned to turn her in, well then, so be it.

Finally, after several more moments of tension, he spoke. "I expected you long before this, Roxana." His voice was low and menacing. "You have put me in a most difficult position."

"I never asked you to wait," she hissed, keeping her voice as low as his. "I could not leave when I had planned."

"Indeed? Having come on a mission of mercy, you should have been able to leave whenever you wished." His gaze pierced hers. "I watched you up on the battlements last night. You were foolish. Anyone could have fired."

Her heart jumped. So he *had* been watching.

"Would you have cared?" The words seemed to catch in her throat; her heart hammered as she waited for his response.

"Aye," he said so softly that she almost thought she had imagined it. "I would have cared." He paused, then spoke again, his voice slightly less cold. "If I had not waited, how do you think you would have gotten back through the encampment? You would have had a difficult time of it—especially if they found you to be a woman."

"They would not find out." She glared at him. "And if they did, I would merely tell them who I am."

"And say you had a message for your uncle, no doubt," he sneered. "Whoever gave you your information, my sweet spy, is cold by several days. Your uncle and I came here from Enniskillen last week. Hamilton feels we are needed here more."

She glared at him. "I am not a . . . spy." Her stomach churned with the dishonesty. She did not like lying to him, but she had no choice. "My only source is you. You yourself said you were headed for Enniskillen."

His features softened a brief moment. "Well, I have no desire to question you further. I want only to see you safely away from here before something happens to you. Come." He took her hand and led her to their waiting horses. His hands smoothed her rounded buttocks as he lifted her up. She felt her senses alive with her desire to be with him, but held her tongue. She could not talk to him of her feelings—certainly not now.

"I will escort you again to the road, and then you, my dear, will return directly to Dublin." He mounted, then took Fire's reins from her, leading her so that she had to sit back in the saddle.

"What if I do not wish to return to Dublin?" She was miffed.

Pausing to look back at her, his eyes blazed. "You will return if I must take you back myself—and you will stay there if I must see you locked in your room."

The panic seized her. She forced herself to control it. "I am not a child, my lord," Roxana hissed. "And I resent your treating me like one. I—."

Sebastian turned toward her again. "No, Roxana, you are not a child; but there are times you act like one—and on those times I shall respond as if you are." He turned his back to her.

She glared at him, wishing daggers from her eyes would pierce his broad shoulders; but he did not again face her.

They rode in silence past the guards as she tried to decide what to say. She truly did not want to part with him angry—if not for reasons of her own, then for her mission.

"Can I not persuade you to let me stay here a few days? I will be good." Her voice softened as she leaned across to touch his shoulder gently. "I promise."

Sebastian lowered his reins and stopped. His eyes met hers now, searing her with his disbelief. "You will be as good as you were at Ardella's, I assume?"

She could not answer.

"No, Roxana, you cannot stay! I will hear no more of it. It would be disastrous for you. I would not be able to control my men, and. . . ." He paused. "I will not see you hurt. Besides, there is not overly much for you to do." A smile touched his lips. "I will not have you clean and cook, as you first suggested." His hand covered hers. She wanted to pull away, but she didn't. "For once, you shall have to trust me. I am doing the best for you."

Roxana felt the pain in her throat again. She could think of nothing to say.

"The road is here, and here is where we part," he said, his eyes upon her. "I am sorely tempted to have one of my men escort you back, since I cannot do it myself."

She stiffened. "It isn't necessary. I made it up here on my own. I can make it back."

"Yes. Well"—he appeared to swallow his dissatisfaction—"I shall just have to hope so. I expect a note from Ardella in the next day or so telling me of your safe arrival." The hint of menace in his voice was enough to send a shiver through her.

It was Roxana's turn now to frown. "That is asking much of your *dear* friend, Ardella. I doubt she will have time to write you, considering her schedule. Indeed, I am amazed she had time to write you at all, with all the entertaining she does." Her caustic tone could not be hidden. She had hoped or expected that Sebastian would ask her to clarify, but he did not.

"Will you. . . ." She paused, feeling foolish for asking, hearing the trembling in her voice. "Would you kiss me good-bye?"

There was an awkward silence. For just a moment, she feared he would reject her, but his eyes lightened and he smiled.

"What is your reason this time?"

Her anger threatened to overwhelm her good sense. "That is not fair! Must I have a reason for everything?"

"I don't know." He paused. "Must you?"

Roxana took a deep breath, then sighed. "Very well. I suppose I deserved that. I—I only wanted us to part on good terms."

"I see," he said, softly. "In that case, yes, my pet, I will kiss you good-bye." He maneuvered his horse closer to Fire and took Roxana in his arms. She suddenly felt safe and secure, there in his hold. For the briefest moment, Roxana was able to forget her fears, to forget Derry, her uncle, the war—to forget all but Sebastian as his mouth demanded her willing response and his lips teased, tormented and caressed her, playing havoc with her senses.

Her arms about his neck, she did not want to let him go.

At last he spoke, his voice husky with emotion. "You do try me sorely, Roxana." He held her again, and she felt enveloped in his desire, thrilling as he touched her earlobe with his lips.

She strained against him, turning to meet his mouth as the blood coursed wildly through her, as his honeyed tongue spun his web about her, taking her excitement higher and higher. His lips sent a path of molten fire down the smooth skin of her neck.

His voice was tight. "Why must I always be the one pulling away from you?"

The same emotion was echoed in her response. "You need not pull away, then." Roxana smiled, not knowing full well what she said, knowing only that she wanted to remain with him, like this, forever. "If you would let me stay—."

His brows knit into a thick line of anger. His eyes quickly chilled again, and she felt the immediate barrier go up between them. She felt the loss and the hurt envelope her.

"So that is your trick," he said fiercely. "I might have known I would get no straight answer from you!"

"But I do want to stay with you!" Yet even as she spoke she wondered how much of her desire to stay was for him, and how much was from wanting to be of service to William.

Sebastian frowned. He was tempted to take her right now—and then to send her on her way. But, no, he would not do that. He would control himself.

"Roxana, look at me."

She refused to meet his eyes. His finger touched her chin, tilting her face upward. His thumb then touched her soft jawline, caressing it, making her weak and shuddery inside.

"You will return to Dublin, Roxana. I will come see you there. And then. . . ." He paused, his voice again low. ". . . if you wish to continue this little game, we can talk there."

Roxana bit her lower lip as she held back her tears. Her tongue was thick. "No," she whispered. No further words would come. Her voice would not comply. She choked back her tears, knowing only that he must not see her cry.

"Go, now," he said firmly, releasing her and handing her Fire's reins. "Go back to Dublin. I will soon see you there." Slapping the thigh of her horse, he stood back as she trotted off.

Roxana's only response was the silent pounding of her heart, and the proud, straight line of her back.

She rode for half an hour, feeling morose and alone. He had rejected her again! She wiped the tears from her eyes. She would never forgive the man. She didn't care if he ever came to Dublin.

Suddenly, a thought struck her and she reined in Fire. If she was not being followed. . . . She turned slowly. She would not have put it past the man to have her tailed, but the road behind her was empty.

Roxana paused only a moment before turning her horse about. Since *he* did not want her, she would return to Derry. She was sure the people there would welcome her. She could not return to Dublin having accomplished only one thing. The least Gilpatrick would expect would be some indication of the number and preparedness of James's men.

Lowering her head to Fire's mane, she galloped back on the road. Sebastian was no longer at the point where he had left her. She kept going.

The two guards that jumped out from behind a rock startled both her and Fire. Pulling her frightened horse to a standstill, she felt her heart pounding as she saw their swords were drawn. Some spy she was—she had not even thought of this before!

"Halt! Who goes here?" The one guard pressed his sword tentatively against her breast. She could feel the blade's weight.

Roxana glanced at the sword. Then her eyes met the guard's. "Let me pass, sir. I have a message for Mr. Sarsfield. 'Tis from the king, himself."

"A message for Mr. Sarsfield." The guard glanced at his companion. "Is that a fact?" Roxana felt herself trembling, knowing that trouble was coming.

"That is what I said." She tried to be brazen, and saw the man smile enigmatically.

"Fetch his Lordship, Tommy," the man with the sword directed.

"Aye," the other responded.

Roxana felt her mouth go dry. "His Lordship? No, you do not understand." She felt the terror creep up. "This message is for Mr. Sarsfield's ears alone."

"Nay, m'lady," the man responded as the

second guard rode off. "The message *we* have is for his Lordship." He grinned. "He told us to watch the road fer ye."

Anger surged through her. So he had not trusted her. Blast that man! Could she never trick him?

"He told us to hold you until he came."

"I believe, sir, you are making a serious mistake. I do have a message for Mr. Sarsfield." She continued to protest, even knowing that she was caught. "He will not want to read his missive with Lord Bristol present. It will be your head, not mine. Let me pass and I will forget it. My uncle will be forced to reprimand you otherwise."

The guard's eyes gleamed. "Bold little cuss, aren't ye? No wonder His Lordship warned us that ye'd try to fool us."

Before she could answer, she caught sight of the second guard returning with Steele. Her heart pounded. What would he do to her now?

Angry at being trapped, she glared at His Lordship. It was his fault. If he had let her stay with him. . . . Her green eyes were sharp as jade as she stared him down.

A smile touched his lips. "I did not expect to see you so soon again, m'lady." There was laughter in his voice. "You must have missed me sorely."

One of the guards guffawed. Sebastian turned his cool gaze to the man. The guard immediately quieted.

"Come." He took her reins out of her hands,

and before she could protest he led Fire over to the riverbank.

What would happen now? Surely, he would turn her in.

Beyond earshot of the guards, Sebastian took her small hand in his larger ones. For a moment his thick fingers stroked the line of her palm. "Roxana, Roxana! What am I to do with you?" He stared up at her now. "If you disobey me one more time, I fear I shall have to inform your uncle of my suspicions."

His hands still held hers, yet she felt herself stiffen. He must not do that! Forcing herself to confront him, she responded, as coolly as she could, "Exactly what is it that you suspect? That I care about starving young children?"

His gray eyes were as steady as stone—solid and hard. He smiled, but it did not touch the coldness of his look. "Do not think you can brazen your way out of this, my precious imp. I am not your uncle, whom you have wrapped about your little finger." He now held her chin while his fingers stroked her neck, creating traitorous responses within her, unnerving her. Yes, that was what he was trying to do. He wanted to unnerve her so that she would make a mistake.

"I suspect, m'Lady Roxana, that you are spying for William—that you have used your good position with your uncle to gain information for the Dutchman."

Her heart fluttered like a trapped bird as she forced her thick tongue to work. "That is preposterous! How *dare* you accuse me of that, Lord Bristol?" The anger in her voice was clear. "I do not think my uncle would approve of your unfounded charges."

His voice was so low that she had to hold her breath to hear them. "My little Roxana, if my charges were unfounded, I would not mention them. What of this delivery you made—and your knowledge of the secret passage?"

"That does not make me a spy. I have told you. . . ." Her mind searched frantically as it floundered for words. He knew. It was as simple as that, and nothing she could say would change his mind. "I have told you, it was . . . for the children."

Seeing her confusion, his tone softened a fraction, but remained insistent nonetheless. "Roxana, you will return to Dublin this day, or I shall tell Patrick everything—from the night rides to this." He paused. His eyes seemed to focus on her heart. "Dear Lord, what a little fool you are, risking your life. I would dearly love to take you over my knee."

Tears choked her voice. "I doubt my uncle or Hamilton would take kindly to the idea that you have let a spy pass your lines. If you think me that, then you should turn me in."

"Touché!" He smiled again, touching his brow. "No doubt you are right. Nevertheless, if you cause me any more trouble, I will keep to my promise. Meanwhile, I shall keep my silence, Roxana. Neither of us will be the worse for it if you leave now." He reached out his hand to comfort her, to somehow reassure her of his good intent—but, angry, she pulled away as if burned by his touch.

Sebastian smiled. "Will you go home?"

"Aye!" she muttered, hating him as she had never hated him before. She truly believed in her cause, but she knew it would hurt her uncle dreadfully if he found out. She wanted Uncle Patrick to know nothing until William was crowned—then she could get him a commission in the new army, if he wanted it. If Sebastian carried through with his threat . . . she knew not what she would do.

Sebastian was silent, regarding her. He took hold of her reins once more. "Since you have already proved yourself untrustworthy, I shall have you escorted."

"There is no need—." Her voice caught.

"Ah, but there is Roxana. I will not have you trying to double back a second time." His eyes narrowed, focusing on the road behind her. Then he looked directly at her. "I pray you have a good story at hand, Roxana, for here comes your good uncle."

Roxana swiftly turned on her horse and stared at the red-haired man fast approaching on his steed. Numbness closed in on her as her stomach tightened in anxiety. What would happen now? She had not bargained for this. She glanced toward Sebastian, biting her lower lip. She prayed that he would keep his word and not speak of his suspicions.

"Roxy, child, what are ye doing here?" Patrick paused his horse and leaned forward to kiss her. "When they told me ye were here, I could scarce believe it. Is there something amiss at Lucan? What are you doing in those old clothes of mine?"

She heard her voice above the pounding of her heart. "Nay, there is nothing wrong at Lucan, uncle. I . . . did but miss you, and I—."

"Roxy, that was foolish!"

"I fear, Patrick, that the girl is too modest," Sebastian interrupted.

She glanced at him. What was he planning? She did not like that gleam in his eyes. He maneuvered his horse closer to hers. His hand touched her knee casually, as if to tell her to be silent.

"Modest? Roxana?" Patrick laughed out loud. "What makes you say that, Sebastian?"

"Well, she is a brave lass. She did volunteer to bring us a message from His Majesty."

"Oh?" Patrick stared at his niece. "In truth, child, that is not what I would have expected of ye. Pray, what is the message?"

"It is in her boot."

Roxana glared at Sebastian. How the devil had he known? Trembling, she wondered what the message from the Reverend Walker was to Gilpatrick. If only she had read it! Now she was truly trapped.

"Well, come now, lass," her uncle stated, impatient. "I have not all day."

"Yes, of course." Her mouth was dry as she unlocked her bootheel. Furious with Sebastian, she pulled out her message and was about to hand it to Patrick when Sebastian took it from her fingers.

After a moment's silence, he glanced up and stated, "'Tis nothing of importance, sir—

only to tell us that there is another regiment on its way to assist us." He stared once more at the note and then, without looking at Roxana, crumpled it up and threw it into the river.

Roxana stared helplessly after the paper, knowing that she could not dismount and attempt to retrieve it. Clenching her fists at her side, she knew she should be grateful to him for going along with her tale to her uncle; yet she was furious.

Sebastian grinned at her.

Patrick, caught up in his own thoughts, did not catch any of the interplay between the two of them. He looked perplexed. "That was foolish of James to send a special messenger only for that. Roxy, what made ye volunteer?" He glanced at Lord Bristol. "Sebastian, there are times when I fear I have not been a very effective guardian for Roxana. I should have had a much firmer hand when it came to raising her—perhaps then she would not be as headstrong as she is now. Ye should have seen the scrapes she got into growing up."

Roxana flushed angrily. "Uncle Patrick! I have never done anything without good reason."

Ignoring her comment, Sebastian addressed his superior. "You are right, Sir. A well-applied hand when the girl was younger would probably have done wonders."

Patrick nodded. "Aye. But what can a man do with a girl of Roxy's nature?"

"You could try marrying her off, sir. Then

162

the problem would be her husband's and not yours."

"Uncle!" Roxana cried, "don't listen to him."

Neither man paid attention to her.

Patrick nodded thoughtfully. "Ye are right there. The girl's nearly twenty, and a beauty like her mother—only I fear she does not have the sweet disposition that my Mary Elizabeth had. What man would be able to handle the wench? She does not have the Sarsfield red hair, but she has more than the temper for it! I fear, Sebastian, she is too headstrong for any man."

"Uncle, I refuse to have the pair of you talking about me as if I were not present!" Her frustration was growing. Never had her uncle behaved like this before. She was humiliated.

Sebastian continued, "Surely, you have had offers?"

"But of course," Patrick acknowledged. "There's been several of the French officers— none of whom she vows she will have. There is—."

"Uncle!" Roxana's fury was rising. "You know there is not a man of them that I can stand."

"Then, there was Lord Berwick—."

"Uncle!" She was fairly shouting now. "If you must discuss me like some animal at an auction"—her temper finally got the better of her—"you might as well have me wed to—to Lord Bristol!" She babbled on in anger, scarcely realizing that she now held both men's attention. "He—he has more qualities in his right hand than any of those men you have yet mentioned."

There was a stunned moment of silence as she saw both Sebastian and her uncle staring at her. Her heart pounded furiously, and fearfully she now realized that they had finally heard her.

"That is an excellent idea," Patrick grinned. "Steele, will you take the girl off my hands?"

Her heart was now in her mouth. They could not take her seriously. Surely they realized she had not meant it.

"Uncle, no! I only said that—."

Sebastian was staring at her, studying her. A smile now touched his lips. He looked her over again—Roxana fumed—as he might a horse he had just purchased.

"Aye, sir, I do believe that I could control the little minx. In truth, it will not be easy, but it will be the most enjoyable task put to me in some time. I accept. Shall we say the first of September?"

Roxana's mouth dropped open in horror. "No! Uncle!" Her eyes went wide. "Uncle, do not do this to me! I tell you, I did not mean. . . ." She faltered. "I only said Steele because—because he was here. Because—Uncle, please," she wailed. "You *promised* me you would never wed me off until I had chosen my own husband!"

"And so I did," Patrick grinned, unrelent-

TAME THE WILD HEART

ing. "But Roxy, I have kept my word. I did not offer ye until ye suggested him."

"But I did not choose Sebastian." She swallowed hard, furious with herself and with them. "I tell you, I did not mean it and you cannot do this to me." Tears welled up in her eyes.

Patrick's eyes narrowed. Tenderhearted when it came to his niece, he was obviously affected by her emotions.

Before Patrick could renege, Sebastian spoke. "Roxana, my dear, you were the one who proposed to me, not I to you. I do believe that qualifies for your uncle's agreement." A sensual smile touched his lips. "Since you have proposed and I have accepted, the honorable thing is to go through with it."

"No!" Roxana cried horrified. "No, I will not! This is a trick. I—I cannot." Grabbing Fire's reins out of Sebastian's hands, tears dancing in her eyes, she clenched her teeth. "I can handle myself well enough, uncle. I need to have no one responsible for me. I need no man to control me. I—."

"I wonder at that, Roxana," Sebastian said. "I wonder if you know what you are really saying."

"Of course I know what I am saying!" She glared at him. "This is your fault! All of it! I shall not wed you—nor anyone else." Jerking Fire's bit up, she reared the horse momentarily and then regained control.

Furious at them, but even more furious at herself, Roxana galloped off.

Tipping his hat to his superior, Sebastian smiled. "You will excuse me a moment, sir."

Himself smiling, Patrick nodded. "I do not envy ye, lad. Roxy is more than a handful for any man."

"I believe I can manage, sir." Nodding again, Sebastian spurred his horse after her.

Chapter Thirteen

IT TOOK BUT FIFTEEN MINUTES OF HARD RIDING for his stallion to catch up with Fire. As good a rider as Roxana was, Lord Bristol was more experienced. His years in the military had given him lightning-quick responses, enabling him to do what many could not.

Roxana had to admit that she was astonished—and even pleased—to see that he had come after her. She was also a little worried. What had she done? It seemed too jumbled for even her exhausted brain to understand.

Her heart was in her mouth even as his pace matched hers. She was not really startled when he grabbed the reins from her, nearly unseating her as he pulled Fire to a halt.

"Get down off your horse, Roxana. We are going to have a talk, here and now."

"No!"

Swinging one long, lean leg over, he dismounted while still holding the reins of her horse. "Get down, Roxana." His voice brooked no denial.

Furious at being told what to do, she stared at the Stygerian darkness of his eyes. It was childish, she knew, but she did not want to talk to him. If she did, she would somehow slip up. She dismounted obediently. Exhausted from the past few days, she knew that she could not get far if she ran—yet she had to try.

Quickly tying the reins through the branches so that the horses would not leave, Sebastian followed her, tackling her just beyond the trees.

"What did you think that would accomplish, my little imp? You cannot run from me. You should know that." His weight was on her so that she could not move; his thumb stroked her cheek, tracing the line of her jaw. Inwardly, she was beginning to melt—but she could not show him that.

He lifted his body off hers and sat up, keeping a firm hold on her still. "'Tis time you learned that your dreams of old—your wishes of an Alexander to come rescue you—are but fantasy. We live not in a world of knights and round tables, or of great empire-building campaigns. We are living here and now in Ireland."

She pressed her lips tightly together, still trying not to look at him—not wanting him to see how much she wanted him to take her into his arms.

"Roxana." His voice was soft, but certain.

"I will be your husband. Whatever you say, whether you like the idea or not, it will be so. Once you are used to it, I fancy you will favor the idea as much as I do. Your uncle certainly does." He winced when he saw her pain, and wished he had not mentioned her uncle.

"Aye! My uncle would favor it! As for me, I favor nothing but the idea of being away from you." The tears were now brimming her eyes.

Sebastian took a deep breath. "That is not what your kisses have told me." His thumb again traced a molten line across her cheek, halting her answer as his finger continued to trace the outline of her mouth. A shudder of anticipation went through her.

She felt a hot sensation travel her body just from the thought of his silver-tipped tongue. "My kisses were . . . otherwise motivated."

"Were they, now?" His voice was still soft but disbelieving as he balanced now on his firm haunches. "That well may be—in part. However, it is not the part I choose to believe."

"Why not?" The tears were now streaming down her cheeks. "Why can't I have my dreams? Miracles do happen."

"Aye!" His voice was tender now. "Miracles do happen, but they do not always happen in the way you think." He paused. "Come, accept the fact. I am your betrothed. Let us kiss to seal the agreement."

She glared at him, trying to continue her anger, and yet feeling her whole body trembling inside. "If I wed you, it is . . . only because of my uncle. It is only for his sake; because it is he whom I love, and he wants this marriage."

"I see." A smile twisted his mustache. "And you have no feelings at all for me?"

"No!" Her protest came too swiftly to be true.

Sebastian shrugged. "Well, that is fine with me."

Roxana's eyes widened. She had thought that would put him off, but it had not worked. None of her tricks were working with him! "You would wed me knowing that I do not love you?"

"Weddings of that nature happen all the time." He released his hands from her but threw one leg over her so that she still could not escape. His hands played with the grass tops and felt their sharpness grazing his palms.

Undecided on what to do, Roxana closed her eyes. "Very well, Sebastian." She took a deep breath, noticing how easily his name came to her lips. Her heart pounded. She did not want to hear his mocking tones, or to know that he was doing this only for her uncle. She wanted him to marry her for her. Tears came again to her closed eyes and seeped out. The only miracle she could think of now happening would be that he would love her and want her for herself—not for her uncle.

Gently, he touched her hair, stroking it lightly. Pulling her close to him, he grazed her brow and hair with his lips. "You are trembling." He wrapped his arms about her to comfort her. "Are you afraid of me, Roxana?"

"Afraid? Of you?" Her eyes opened. "Of course not."

"Good." His fingers again stroked her cheek and felt the wetness of her tears. He leaned over to kiss her eyes closed. "I promise, Roxana dear, you will not be hurt. I hardly fancy the brave Roxana being afraid of me," he joked lovingly as he nibbled her ear.

He was mocking her, she thought. Her anger surfaced again and she stiffened.

He was holding her in so tight an embrace that she could not move away from him. He smiled and kissed her nose. "Look at me, Roxana. I wish you to see me—to think of me and not some mythical prince."

How could she tell him that she did think of him—only of him?

His lips burned hers. Her stomach tightened. His hands stroked her hair, soothing her. He drew her head forward, gently, tenderly. "Roxana, my little imp," he whispered huskily as his mouth grazed hers. Again, he gently nibbled her ear, sending shivers through her. He outlined it with his tongue, his mustache grazing her sensitive skin.

Her tears were falling. He kissed them away, holding her close, comforting her, loving her, exciting her. She could not help herself; she did not want to help herself. Her arms went about his neck, tightening. She could feel his breath warm and soft on her skin. She sensed his desire rising, firm and hard, and she felt the warmth of her own desire.

Each of his movements heightened her sensations. She wanted him, and she knew it—even as his mouth captured hers, possessing her. His tongue entered, feeling her velvet. Gently, he lowered her back onto the soft grass. His hands stroked her, touched her, ignited her; His calloused palms brought up the senses of her creamy white skin. Mindlessly, she surrendered to his touch. She felt nothing but his arms sheltering her, comforting her. Roxana was only vaguely aware that her shirt had been loosened and raised. She grew languorous with his love, while his tender hands traced her breasts. His calloused palms rubbed the sensitive nerve endings. He lowered his mouth to suck, tease and pull her into a flood of ecstasy, while his other hand drew circles of tender love about her other nipple. Her senses spun. She moaned as she tried to think, tried to stop this onslaught.

Gently, his hands moved between her thighs, and she could feel the heat as she strained closer to him, begging him to touch her, grasping him, clawing at his back with her fingers.

"Roxana," he muttered, making her name sound as soft as the wind through willows. Once again, she allowed her hands to caress and touch his hard sex and soft secrets beneath.

Sebastian groaned, as his mouth sought hers in a mutual passion and his hand slid to the softness of her sex.

"Will you . . . will you . . . ," she began, her fingers digging into his strong back as she felt her hunger demanding and insisting more of him. Suddenly, he moved slightly away from her.

His hand now gently stroked her cheek, her hair. "Nay, Roxana, I will not have you now. Not like this. I only wanted to show you that marriage will not be as difficult as you fear."

"But I. . . ." She wanted him desperately—but surely he knew that.

"We will wait until the right moment." He tenderly pulled her shirt down and tucked it again in her breeches, his hands pausing just a moment at her soft roundness.

Confused, Roxana lowered her eyes. She could not look at him—not now, not after the way her body had betrayed her. He had made her want him—only to have him reject her yet again. Had she done something wrong? Maybe he was purposely driving her wild? Maybe he thought she had tricked him into the marriage proposal?

Even as she tried to deny it, she knew that she didn't have to mention the marriage. She knew that she had allowed her emotions to get away with her—hoping he would notice, and now afraid that he had.

He touched her chin, drawing her out of her thoughts, directing her tearful eyes up to him with gentle fingers.

"I want you to tell me that you love me," he said softly.

Was it love or just desire? Confused, she knew not what to say. Unashamed tears spilled on her cheeks again. She wanted him to hold her, to have her, and yet she would not betray her feelings when he was only using her for winning her uncle's approval.

Why in the world did he want her to say she loved him? For his own knowledge of conquest? The lump choked her constricted throat. She knew her pride would not allow her to admit her love until he did.

Slowly, she shook her head. "I—I cannot."

"Oh, Roxana," Sebastian sighed. His eyes were again on hers. "Realize this," he said as he assisted her up. "Your uncle has more than a right to wed you to whomever he chooses. You are indeed lucky he has let you run him all these years—that he has not chosen someone else to take you in hand. If I do not wed you, someone else will—and I doubt that someone will have the tolerance for your night rides and other mischief."

She wanted to call him a blackmailer, but in truth she could not. The fault lay not with her uncle but with her own impulsive tongue. She supposed she had best take responsibility for that.

Glancing up, she said quietly, "You have made your point." She sniffled back her tears. "Does it please you to humiliate me? To have me beg?"

Sebastian said nothing. His gray eyes were like steel spikes staring into her heart, dividing it and conquering it.

She took a deep breath. "I will wed you, as you wish."

Sebastian shrugged. "You must tell me that

you love me as well, or I will assume that you wish our marriage to be in name only."

Blankly, Roxana stared at him.

"Come now, my imp, don't play the innocent." He realized that he was being harsh with her, but she had to know exactly what she wanted. She had to admit it to her heart and to him or she would forever hold the grudge against him. "Most court marriages are for show only. If that is your wish, I shall not bother you."

Stunned by his words, confused, knowing that even now her body cried out for him, she glared at him, feeling the jealous monster cutting her deeply. "What does that mean, exactly?"

His mysterious smile puzzled her. "My dear, you yourself have said that there are many women in Dublin alone who desire my presence. Lady Conway, for one." Sebastian paused, letting the words sink in. "Except for the first night, I need not bother you at all." He paused again. "If that is your wish, my little Roxana, I shall oblige you."

Her mouth went dry. Furious at the way her own body was betraying her, she knew that she craved his touch, his kiss. It irritated her.

"Are you telling me"—her voice was hoarse with the fear that she might lose him now— "that you would have a mistress?" She took a deep breath and felt the anger harden in her. "Lady Ardella Conway could not fit you into her schedule!" She felt the jealousy curdle her tastebuds. Wishing she could control it, knowing she could not, she continued recklessly,

"That is, unless you wish to join her other lovers! But, of course, Lady Conway is not the only one who is available to your charms, is she? There is Lady Melfort, Lady Tyrconnel . . . and numerous other French ladies at the court." Her green eyes were now sparkling dark with anger. "You had best understand this, Sebastian Steele, Lord Bristol or whatever other name that fool of a king James wishes to give you: if you wed me, if you are my husband, then you will not make a fool of me with Lady Ardella Conway, Lady Melfort or anyone else."

Sebastian stared at her for a moment more, and then threw back his head and laughed—though not without gripping Roxana's arm so that she would not bolt. Finally, he calmed enough to speak. Still grinning from ear to ear, he said, "Roxana, you are precious. I can see that I shall never be bored as your husband."

He coughed back another laugh as tears of amusement sparkled in his eyes. "Very well, my sweet wife-to-be, I will do exactly as you wish." He bowed low and took her hand, kissing her fingers. Did every touch have to excite her so? "I will always do as you wish." His voice was so low that she had to lean forward to hear him.

Sebastian took advantage of her movement. Once more he kissed her lips, making her blood flow faster, sending it pounding through her brain.

Weakened, she stared and felt the knot in her throat. She had the sense that he somehow had gotten the better of her just now; yet in her heart, Roxana knew he had not tricked her.

She looked up into his eyes, conscious for that moment only of how she did love him, but still uncertain of his affection for her. He was still her enemy and she still worked for William. She knew she would have to be doubly careful thenceforward—yet it would certainly make her life more interesting.

Aware that he was watching her intently, she found her voice to speak. "What . . . what happens now?"

"Now?" There was still amusement in his voice. "Now, my lady love, we mount our horses and I procure you an escort back to Dublin, where you will stay until I come for you."

"No!"

"Yes!"

Their eyes battled for a brief moment. Roxana realized that he was not one to be crossed. She sighed. "May I at least stay at Lucan?"

Sebastian brushed a loose curl from her face. Tenderly he answered, "Aye, my lady, you may stay at Lucan."

With his help Roxana remounted, and waited patiently as he did, as well.

It seemed, she realized as they guided their horses back to the camp, that she had met her match—at least for this day.

Chapter Fourteen

IT SEEMED AS IF THEY HAD BEEN RIDING FOREVER. Obviously her escort was in no hurry to get back to the siege—especially since Steele had given him several days' worth of provisions, and better fare than he would have had if he'd stayed with the others. He did not know who this lad was, but Sebastian Steele had asked him especially to accompany the youth to Dublin.

They camped for the second time, even though Roxana wanted to continue. The city was less than a few hours away, but the soldier refused. Finally, admitting her own exhaustion, Roxana agreed to rest.

Her stomach growled as she nibbled on the hard bread and cheese. Tired of the silence, she searched her mind, trying to find something she could discuss with the man—but Sebastian seemed to be the only topic that came to her mind. "What is Lord Bristol like to work for?" she asked finally.

The soldier, a lad not much older than Roxana, grinned. "There's not a one I'd rather be with but Sebastian Steele. Right good they are to us. 'Tis jealousy I hear from my friends in the other camps. His Lordship does get us the best of the food available. Mind, that ain't none too great, but when me friends have none, whatever he gets us is more than welcome by us."

"Does he eat what you eat?"

The soldier glared at her. "But of course. He wouldna have it otherwise. Sleeps out with us, too, he does, though I hear that others have their own special tents with servants and the like. He's like a father to us, he is."

"Surely. . . ." She paused. "Has he not faults?" Roxana held her breath, feeling the hard bread on her tongue.

"Ye mean does he womanize?"

She nodded. He paused to think while Roxana felt pain stab her heart. She watched the soldier's eyes, wondering what the man would say if he knew she was female.

"Tell the truth, I canna say. His Lordship don't allow none of us to have women, so I doubt as he does."

Roxana felt the relief wash over her.

Suddenly, she rose. "If you do not mind, I'll go on to Dublin on my own."

"But his Lordship said—."

"It's all right, believe me. He only wanted to see that I returned safely to . . . to my home."

The soldier grinned. "That does sound like

him. Never did I know one to care about us men as he. Even if William offered us all full commissions, I doubt as any one of us would depart."

Roxana felt pride swell in her heart. Well, if she must be associated with the man, at least she had reason to be proud.

Pulling out her purse, she handed the soldier some coins. As far as Roxana was concerned, anything from James's treasury was worthless; but the lad seemed grateful.

"I know that Lord Bristol has already paid you to escort me, but I want to thank you also. I can get on from here by myself."

The lad turned to stare at her. "But ye'll be going on yer own?"

Roxana shrugged and nodded. She needed to meet Gilpatrick and give him a report. It would not do to have one of Steele's men with her, no matter how young or innocent he might be.

After a moment, the boy shrugged. "Well, 'tis fine with me, as long as ye say nothing to his Lordship. Not a one of us likes to chance his rage—right bearish he be."

Roxana nodded and forced herself to smile. "I shall say nothing," she responded. Mounting before the lad could change his mind, she quickly rode off.

Reaching Dublin, Roxana left a message for her contact to meet her within the hour.

Gilpatrick was not pleased at her early return, but said she had done well with the food and the messages to Derry. She waited for further questions about how she had gotten past the guards or whether there were any return messages, but none came—and she did not offer the information.

"What of Steele?" Gilpatrick seldom used Lord Bristol's title since it had been given by James and was not recognized by William. "Will you continue your watch over the man?"

Roxana pulled her cloak about her to protect herself from the misty chill of the river. As his wife, she no doubt would continue the job. Slowly, she nodded and glanced toward the depth of the dark waters.

"He—he is said to return in one week's time to Dublin. He . . ." Her voice choked as she felt a distance between herself and the words. "He is, they say, engaged to wed the Lady Roxana Alden, Sarsfield's niece." She faced the river now, afraid that her own emotions would betray her.

"Is that so?" Gilpatrick was interested and moved to step beside her on the bridge. "Why seem you so sad, Alexander?"

She shook her head. "'Tis nothing."

"Come—did you fancy Lady Roxana yourself? Charming wench, she is, but I doubt anyone save Steele could handle the girl. 'Tis said Lady Roxana is a regular she-devil, Twisting her uncle about to get her way. Cool as ice that one. Not a man can come near her—not even James himself!"

"Perhaps the Lady Roxana had reasons for what she has done." Roxana's voice was hoarse with fury. "Perhaps no man has treated her as he should."

Gilpatrick stared hard at his contact. "What is affecting you, lad?" His concern seemed genuine.

Realizing that she had very nearly gotten herself into trouble, Roxana shook her head. "I do not think folks should judge, lest the true story be different."

Gilpatrick shrugged. "Well, it does not matter to me, as long as you follow Steele for us. Next week?"

Roxana would not trust her voice. She nodded.

"Then it is set, unless I hear from you sooner."

Gilpatrick left Roxana alone on the bridge. She felt the dampness chilling her heart as she stared into the dark waters. So that's what they said of her. Was what she heard about Steele true, too? She quickly moved away to her horse. She was sure the gossip she had heard about him was correct. He had even confirmed it, had he not? She bit her lower lip, and wondered what marriage to the man would be like.

While Gilpatrick was glad to see Alexander, Lady Ardella Conway was not glad to see Roxana, especially when the news filtered back to her that Roxana had "trapped" Bristol.

"If you think he will stay faithful to you, Lady Roxana, you are indeed a child," Lady Conway said spitefully.

Roxana glared at her hostess. "I think 'tis you who are mistaken." Her beribboned green satin gown moved gently in the breeze of the bright Irish day—one of the few bright days they had had all this gloomy summer. "Sebastian has assured me"—she felt the lie flutter in her own heart—"that he will always be faithful to me."

"Of course he would zay that, you dolt! Do you not think His Majesty did not zay the same to Queen Mary of Modena?" Lady Conway smiled and laughed. "If he is faithful to her, then I have lain with a ghost!"

Roxana winced at the mention of James. "I care not what you say—only what my heart tells me. Sebastian will be true to me." Within her, Roxana vowed she would see that he was!

The smile remained on Lady Ardella Conway's painted face as Roxana paused by the coach door, glad at least to be returning to Lucan.

"I give you one month of marital bliss, my sweet innocent; no more. After that, your good husband will go where he is most pleased." Her hard blue eyes looked coldly at Roxana, then glanced up to her chambers. The meaning was clear. Lady Conway continued, "He'll not settle for an untried innocent like you when he could have one that he *knows* will give him pleasure."

Roxana felt her stomach churn. The idea of Sebastian being with this woman was more than she could bear; yet through her trembling rage, she managed to keep her calm. Matching Ardella's cold stare, she responded, "He would not have offered for my hand, m'lady, were he not already well pleased with me. I am a quick learner—my husband will have no complaints of me."

Giving the widow a cool smile, Roxana stepped into her carriage and felt the rush of her blood in her ears. "Good day to you, Lady Conway. No doubt, we shall meet again."

Leaning her head back on the seat cushions, Roxana took a deep breath as the tears stung her eyes. If only Sebastian had truly offered for her! Well, he had not—not in the way she had hoped he would—and, no, he was not at this moment pleased with her. She sucked in her lower lip. Nor was he likely to be pleased if he learned that she continued her efforts for William. But what could she do? She could not allow James to be king of Ireland.

Her head began to pound with fearful anticipation of her wedding night. Lady Conway was right; she was an innocent. She had heard from many of the servants that the first time was seldom pleasant, but Sebastian had told her that he would never hurt her.

She swallowed back her fear and stared out at the now desolate countryside. She would have to trust him in that.

It was not a week but a full month before the siege ended. On July 31 the ships decided they had waited long enough. Blasting the dam, they had made their way down the Foyle, much to the relief of the folks at Derry.

Roxana, along with the other faithful, cheered—but she did not cheer the fact that her uncle would soon be coming home for a bit of rest, and that he would be bringing with him Sebastian Steele. But, of course, one could not have a marriage without the groom.

She found herself thinking constantly of Steele—with every clash of thunder, with every sunrise, with every drop of rain. Was he her Alexander?

Her heart hammered even as she slowly turned for the dressmaker to adjust her wedding gown. She wished she had held her tongue that day, for then he might have truly offered for her on his own. As it was, she knew of no reason why they had to go through such a farce.

If he loved me, she thought to herself, that would be an entirely different matter. Tears shone like brilliant emeralds in her eyes. But the truth was that he would not say he did. He would marry her simply from desire for her body, and for her uncle's good favor. Was that not reason enough for Sebastian Steele to put up with her? She swallowed her tears.

"What is that, m'lady?" the dressmaker asked, her mouth filled with pins.

"'Tis nothing." Roxana squeezed her fist to stop the tears.

"Have I pricked you, m'lady?"

Roxana shook her head. "'Tis nothing. Pray, continue."

The dressmaker shrugged. She had heard that the Lady Roxana was a bit odd at times. "'Tis just nervous, ye be. I can tell. 'Tis natural, m'lady, especially with a man as well versed as his Lordship."

Roxana closed her eyes, wishing the woman would be quiet.

"'Tis not every day that one weds a man like Lord Bristol. A handsome groom he'll be. Many a woman, I vow, does envy ye."

"Aye," Roxana responded dryly, her heart pounding. Even now the words of Lady Conway rang in her ears. She would keep him more than a month—she would keep him forever! If he vowed to her, then she would not let him be with another.

"And a lovely bride ye'll be, too. Why, even His Majesty will be pleased."

"No doubt." The taste was sour in her mouth.

"'Tis monstrous good fortune that his Lordship is so blessed by His Majesty. Imagine, to have the king himself at yer wedding—and giving ye the party and all, after!"

Roxana would say nothing against James but, "Aye, it was monstrous fortune." James would give a party with any excuse. She thought of her new friends in Derry, of all those wide-eyed children eagerly grabbing at the dried beef she had brought. She thought, too, of the soldiers—such as her uncle—who even now laid down their lives for that fool. She remembered the poor of the land, who could, after the burning of their crops, barely subsist. Their only means of living had been taken by James, and she wondered how the man could be so insensitive.

She wanted to be wed in the small chapel at Trinity, but that had been made into a powder magazine. Her next choice was to be married

186

at Lucan, and give to the poor whatever food the wedding might have used. Besides, did Sebastian think she'd be able to eat a morsel on the day she would become his property? Even though she loved him, the idea of having to obey him forever wreaked havoc with her—especially since she feared Lady Conway would make good on her threat. As he himself had pointed out, there were few court marriages that were in fact true marriages built of love and loyalty.

She turned once more with relief, knowing the dressmaker was nearly done.

The woman stood to take a good look at her handiwork. "Were he not already in love with ye, he should fall in love with ye now!"

Roxana inhaled sharply, feeling her heart skip a beat with the momentary hope. The glance at her image in the table mirror revealed a woman she had never seen. Her dark hair was piled high, and the creamy seeded ivory satin gown set off her smooth, pale skin. She *did* look lovely. Would Sebastian fall for her charms? Could she make the man love her—after the marriage?

Taking a deep breath to steady her leaping thoughts, she decided that was exactly what she would have to do. She would make him love her. She would be the ideal wife . . . at least for a time.

She thought then of her next report to Gilpatrick. It was due soon, and she had naught but gossip to tell him—none of it confirmed.

Her heart pulled apart. She realized that whatever she now said might put her husband's life in danger. If only she knew that she could make him love her—then she would give up working with Gilpatrick for Sebastian's sake. Tears stalled in her emerald eyes. Yes, if he loved her, she would quit her work for William.

As soon as the dressmaker had left, Roxana quickly slipped into her pale blue morning gown and sat down at her writing table. She had decided to write Sebastian, to tell him that she truly did want to be a good wife and to admit that she bore love for him. Perhaps it would inspire some sort of confidence from him. But though her wit be quick when it came to chatter at court, for the life of her she could not now think of anything to say!

The knock at the door disturbed her. She wanted no interruptions, not while she was trying to compose this note. She needed to plan her strategy.

"I want no lunch, Maggie," she called. "I am not hungry." She returned her attention to the quill, ink and parchment by her hand.

Her mind would not work. Perhaps if she started. . . .

"My dearest," she wrote . . . and stared at that. Nay, it was too formal. Besides—she frowned, heavyhearted—Sebastian would no doubt suspect she had a motive or two behind the missive. Tears sprang to her eyes and stung her cheeks. Indeed, she did have a motive. She wanted him to love her. Was that a crime? She wanted some assurance that he would be faithful.

The tears dripped onto her parchment, splotching it. She would have to get a new sheet. She sniffled and wiped the tears with the back of her hand.

"'Tis a powerful pent-up well of emotions that makes you cry so."

Startled, Roxana turned from her window seat, her heart in her open mouth. She stared at the figure before her. "Sebastian! I—but you were not expected until the week after next!"

Nodding, he approached her. "That is true, my sweet Roxana, but I told your uncle that I had need to speak a few words with you. He has retreated now to Sligo since MacCarthy has been wounded and captured at Enniskillen."

"But I—but we. . . ." Roxana swallowed her anxiety. "You should have written first. Anyway, you should not be here, in my room like this. I am. . . ."

"What is wrong, Roxana? Why should I not be here?" His gray eyes clouded over. "I have already on more than one occasion been in here."

"I know that, but—." Why was she acting like such a foolish maid? He was right. There was no reason; and yet, even while she had been thinking of him, it seemed that being confronted with him in person was more than her courage could bear.

"What is it you do, my little imp?" He took a few steps forward. "Do you still continue your work on behalf of William?" His eyes narrowed so that daggers of ice seemed to come from them.

"No! I. . . ." She swallowed hard, stepping over to her desk so that he would not see her letter.

Even as she did it, Roxana knew that it was the worse thing she could have done.

"What is it you hide, Roxana? A missive to your contact?"

"No!" The horror came straight from her throat. "'Tis nothing."

Sebastian reached behind her and grabbed the parchment before she could say anything more. He read the two words. His face was like a thunderstorm; he seemed close to violence. The anger in his eyes frightened her.

"Who is this to, Roxana?" he demanded. His voice was soft but venomous.

"No one!" Roxana forced herself to turn from his stare and face the window. The only sound in the room at that moment was the beating of her heart.

"I find that hard to believe. You make love to a ghost? Come, girl, don't play me the fool. Who was this to? Who have you been seeing? Am I to remain faithful while you dally with one of William's men?"

"No!" Her voice was hoarse with fear and with anger. How could he accuse her of such! "No! You do not understand."

"Then, tell me." His arms folded across his massive chest—much as they had on the morning she had come from Derry. "Tell me, then, so I might understand, Roxana. I would dearly love to understand you, my little paradox, before we are wed, but I fear that is impossible." He glanced at the parchment still in his hand.

Roxana closed her eyes to blink away the tears as they scalded her cheeks.

The softness of his voice scared her. "Who was this message to, Roxana?"

She swallowed hard. "You," she whispered. Her voice sounded like trumpets in her ears, but in truth it was barely audible. She opened her eyes.

He stared at her, fearing that he had not heard correctly.

She licked her lips and repeated it slightly louder. "You."

His gray eyes went wide. His tone was softer this time, but still disbelieving. "Say that again."

Roxana took a deep breath as she tried to steady herself. She felt her irritation rising now, and was sure that he was baiting her. "I said, 'You'!" she screamed. "You! You! You! The letter I started was to you, Lord Bristol!"

Roxana could not have stopped the tears now, even if she had wanted to. Sinking down onto the window seat, she began to sob. "The letter," she choked, "The letter was to you. To tell you. . . ." Her tears overwhelmed her again.

"To tell me what?" He was beside her now on the window seat, holding her, attempting to comfort her. "My little imp, I am sorry if I wrongly accused you." He felt his own throat constrict as her tears wet his shoulder. He continued to hold her, stroking her hair.

"I . . . wanted to tell you . . . that I. . . ." She couldn't get the words out. Frustration made the tears come again. She could face the worst of dangers, she knew, but to have him angry with her was somehow more than she could bear.

"What is it that you wanted to say?" His tone was tender again as he held her and lifted up her chin. Gently his lips lowered to hers, kissing away her tears. They rested a moment—no more—on her mouth, tantalizing her. "Tell me, my sweet, what was it?"

She stared at him, still unable to speak, and then leaned her head against his shoulder. Her fingers reached up to stroke his neck. "Tell me why you've come," she said. Was he intending to call off the wedding? She prayed not.

Trembling, she waited for his answer.

Sebastian grimaced. He wondered how she would take this. He wanted to tell her that he loved her, but he did not know how she would take it.

"Very well," he sighed. "'Tis about the wedding, dearest girl. I do know"—he paused to glance down at her, to see her eyes as she looked up to him—"that most women wish to have big celebrations for their marriage. However, you, my precious, are not like most women. Therefore, I thought you would not mind if we wed simply in the chapel here at Lucan. I do not think that His Majesty will be pleased with my decision, especially since I have asked that whatever food the king was going to offer for the buffet be given to the soldiers, but I hope that you will understand. Had we been married at another time—." He was watching her and saw her mouth drop open slightly.

Roxana could not believe what she was hearing. She continued to stare at him, continued to feel the warm comfort of his arm about her. Had that not been her hope and plan exactly? Her heart leaped with the joy of knowing that in Sebastian she had found a man who, while they might disagree the merits of James's kingship, seemed her soul mate in so many other ways.

"Well?" He continued to stare into her pools of liquid green. "Is that acceptable to you? His Majesty told me you would have a fit and disagree violently."

"His Majesty is wrong," she said softly, sitting upright. Her eyes now reflected her happiness. She took his larger hands in hers. "You are right about the food, about the chapel. 'Tis my wish completely."

"You go along with my decision then?"

Smiling, she nodded. "Aye. I would not feel right indulging on that day when so many have so little." She lifted her eyes to him again, "That was what I wanted to write you about, but I feared you would not approve."

"Not approve? You know me very little, then, if you think that I rejoice in the hardships of others."

Her heart fluttered as she acknowledged, "Aye. I know you . . . very little."

He drew her into his arms again. "Then I must correct that soon. You must have plenty of opportunity to know me." His lips touched her brow, her nose. "Was that the only message you had for me? Was there nothing else?"

Roxana felt the blood rushing to her cheeks. In a small voice, she began, "I wanted to tell you. . . ." She paused, trying to will her courage up, "that I do love you—sometimes."

Laughing, Sebastian hugged her to him. "Oh, Roxana." There was tenderness in his tone. "Well, I must be content with 'sometimes' for the present. I hope we will soon change that to all times."

Her heart thudded. "Do you truly wish that?" She lifted her eyes to his.

There was a tremulous moment before he smiled and grazed the hollow of her cheek with his thumb. "Always," he said gruffly, allowing his lips to meet hers. "Always, Roxana. Sometimes I wish I could be with you always, to hold you forever." His lips grazed her hair. "Even when I am furious with you, I cannot hide my feelings for you."

Roxana's heart barely seemed to beat. Surely, she was dreaming all this. Surely, he was not saying that he loved her. Nay, it could not be. Yet, as he kissed her again, she felt herself lost in her sense of him. She would win his love—and would keep it. She knew that she could do that.

It was only after he had left, after she was again alone with her thoughts, that Roxana realized the truth. For all his tender words,

Sebastian had not yet told her that he loved her.

With Sebastian in residence at Lucan, the days seemed to fly by. Whatever his motive, Roxana could not fault him as a suitor. He was almost too perfect—keeping somewhat aloof, politely regarding her.

Roxana found his distance irritating. Why was he doing this to her? Why was it, too, that she could think of nothing but him? At the oddest moments her mind would relive his touch, his feel, his smell, remembering how his lips had met hers. She would look about, expecting to see him, and he would not be there.

In time she almost wanted to scream from frustration. What was this man doing to her? Did he know how she hungered for the sight of him, for a touch from him? Why was he staying here at Lucan if not to be with her? Was it only for appearances—was that all he cared about? Her fists clenched. She could not let him guess how much she wanted to be with him, how much he was tormenting her.

Controlling herself, Roxana was determined to bide her time, determined to ignore him if she could . . . yet she found herself walking more and more in the gardens where he often strolled.

"'Tis but two days more, my imp," he told her one evening. "Do you believe you can wait?"

"Of course I can wait!" She glared at him, angry that he was causing this reaction within her, angry with herself for falling into his trap of wanting him more with each day, and angry with herself for being frightened of the coming night—of the coming moment when she would lose control and become totally his.

"I suppose you will expect total obedience once we are wed," she fumed, still furious from the way his kisses had ignited her just a moment before and had then been withdrawn.

Sebastian threw back his head and gave an ample laugh. "That would be nice, but it is not in my hopes for now, Roxana."

"Good." She stood, moving away from him, staring out at the darkening river, fearing that if she remained too close to him she would throw her arms about him and beg him to get the deed done with now, to get it over with so she would not have to worry more. How could she want something so much and yet dread it so much? It was not natural!

He stepped up behind her so that she could feel his warm presence. His arms went about her, encompassing her for a sweet, wonderful moment before he spun her about. "There is but one thing I require of you, my lady."

"What is that?" Her trembling instinct told her that she was not going to like his decision overly much.

"I ask, my sweet precious. . . ." He stroked her cheek, inflaming the fires that already burned. His voice was soft, but full of meaning. "I ask that you give up your spying for William."

"I—."

"Nay, Roxana. Do not lie to me. You know I hate dishonesty. Fire has been gone from his stable two of the nights since I have been here with you."

She flushed. How dare he check up on her! "You have no proof that it was I who rode Fire those nights, or that I rode him anywhere on William's business," she hissed. "And even if I had, it would be from obligation—a sacred vow I made. I will not give it up. My mother—."

"Roxana, your mother would not want James hurt—and well you know that." He drew her into his arms. "Come. Tell me you will drop your dangerous mission." His lips grazed her brow, her hair, making her nerves vibrate in awareness of him. He held her so tight that she again felt the hardness of his desire, and felt her own desire for him creeping up with the rush of her blood and the warmth that was flooding her.

"Sebastian, I. . . ." she could not speak.

"Nay, Roxana. I want no excuses. I want to know only that you will give up this dangerous work." He lifted her chin with his forefinger. "Melfort is right. James should retire, but he will not—not with Lord Tryconnel urging him on. My pet, we both know that in the long run, William will win."

Roxana felt her heart stop. Her eyes opened wide and her mouth dropped as she inhaled sharply.

"You agree with me?" Her eyes were still

wide in wonderment. Would miracles never cease? His words spun in her mind as she tried to think. "If you know William to be the true king, why then do you stay here? Why do you fight for James?"

"Roxana—." He paused. "My darling Roxana, 'tis not as simple as that. My commission is with James. It is a matter of honor, not only for me but for my family, as well. In truth, yes, I once thought James the better of the men—but seeing him here, now, running the war, ruining the war, has made me see that he truly has no spine, not as a king. I can only hope that William will be better. But my honor, pet, 'tis my honor that is pledged to James, at least until the end of the war. And I am also pledged to your uncle. You know that as well as I do. Your uncle will not say nay to James."

Sadly, Roxana nodded. She knew all too well. The pulse in her neck pounded. Sebastian's confession was one she had never expected.

Tears stung her eyes. "But do you not wish this farce of a war over as soon as possible?" She swallowed the pain. "Men"—her voice came out strangely—"men, women and children are dying because of James's pride."

"Aye, my sweet." He gently brushed her tears away with his linen. "I do know. I just do not wish you to join those who are dying. I do not want you placed in any position that will be of danger to you—as in Derry. You must promise me, my pretty one." His hand was again on her hair. He held her close, confusing all her thoughts. Was he telling the truth? Only a short time ago she would have given up her work for him, for his love . . . yet now she knew not what to say.

The tears scalded her eyes. She shook her head, feeling his comforting warmth surrounding her. "Do not ask me that. I want . . . I want to be a good wife to you." She felt the words come from some other source. "Yet 'tis true that"—she swallowed hard, her hands pressed against his chest—"that you have not yet told me. . . ." She paused again and stared up at him, seeing him through her bleary vision; her voice was barely audible now. Sebastian had to lean close to hear her when she asked, "What are your feelings for me now?"

He was astonished. "How can you ask that, Roxana? My affection for you breaks all bounds." He smiled. "Despite your headstrong ways."

"Then"—she hated herself for her timidity, as well as for being the one to ask—"Then do you love me?" The tears sparkled in her eyes.

"Aye, my little imp," he said gruffly. "I do love you." His eyes were tender; his lips bent to graze hers. Then he added, "Will you give up your spying?"

The heavy chill settled around her heart, but she nodded. She had promised that if he said he loved her, she would give it up. . . .

His lips devoured hers again, and she felt herself flying free on their mutual pleasure.

It was only after he left her that she began to doubt. Had he said he loved her only because she had asked, or because he wanted her to give up her assisting William? Or did he truly mean it?

Back in her room, she stared out to the darkened river. Well, she would keep her promise to him—at least, she would try. On her next ride to meet Gilpatrick, she would resign.

Chapter Fifteen

ROXANA DID NOT THINK THERE COULD BE A more nervous bride than she. She wished now that she'd had the courage to call the wedding off. Lounging in the hot, sudsy water, her hair piled on her head as Maggie scrubbed her body, Roxana closed her eyes, trying not to think of the coming night.

"'Tis a shame yer mama did not live to see this, Lady Roxy. She'd have liked his Lordship —him being a James man and all."

"Yes," Roxana said, tasting the bitterness. "I have no doubt she would have heartily approved of Lord Bristol."

There were several more moments of silence. Maggie awkwardly spoke once more. "Ye do know what is to be this night, don't ye, m'lady?"

Roxana glanced at the older woman and bit her lower lip. She wanted to say that she did, but truly she had only the vaguest of ideas.

"I—I believe that I know all that I want to know."

Maggie knew her lady better than to take the rebuff. "Well, since as ye donna have a mother, and since it would be unthinkable for the Master to speak with ye on it, I only wanted to be sure. 'Tis not the most pleasant of moments for a woman, lass; but if yer man be loving and gentle, as I'm sure his Lordship be, it will be fine. After. . . ."

Roxana felt herself trembling despite the heat of the water and the roaring fire. Her eyes widened. "After what?"

Maggie patted the girl's hand. "I only meant to say that the next time it won't be half as bad."

Roxana's throat was dry despite the steam of the bath. "What if there is no next time? I mean"—she frantically searched for words—"what if I disappoint him? Oh, Maggie!" Tears choked her voice. "I know I shall ruin everything. I know he shall hate me," she sniffled, "and leave me. There are . . . so many . . . better than I."

"Hush, lovely." Maggie patted the girl's damp dark hair and took her into her motherly arms. "Lord Bristol will not leave ye. He not be that type o' man. You remember how he cared fer ye in yer illness. Mean as he can look, 'tis a heart of love that man has. If ye'll only follow as he says, ye'll not need to worry."

Silently Roxana rested her head on Maggie's plump shoulder. She did not know if she could follow his instructions. So far she hadn't had much luck in doing so.

"Here, lovely, why not have a small drink o' your uncle's brandy. It will relax ye and keep ye from being all nervous. I'll be back with yer dress in a minute."

Roxana nodded, eyeing the glass as she accepted it. She stared into the amber fluid and then gulped it down in one swallow, feeling the hot fire course through her gullet. For a moment she gagged and grasped the side of the tub. A trick! Sebastian must have told Maggie to do this—to kill her!

After a moment the fire subsided, to be followed by the warm, mellow glow. For a moment more, she fought her fears.

Maggie was right, Roxana thought, leaning back against the smooth brass of the tub. The drink *had* relaxed her. She poured herself another, reaching over the furry rug, not caring that she dripped bubbles or that she nearly spilled herself unceremoniously out of the tub. Maybe, her slowed mind thought, maybe if she had enough, she would not even feel the pain that Maggie spoke of.

The glow again was warm. The hazy sense of peacefulness mingled with her tears. Why was she such a coward? The tears continued to drip down into the water.

By the time Maggie returned, Roxana had consumed nearly half the decanter of brandy. At least her nervousness was gone. In fact, everything was gone. Glancing at the bed, she knew that she would dearly love to have crawled back in there and slept, and slept, and slept more—much to the dismay of her nurse.

"Come now, lovely." Maggie guided her tipsy mistress, now dressed and ready, to the waiting coach.

"Where are we going, Maggie?" Roxana slurred, her mind numb as she allowed herself to be led.

"To yer wedding, lass. To the chapel."

Roxana stared at her servant, not comprehending. "Wedding? Me?" Her disbelief was obvious as her eyes widened. "Who is it that I am marrying?"

"You are marrying me, my sweet," Sebastian said, frowning as he took her arm firmly and assisted her into the carriage.

Roxana stared at the handsome, craggy face looming close above hers. She blinked as she felt a jerk in her heart, and a moment of lucidity broke through her alcoholic haze.

"Oh," she said simply. From the far reaches of her brain, she heard herself speak. "Maggie says you will teach me all I need to know. Will you do that?" Her eyes were wide. "I do not think I will be a very good pupil. Oh, I can be—to be sure," she giggled, "but none of my tutors stayed long." She grinned up at him and giggled again. "They all left in a huff." She made a face and wagged her finger. "They told uncle that I was not worth all the money he might pay them." She giggled again and looked up at Sebastian, this time more serious. "You're going leave too, if I don't listen to you, aren't you? But I can't listen to you all the time. Wouldn't be much fun, would it?" She grinned mischievously.

Sebastian scowled as he struggled to keep from laughing. "Roxana, how much have you drunk?"

"Drunk? Me? Why only this little bit." She pinched the air in front of him. "Just this teeny bit." She grinned. "Maggie said it would relax me. But I wasn't nervous. Oh, no." Her mouth formed a big O. "I am *not* nervous. 'Tis perfectly. . . ." Her hand swept the air before her. "'Tis perfectly natural."

"Yes, Roxana." Sebastian grabbed her hand, still frowning. "It is perfectly natural." He scowled at Maggie.

"'Tis indeed sorry, I am, yer Lordship, only m'lady was in a frightful state, and while I was off—."

Sebastian sighed. He had tried so hard to show Roxana that she had nothing to worry about, but he supposed her fears were natural.

"Never mind," he told the servant, as he touched Roxana's cheek and drew her attention toward him again.

Maggie pressed her lips in continued worry as Roxana directed a childlike gaze at Sebastian. "Will you teach me everything—even if I am very, very naughty?" She took a deep breath, almost as if she was afraid of his answer.

The smile curved his mustache, making

him seem even more roguish. "Aye, my sweet, I will teach you, even if you are very, very naughty—but I believe you will be a good student."

"You think so?" Her wide-eyed gaze was still upon him, and even through the haze she heard her heart beating faster.

"Aye." His eyes met hers, and his lips grazed hers gently for just a moment.

"Begging yer pardon, my lord!" Maggie exclaimed. "Yer not to do that. . . . I mean—." She backed down, flushing.

"'Tis all right, Mag." Sebastian gave her a crooked smile. "You are correct in reprimanding me. It seems that, drunk or sober, she holds a charm for me that no other woman has ever held. It quite makes me forget my manners at times."

"Well, I'm glad to hear that, my lord, though I fear she does believe ye do not truly love her. 'Tis beyond my powers to convince her of such."

Sebastian glanced keenly at the maid. "Yes, that is beyond your powers . . . and it is something that Roxana will just have to learn." He leaned his head out of the coach, calling up to Dory, "Let us start! Patrick awaits us at the chapel."

Nodding, Dory clucked the horses.

Jerked by the sudden motion, Roxana fell backward into Sebastian's arms. She grinned up at him and remained there the whole of the short trip to Lucan Chapel.

* * *

Roxana barely heard the ceremony. She was conscious only of Sebastian's strong arm at her side—holding her up—and then of the tenderness of his lips as the priest finally allowed him to lift her veil and kiss her.

Her heart flew as he swooped her up into his arms and carried her down the aisle. Content, she laid her head against his strong shoulder. She smelled his scent, and felt the rapid beating of her heart against his.

She continued to cling to him as they passed her uncle, who was foolishly grinning, shaking the hands of the guests and neighbors. They were disappointed that there was to be only a small party, but they had to respect the wishes of the bride and groom. Roxana heard her uncle assure them that there would be celebrations aplenty when the couple returned to the city proper. For now, the king was still concerned with Schomberg's planned attack near Dundalk.

Several well-wishers accompanied them back to the hall. Expecting this, Patrick had ordered a moderate spread laid out. Looking at the lavish food, modest though it may have seemed to the guests, Roxana could not help but think of the soldiers dying of hunger. The sweet haze of the alcohol was leaving her— much to her displeasure—and the dull ache of fear was returning.

She paused in front of the pastries and glanced toward Sebastian, now speaking in the corner with her uncle. Were they discussing her? Probably. At this moment, she did not feel very married, but she knew that she most assuredly was.

Maybe if she had a bit more to drink. . . . Her hand closed over the brandy decanter just as another hand closed over hers.

"I believe you have had enough for one day." The warning tone of his voice made Roxana turn to look into the stormy gray eyes of her new husband.

"But I—." She swallowed hard. Maybe it was the liquor, but suddenly she forgot her vow to be a perfect wife to him. She was determined now to show him that he could not control her as he might an ordinary woman. "No," she hissed, "I have not have enough! I want another cup."

She turned from him—a mistake, she would soon learn—and started to pour.

The decanter left Roxana's hand before she could cry out, and firm fingers gripped her shoulder. "I think, my sweet wife, 'tis time you and I retire."

Startled, she glanced up quickly. Her heart hammered. Frantically, she glanced about for Uncle Patrick, hoping that he would save her.

Sebastian read her mind. "Your uncle is involved with his friends right now. I am sure he will understand when he finds us gone."

Roxana swallowed hard. Never before had she dreaded something so much. What if she failed? What if he left her?

"Well, do you walk, my love, or do I carry you?"

She tried to move, but could not. She would

rather have faced a line of fire than this moment. Color rushed to her cheeks. She recalled all the many nights when her mother had cried out in pain, when James's dear friend Lord Stuart Alden had taken and abused Mary Elizabeth. "Please," she pleaded, "can we not wait a bit—until more have gone, or. . . ."

"Roxana." His fingers stroked her cheek, heightening her senses, making her heart pound the faster as he stared into her green eyes of liquid fear. His voice suddenly took on a mocking tone. "Can it be that you are afraid to be alone with me?"

She swallowed the pain in her throat, unable to take her eyes from him.

"Afraid? Me?" Her voice sounded high, even to her own ears.

His mustache lifted slightly with his smile. An amused tone crept now into his voice. "Yes, imp. I believe you're afraid of me."

Her wide eyes betrayed her fear more than her voice had. She tried to shake her head in denial but her neck would not move. Nothing about her seemed to move except her racing heart.

His hands touched her neck as the fires rushed through her nerves. "You need not worry, my dove."

For the moment, their eyes locked again.

Without another word, he bent and swept her up into his arms.

"Sebastian!" she protested.

"Be quiet, Roxana," he whispered in her

ear, nuzzling it slightly, creating sensations that she could not deny. "Your friends all think us to be a happy couple. Let us not disappoint them."

Through her veil of fear, she heard someone clap. How dare they! She squirmed in his arms to see who it was, wanting to give them a scathing look, but Sebastian held her fast. Soon, others had joined the clapping.

Even while holding her, Sebastian managed to salute the crowd. "Smile, Roxana."

Forcing herself to turn, she gave a tremulous smile. "Good girl." His lips grazed her cheek as she felt the rush of blood.

All too soon they were in the silence of the dimly lit hall. Even with the warmth of his arms, she shivered. He held her closer as he carried her along the passage.

In her room, the fire had been lit and was now blazing brightly, but Roxana continued to cling to his neck.

With a playful kiss to her ear, Sebastian let his lips wander across her closed eyelids, trailing molten heat down her neck. She felt herself relax slightly, despite her fear. Untangling her fingers from his hair, he laid her down on the new feather comforter and disengaged himself.

His hand touched her brow. "Shall I call Maggie to come help you undress, my pet?"

Her voice would not come. It was only with effort that she managed to shake her head.

"No?" He lifted a brow. "Surely, you don't expect to get out of that contraption yourself, do you?"

Mesmerized by his eyes, Roxana stared at him. She didn't know what to think.

With a sigh, Sebastian sat on the edge of the bed, cuddling her in his arms. "My pet, the fear you are feeling is only natural. I do promise that I'll not hurt you."

Roxana felt the tears come to her eyes. She did not want him to think her weak; she wanted to stop them—but the tears came anyway.

Tenderly, Sebastian kissed her. His mouth found hers; his gently probing tongue parted her lips, tasting the sweetness that she offered.

Even for all her fears, it was impossible not to respond to his experienced hands.

Quivering inside, she felt all the nerves tense in her stomach. Her arms slowly went about him again—this time not out of fear, but out of a wild flutter of the wings of desire.

Slowly, he pulled the pins from her hair. Her dark glossy curls tumbled loosely over her shoulders, contrasting their brilliance with the alabaster of her skin.

Inhaling the masculine scent of cleanliness, leather and tobacco that was his alone was like an aphrodisiac for her senses.

"Have I told you yet how breathtakingly beautiful you are, my darling?" His expert hands undid the hooks of her gown.

"No." Roxana managed to find her voice amidst her floating senses.

His hands moved toward yet another clasp. "'Tis true, my Roxana. You are— exceedingly." There was a huskiness in his voice, a look in his silver gray eyes that sent her pulse racing.

She watched, hypnotized, obeying him fully, as his hands guided her to her feet for a moment to remove her dress. He bent his head then to kiss her exposed flesh and the tops of her breasts. Roxana shuddered.

With each movement, with each touch, she was becoming less fearful and more aroused —but what was she to do? Feeling at a loss, she continued to stroke the smooth velvet of his coat, then his back, his neck, entangling her small hands in his curls, amazed at everything.

His whispered words of love filled her head as he now kissed her all over, carefully avoiding her special areas, tantalizing them with this closeness until she ached to have him touch her there . . . everywhere.

"I want you, Roxana, my little wife. I want you more than you will ever know." The deep timbre of his voice brought echoing vibrations from somewhere within her as her hands again went to his hair and her lips kissed his as fully as he was kissing her.

Her hands stroked him, petted him; she heard his low moans—or were they hers?— and quick breath as she touched, explored parts of him that she had not dared imagine.

She allowed him to lead her, to be the aggressor, to teach her—and a good pupil she was. From beyond her mind, she heard her own moan of pleasure as his lips ignited tiny flames of fire—more so than ever before.

Suddenly, he moved away and stood. Distraught, she protested. "No, don't go away!" Had she done something wrong that he was now leaving?

"Hush, my precious." Sebastian put a finger to her lips. Standing before her, he began to shed his garments.

With the firelight glowing behind him, he appeared a golden god—or a satanic devil. Whatever he was, Roxana could not help herself, could not keep her eyes off him—his broad chest, his lean arms, and his hard, muscled body with the sleek, narrow hips. His skin was golden, either from the sun or from heritage. Dark hair bloomed on his chest and trailed over his belly to thicken in a darker grove between his thighs. She scanned his long, lithe legs, but her eyes could not help returning to the darkness between his thighs, to the evidence of his desire proudly wanting her.

He stepped forward slowly, realizing that this was a new experience for her, realizing that he would have to move with caution to give them both the most enjoyment possible.

Roxana continued staring at his maleness. Her eyes widened in surprise as, mesmerized, she stretched out her hand to touch him. For a brief moment she recoiled, but then, like a curious kitten, she approached again, feeling the baby-fine softness and contrasting hardness along its length.

A small frown creased her brow. Glancing up at his eyes, she trembled.

Forcing himself to remain conscious of his every movement, he asked, "You would like a drink, perhaps, my love?"

Unable to take her eyes from him, she swallowed hard and nodded.

It was true that before he had forbade her drink, but now, he saw her fear. He would not make this difficult for her.

Roxana swallowed one sip of the brandy and felt the fire burn her throat. Gasping hoarsely, she said, "I need no more."

"No?"

"No." She looked up at him and smiled slightly, trying to keep up her confidence. "You said you would not hurt me. Though I can hardly believe it, with that . . . yet"—her eyes met his again, trusting, loving, willing him to continue—"I believe you."

Like a foolish boy, Sebastian grinned.

His beauty still exposed and ready, he again approached her. Standing in front of her, his hands touched her hair, stroking her. Once again, Roxana's fingers began their delicate exploration as he spoke thickly. "I love you touching me, my darling. You are a wondrous lover."

He moaned softly and pushed her back on the soft bed, then took her into his embrace so that her nakedness matched his, so that every part of their bodies touched.

Roxana felt the stimulation of his touch as his hands slid over her, as his roughened palms grazed her breasts.

Greedily her mouth took his. Roxana responded as his hands continued to heat her flesh, finding each womanly curve and making her body his alone.

With the fire inside her growing, with the hunger now begging to be sated and the curiosity forcing her to abandon her fears, Roxana pressed herself against him, allowing the delight to escape her lips as his kisses covered her body.

Sebastian's mouth now found the roundness of her breasts; she trembled with pleasure, groaning as his mouth closed over first one nipple and then the other—kissing them, sucking them, teasing them until she thought she certainly would die of frustration. Surely, she would go mad if he didn't do something now. The ache within her loins was almost unbearable. Pushing herself toward him, she pleaded, hoarsely, "Please, Sebastian. . . ."

"Please what, my imp?" He teased and sucked her other nipple.

Unable to think but wanting to retaliate in kind, Roxana reached down to take his hardness in her hand. Stroking him, playing with him, she allowed her fingers to tangle in his hair. He groaned blissfully and lay back, yielding to her play, and yet availing himself of her own secrets as his fingers rhythmically stroked her moist lips, causing her to gasp as the wet sensation flooded her.

Growling with delight, he laid her back on the bed and allowed his lips and tongue to tease her sensitive flesh. His hands held her hips firmly as she squirmed in exquisite pleasure, drawing her nearer him, arching her body. She gasped in spasms of wonderment.

From the depths of her mind, Roxana knew she could no longer fear something that was so beautiful. She knew that this was not yet all; but already she felt so gloriously happy.

Drawing her up beside him, Sebastian held her for a brief moment as her body continued to undulate with his touch. His hands strayed the length of her body, her back, her breasts, and settled again between her legs as he pressed his fingers inward, exploring and delighting her with his movements.

"Oh, Sebastian," she whimpered, unable to control herself, pleading for him to continue, hating him as he withdrew his hand again, tantalizing her, teasing her.

Her world was filled with him now. She knew that, from this moment on, no matter what happened between them, he was her husband and she would live and die for him. She sensed that only he would be able to fulfill her as she was being fulfilled now.

He rose over her suddenly.

"Now?" Her voice was thick with emotion as a tinge of fear returned.

Nodding slightly, Sebastian's hands again parted her velvety smoothness. He guided himself slowly and gently into her satiny sheath.

Roxana gasped, feeling her eyes open wide with the slight pain as again he pushed gently. His mouth closed over hers. His darting tongue tasted her sweetness and demanded her response, divorcing her from her fears, dwarfing her momentary pain as he pressed forward. Instinctively, she arched her hips for him.

Relenting for just the moment, he kissed her brow. "Are you all right, my darling?"

Roxana swallowed her pain and nodded, entwining her fingers in his hair, pulling his mouth over hers again. Tears stung her eyes for that second. If this be love, then the pleasure of those few moments before were worth the pain now.

Sebastian beamed a smile at her as he again kissed her deeply, thrusting slowly, gently, gaining momentum with his hips so that Roxana had soon forgotten the pain as she moved her hips in time with his.

His hands stroked her breasts rapidly as his thrusts became less gentle and more insistent. Roxana, already wild with pleasure, pushed herself even closer to him, straining to feel him. It was almost as if she were about to explode, as if she were about to fly on the wings of an eagle, soaring higher and higher.

Suddenly, he plunged his total length into her, his thrusts taking her deeper and deeper into her desire. Roxana moaned with pleasure as her hands pulled and entwined in his hair. Distantly she felt herself scratching his back, stroking his round, hard buttocks. She wanted to scream as she felt herself being lifted away from her body.

Sebastian's mouth pressed down on hers,

consuming her with his flame as each sensation heightened her pleasure. Briefly, he raised his head. "You are wonderful," he whispered hoarsely. Then he released all his passion, and together they tumbled down from the marvelous heights—bonded forever.

His breath was ragged as he kissed her brow. "I thank the Lord that you are my wife and not someone else's. I would hate to have you waste that passion." Grinning, he kissed her again and rolled off to close his eyes. His arms went about her, holding her, cuddling her as she, too, closed her eyes.

It was several moments before either of them spoke again.

Nestled against his warm body, Roxana rested contently. She knew not why people had scared her so. The warm glow of happiness she now felt had made it well worth the small pain and the wait.

Her fingers teased and toyed with his dark hairs as they lay curled and damp on his flat stomach.

"Roxana?"

"Um?" she asked, contently continuing with her play.

"Are you all right, my sweet? Did I hurt you?"

Roxana glanced up at him, a huge grin spread across her face. "I am fine. I do readily admit that my fears were exaggerated."

"In truth, my dear, in many cases the pain is not exaggerated. Not all men want their loves to enjoy it as they themselves do." He rose up slightly on his elbow to kiss her brow, then pushed her damp curls from her cheek. "You did enjoy it, did you not, Roxana?"

She nodded. Her eyes sparkled as her small hands touched his roughened cheek. "But pray, why is it that you are constantly calling me Roxana? Do you not like the name Roxy?"

Sebastian smiled. "I did not have your permission to use it."

"But of course you do!" In the warm afterglow of happiness, Roxana wondered if she was betraying too much of her feelings for him. Did he want her love, truly, or . . . ?

Self-conscious, she lowered her gaze. "You are, after all, my husband. You may call me"—her hand grazed his hairs again—"whatever you wish." Her heart was pounding.

"Even if I call you Lady Bristol?"

She shrugged as coolly as she could. Glancing up at him, she felt the barrier break apart her happiness. "If you so desire. It is, after all, the title given you by your king."

"My king? Not yours?"

The emerald green flashed in Roxana's eyes. "James will never be my king. I tolerate him because of my uncle . . . and now because of you."

"I see."

There was an awkward silence. Roxana wanted to cry for the obstacles that still separated them. Determined not to dwell on them —to think only of the beauty of the moment they had just shared—she turned away from him and lay her head back down on his chest, feeling the roughness against her cheek.

Silently, she continued her play again with the tiny hairs, following them as they trailed down. She wished she could read his mind. She wished she knew what his silence meant.

Her eyes strayed down and focused on his manhood as it began once more to rise proudly.

"Look!" She sat upright and pointed. "Is that wondrous? Did you tell it to do that?"

Sebastian smiled at her astonishment. "Aye." He gave a low laugh. "It is rather wondrous. And, no, I cannot always control it."

"Does it always return again?" she asked, eager for his answer, glad to have something to discuss other than who might best be king. "How many times does it come back?" Playfully, she asked, "Is there a law that tells one how many times one is allowed to be with one's husband?"

Sebastian laughed as he drew her to his arms. "Nay, my sweet, there is no law. We can be together as often as circumstances allow." He grinned. "As to how many times it returns—well, that depends."

"On what?" she asked suspiciously. Did he mean to trap her into another form of obedience?

The throaty timbre of his voice thrilled her. How could she ever have not desired him?

"It depends, Roxy, on how well you do love him."

"Oh!" She reached out to stroke his erectness, feeling it harden in her hand. "There is no question of that." Stroking him again, she asked, curious, "Does this not hurt you?"

His answer was to pull her forward in a kiss. His tongue darted into her mouth and she kissed him deeply. Sebastian whispered, "It hurts only when he is away from the one he loves."

She grinned. "Then we must not let him be away too long. Tell James that you resign your commission and wish to stay only with me." Her fingers entwined his hair; she returned his kiss as his hands roamed her body, pausing to excite her.

Each sensation heightened by his touch made her breathless. "Maggie . . . says . . . that it will be better the . . . second time. Is . . . that a fact?" Her desperate mouth sought him, searching for him as she tried to quell the rising hunger within her.

He touched her cheek softly. "We can only know that if we try, Roxy."

Eyes gleaming, she nodded, surrendering to his touch. His mouth gently opened hers; his golden tongue explored, tasted and carried her with a fervor that sent her senses spinning. With tender roughness, he possessed her breasts, her belly, her inner thighs. Roxana could think of nothing but her hungering need for him, her desire to please him and bring him the same pleasure he was bringing her.

As his hands moved between her thighs, rising upward, she inched higher, responded to his touch, feeling the passion in the catch of his breath, seeing it in the deep gray of his eyes.

Softly, so softly, he whispered to her of his love. Roxana pressed herself urgently toward him, straining, wanting to believe in what he said, and yet still doubting, wondering if this was not being said for reasons other than love.

She pushed away the fears as their passions grew, as she sought him with her lips.

"You are a passionate wench," Sebastian whispered hoarsely. "It will be interesting to see how much you learn in the next few months."

Hugging him, Roxana laughed as she traced the hard line of his jaw and the outline of his lips with her fingers. "In these lessons, I assure you, I shall be the most excellent pupil you have ever had. If only. . . ." She paused as Lady Conway's words echoed in her mind. "If only you never desert me." Tears of uncertainty now shimmered in her eyes, mingling with her tears of passion.

Sebastian's arms went about her, loving her, comforting her. "My sweet Roxy, you need never fear on that as long as you remain honest with me."

She swallowed hard and nodded, feeling the uncertainty still there. She had yet to face the matter of telling Gilpatrick that she was quitting.

Throwing her arms about his neck, she responded to him with all the wild abandon of her primitive instincts. As she undulated her body on top of his she felt the rising of his desire as he held her roundness.

She knew when he was ready this time, and rolled over to welcome him in. Ravaged by her hunger for him, Roxana was conscious only of immediate pleasure this time as he put himself between her opened thighs. Unashamedly she devoured him with her passion, arching higher and higher, straining to be part of him. Her eyes closed, her lips parted with a gasp.

When he brought her over the top, he heard his breathing become more labored than before. "You keep this up, m'lady, and you will wear me out before the week's end! Then I shall surely be of no use to His Majesty."

For all her pleasure, she could not help but feel sad.

"Even your brow creases beautifully, my Roxy."

He took her hand and kissed her fingers individually. She took a deep breath as they lay together, his long legs entwined against hers, her head on his shoulder.

"I do love you," she admitted, "even if you do not share all my beliefs—but pray," her voice trembled, "do not mention his name, even in jest."

Sebastian tousled her hair. "It will be as you wish, my dearest wife. Come now, let us sleep, for no doubt your uncle and I will have much to discuss on the morrow."

Roxana pressed her lips together and nodded.

Curling up beside him, she lay her head on his chest again, listening to the beating of his heart, the steady sounds of his breathing. She sensed when he fell asleep, and then let the tears fall from her eyes. Quickly she brushed them away, lest they touch him. She had not lied to him. The hurt she felt now was not physical. The pain that wounded her so deeply was emotional.

It was bad enough to have her dearly loved uncle fight on the wrong side, but now she was married to a man who also fought for the lost cause.

Sighing, she wished the war were over . . . and she wondered how long she could keep her promise to her husband.

Chapter Sixteen

ROXANA, NOW LIVING IN THEIR DUBLIN TOWN-
house, found herself thinking constantly of
Sebastian, wanting to have news of him—and
her uncle, of course. Was he well fed? Was he
exposed to the chills of the river and mists?
Her worrying could accomplish nothing, and
she wished she could see him more often. It
was now January, and he had only managed
to return to the city twice—hardly enough to
consider him a husband! At least, not the one
she had expected. She could not help missing
him. Her body missed him!

There were now but two thousand men to
protect Dublin, yet James did not seem worried. Under pressure from the Irish, His
Majesty had given Lord Nagle the post of
secretary at war, once held by the now absent
Lord Melfort.

Roxana did not think Nagle would fare any

better than his predecessor. The man was a decent lawyer, but he knew less about the military than Roxana herself.

Her desire for news, despite her promise to Sebastian, kept her in the middle of things. Why was it that Tyrconnel was instructing James not to concern himself with the weapons that had recently arrived from France? Did he think that things were going so well that they would not be needed?

It worried Roxana to think that Lord Tyrconnel might be right. Encouraged by the supplies coming from France, James had offered forty shillings to any man of William's who would join him—and several had defected.

Pacing the floor of the townhouse, her cup of tea cooling on the marble table, Roxana knew that she could not continue this idleness. Why, she was becoming half-crazed with fear. If something were to happen to Sebastian, she did not know what she would do. If she kept busy, at least she would not worry about him so much—and perhaps she would not miss him so much.

True to her word, Roxana had told Gilpatrick she could no longer continue her activities. She'd made up an excuse about illness in her family, and had hoped that in time she would have an opportunity to explain the truth to William. It would be easy enough, though, to go back now.

Roxana turned her thoughts to the campaign. She knew that many of Schomberg's men had succumbed to fevers and chills. She feared that, despite James's bragging, his forces fared no better, and she worried about Sebastian and her uncle on this account, as well. William's forces had taken a small victory at Boyne and Jamestown on the Shannon, but it could mean little to the men on either side who were now dying in the tents, feeling life slip away because of fever.

"Oh, Dory," Roxana sighed as she spun about. She heard the heavy satin swishing as her dress flared. "If only we had medical supplies to give the troops. It was downright cruel of Berwick to capture those supplies in that raid." She turned again in obvious frustration and boredom. "I want to help, but instead I must sit by idly as I promised his Lordship. I must wait for the dressmaker like a good girl." Her voice was high-pitched with irritation. "You would think James would tire of all these parties, would you not? Considering the riots and unrest that this city has seen, you would think the king would be concerned. I would rather be starving and fighting up north with Sebastian and my uncle than be here!"

She sighed again and sank into the chair for one moment, toying with her teacup before rising again to go to the window. Opening it once, she quickly shut it. "'Tis the stink of luxury and corruption that I smell here." She glanced now toward Dory, who scowled as he sipped the tea that she insisted he drink with her. They had long ago healed the rift caused by his support of Sebastian, but his reserve was still there.

"It was your choice, m'lady. You agreed to his Lordship's demand."

"Nay! It was not my choice," Roxana protested, trying to disown her responsibility. "Do you think he would have wed me if I had not agreed?"

Dory gave a lopsided smile. "I believe his Lordship would've wed ye no matter what ye said." He paused. "Begging yer pardon, m'lady, but there are times when I find ye most confusing. With one breath ye hate the man, and with the other ye love him to distraction. 'Tis but one you can choose."

Roxana glared at him. Why was it that Dory was always making her think? Clenching her fist, she grimaced. Then, releasing her fist, she sighed. "'Tis true, Dory, I do love him. That is the trouble. I do not love the king he supports, nor what that man has done to my country. Dory"—her voice was hoarse—"you must believe. I do love Sebastian, though I do not believe he always loves me. He is so"—she searched for the words—"so disapproving at times. The promise I have made to him is not a promise I can keep. 'Tis not fair."

"Do I locate Gilpatrick, then?" Dory stood.

There were tears in her eyes. She knew that Sebastian would be angry, and she hated that—but this was something she had to do. "Aye." she swallowed her pain. She would help William's sick men—surely Sebastian would not begrudge her that.

Turning again toward the window, she knew in her heart that Sebastian would not approve of her involvement, whatever her cause. She prayed he simply would not learn of her renewed deceit—and vowed that nothing she would say or do would bring harm to Sebastian or her uncle.

Roxana informed Gilpatrick that Louis XIV was preparing to send seven thousand men, and she added that Lauzun—that crafty duke —was also returning. Disguised once more as Alexander, she asked Gilpatrick if she could help to get medical supplies, and was horrified to learn that she must get the information from Berwick.

"'Tis he ye must approach. If ye can lead us to the supplies, ye'll be well rewarded, Alexander. We have found that the best way to get information from Berwick is through women. Drunk though he may get, he does keep his senses with the men. 'Tis only with the women that he reveals his true self."

"Like father, like son," Roxana commented.

Gilpatrick nodded. "Have ye a woman ye trust?"

"Aye." Roxana nodded. "I know just whom to use."

A smile touched her lips. She despised Berwick, yet he had once offered for her. Would he not be interested now in "talking" with her?

"I will have the information for you within the week."

Gilpatrick saluted. "It is good to have you back, Alexander."

She waited there until Gilpatrick disappeared into the mist and turned again toward the river, feeling a faint thrill.

Never before had she been so full of excitement. She knew that now she would truly be useful.

For a moment, she thought of her dear husband. How she longed for him, to have his arms about her, to feel his lips on hers. . . . She sighed. It was better that he remained where he was, for now. She knew that he would never tolerate her flirting with anyone —especially a womanizer like James Fitzjames, the duke of Berwick.

With renewed interest, Roxana saw the dressmaker once more, this time altering the gown she would have worn by adding a plunging neckline that astonished even the dressmaker.

"M'lady! Ye cannot wear that—not without some other covering."

"Oh, I shall have other covering." She smiled at the woman, fingering the laces. "You may put a bit of that here."

The woman flushed. "M'lady, what will Lord Bristol say when he finds out? I fear he will send me away! With his temper . . . m'lady, it is a known fact that his Lordship is quite possessive of ye—why, nary a man can speak to ye for fear of getting a dagger cast into his heart."

Roxana nodded, feeling a shiver go through her. "You need not worry, Eloise, my husband will not know about this gown. Besides, with the shortage of fabric in Dublin, I would think this would please you." She paused. "No, Lord Bristol will not know. He is too busy with his fighting to think on me. 'Tis seldom that I have even seen him since this new offensive has started. There are times when I do not even believe myself to be married." She glanced at the woman. Would the dressmaker's tongue carry her words to the right places? "While others come frequently home to see their wives and family and to dance on James's attendance, my husband would rather have the company of his men."

She noticed the woman's startled look, and quickly corrected herself. "Not that he favors men! 'Tis only that . . . he is more concerned about the war effort than he is about me." There, that should start some gossip. Sadly, she felt most of it was true.

"Very well, m'lady," said the dressmaker, resigned. "But I've warned ye."

Dory also protested when she informed him of her plans. "'Tis not right, m'lady. 'Tis far and away the most dangerous thing ye have yet done. What happens if the duke discerns your questions?"

She glared at him. "I will manage."

"There is always a first failure, m'lady. And consider the man's reputation! Ye can handle my lord, as he does love ye—."

Roxana sighed, squirming in her seat. "I can handle Berwick, as well. As for Sebastian . . . if he loved me as you say he does, then why does he not come to me more often?"

Tears came to her eyes. "I have played the simple wife, waiting for him. Where has it gotten me? I must do something on my own to stop the suffering and end this war—or to assist William, if I can. Why must I sit at home when perhaps I can spare a life or two?" Her heart pounded so quickly that she could no longer speak. Tears stung her eyes and poured down her cheeks in hot streams.

"Ah, lass," said Dory softly. "Does my lord know but a fraction of how ye love him?"

Roxana shrugged. "If he does not"—she forced herself to smile—"he must be a fool."

"Aye. He may well be one and not know it."

"You will help me, then?"

"Did you think I would not, m'lady? Perhaps between us we will save one or two lives."

Impulsively Roxana fetched them each a cup of tea from the table. Tears still in her eyes, she raised her cup to his. "To William," she whispered, "and Sebastian."

"To William and Lord Bristol," Dory echoed.

It was the dressmaker's warning that Roxana recalled as she prepared for the ball. She had been feeling skittish all day, and now she thought again of Sebastian.

She stared at herself in the mirror, conscious of her discomfort. Did she actually dare go dressed like this? Her gown was cut so low that it nearly exposed the rosy red nubs of her breasts, and the fabric was strained so tight that they appeared more massive than they were. Others, such as Lady Conway, dressed this way, but she was not others. Maybe Dory was right. Maybe she should not wear this. But she had to—she must show Berwick that she wanted to be with him; she had to tantalize and tease him as the other women did.

Self-conscious, she adjusted the generous rows of lace that barely kept her from being exposed, and then turned, noting how the train of the petticoat followed her. She had to admit that she liked the effect of the black translucent next to her pale skin, with her dark hair and green eyes. She almost wished Sebastian could see her now, and then hastily threw the thought away. No, she did not want him to see her like this—at least, not at this moment.

She studied herself a moment more, deciding on a star or a moon for her face. These things were silly, but Berwick liked his women dressed in the height of fashion.

Crowning her hair with the emerald tiara, she forced herself to smile. Candlelight caught the sparkles of the emeralds against her throat and dangling from her ears. If only there were some other way to get the information without damaging her reputation so much. She prayed that the gossip would not travel up north, else she would have some explaining to do.

Just thinking of Sebastian again made her long for him. Her face flushed with desire. She fanned herself to keep down the heat and liberally applied another coating of that

ghastly white powder. Choosing the moon—
for her moonlit rides—she placed the silhouette on her cheek.

Startled, she stood at the knock.

"I am coming, Dory," she called in response. She pulled on her cloak, took one
more look at herself and decided that it would
have to do. Without standing on ceremony,
she flung open the door . . . and stared into
the dark eyes of her dust-encrusted husband.

Her mouth dropped open slightly. "Sebastian!" Her heart beat quickly in momentary
terror, until her wifely emotions overcame
her. "Sebastian, are you ill? Are you hurt? Is
my uncle well?" She could think of no other
reason for him to have ridden pell-mell from
the north as he obviously had. Taking his
arm, she led him into the sitting room.

He eyed her strangely. "We are both well."
He continued staring at her.

She flushed. "Then why have you come?"
Realizing how strange that sounded, she hastily recovered. "I mean, you seem to have
ridden here as if the devil were on your tail
and I—it startled me." She leaned over to kiss
him gingerly, aware of the frown still on his
face, of the anxiety rushing through her. "I
am happy to see you, Sebastian." Receiving
no response, she drew back, hearing her heart
pound as her stomach tightened. "I did not
expect you this night." She gave a forced
laugh. "I vow the other wives will be quite
jealous."

"What is wrong, Roxana?" His all-knowing
gray eyes seemed to stare into her.

"Wrong?" She felt the flush coming to her face under the white paint. "Why, nothing is wrong. I told you. . . . I am just surprised to see you. I was on my way to the king's ball this very moment. In fact, I thought you were Dory coming to fetch me."

"Ah, yes." His cold gray eyes assessed her. "The King's ball. I suppose that explains your face."

She waited, wondering what to do now.

"There was a time, not too long ago, when you would have hugged me the moment you saw me." He paused. "Tell me, Roxana, have you been well?" He drummed his fingers on his knee. The material of his pants was wearing thin. She became conscious of the expensive fabric she had put into this gown. "I am well," she said softly. She averted her eyes.

"There is nothing urgent that you must tell me?" His hand reached out to stroke her cheek, drawing her eyes toward him as the fires began to burn within her.

She forced herself to resist him. With a coldness and calmness she did not know she had, she stated, "Nay, Sebastian, there is nothing I need to tell you." She looked directly into his eyes boldly and softened her tone. "I am glad you are safe and well." It took all her power to keep from kissing those fingertips, those hands, that face that gave her such pleasure. Pain stabbed at her heart as she saw the hurt and sadness in his eyes.

He took his hands from her. "What then of the message I have received?"

"What message?" The words caught in her

throat. Surely, the gossip could not have reached his ears already.

He pulled out a crumpled note. "'Tis from Dory. He says as I should make haste to return, as you are in sore need of me."

Forcing herself to give a laugh, she glanced into his eyes and noted the concern there. Her heart leaped with desire even as she mentally cursed Dory. "Sebastian, there is never a moment when I am not in urgent need of you." She touched him playfully.

Grinning, he leaned over to kiss her lightly on the mouth. "And I you, my Roxana—but why at this moment? Why did Dory write, and not you?"

Roxana shrugged. "I do not know why Dory sent that missive. I only know that I long for you day and night, and I constantly worry about your health and safety. I would be much happier if you would let me be with you."

"Nay, my sweet Roxy." He softened as he stroked her cheek again. "You would not be happy there. I would be too concerned about you to lead the men well. Well, since I have come, I might as well stay a day or so. 'Tis good to feast upon your beauty again, Roxana."

Roxana was melting with desire for him, and yet she was torn, as well. Damn Dory! Yes, she wanted Sebastian to stay—but not this night. Not at the cost of the plan. She needed for Berwick to believe she desired him—but if he thought so, then Sebastian would no doubt believe it, too. How could she flirt with James's son and yet have Sebastian be with her, love her? For just a moment, she released her fears and, putting her arms about him, kissed him.

"What are these tears I feel, precious?"

She swallowed hard. "They are but . . . tears of joy that you are well, safe . . . and with me."

"Oh, Roxana." His voice was husky as he kissed her deeply, fumbling with her cloak, heightening her passions as his hands covered her body. Her blood coursed hotly through her, but she could not give in—not now.

Pulling away abruptly, she babbled an excuse. "I mustn't. I'll be late. Berwick will be angry."

"What is this?" His eyes narrowed to daggerlike slits. *"Berwick?"*

Roxana flushed, and stammered, "I have promised him the first dance this night—and —I did not want to be late. I do hate to disappoint people."

"Is that a fact?" His eyes met hers. He touched his hand to her cheek again. "Well, you would much disappoint me if you do not continue what we have now started."

Her heart hammered. Her body wanted to continue, but her mind screamed no as she thought of the dead and dying men of William's troops—soldiers who needed the medications that Berwick had confiscated.

Resolutely, she shook her head. "'Tis a promise I have made first." She bent over once more to kiss him, to show him of her love. If only he truly knew how much she wanted to stay with him—now and forever. If only she could confide to him her mission this night! But, alas, he would not understand and he would surely forbid it.

"Will you come to the ball this night?"

Sebastian grunted. There was a weariness and a coldness in his tone that still hurt her deeply. "Aye, I suppose I must. The king will have my head if he learns I have been here and did not appear. You go along as planned, Roxana. I shall follow later and find you after I have washed off some of this gravel. And I trust I will not find you in the arms of Lord Berwick."

He stood and turned away from her, dismissing her. Roxana remained for a moment longer, feeling cold and alone. Tears sprang to her emerald eyes. She breathed deeply and brushed them away.

At the door, he turned. "'Tis most strange, Roxana, but I do not recall you being such a social butterfly before we were wed."

He was right. She was not then, nor was she now. "I have changed," she said simply, her voice barely a whisper as she tried to hide her emotions.

"Aye." His gray eyes cut her to the quick. "You have changed."

She continued to sit there for a moment more after he had gone. Finally, she could not put it off any longer.

Taking another deep breath, she steadied herself and pulled the cord so that Dory would fetch the carriage.

After this night, she vowed, she would

again be his loving wife—but she needed to learn where William's supplies had been hidden in order to save the lives of the ill men—even if it meant ruining her own life.

"Dory! Dory!" Roxana cried. "Why did you do it? Why did you have to summon him? Why just now?" She'd had Dory stop the carriage by the river, and now the tears rolled down her cheeks. "You should have seen his face." She sniffled, not wanting to ruin her carefully applied patches and makeup. She vowed that she would never use it again after this night.

Her voice choked. "He believes . . . I have changed. . . . He believes that"—the pain was so great she could barely swallow—"that I do not love him."

"Oh, m'lady! My Lady Roxy, I be deeply sorry. Sure as I'm Irish, I thought I would be doin' ye a good turn. I sent the note just after Lord Humphrey did come home, and his wife were gloating to ye. Ye did seem so sad, and ye did say that ye wished his Lordship would return for a day or two, since all ye had from 'em were letters. Well, ye were so upset that day, I got me boy, Charley, to write him. You taught Charley his letters yerself, remember?"

Roxana nodded, still feeling the lump in her throat, the hammering in her heart, the tears prickling her lids.

"Well, it weren't but two days later that ye met Gilpatrick." Dory hung his head. "I clean forgot about the letter 'til just this very moment."

"I see." She sighed heavily and dabbed her eyes with the linen. Shivering, she glanced out at the dark waters of the river. Her heart was heavy, her voice slow. "Well, what should I do?"

"Ye only have two choices, m' lady: to go as ye've planned—."

"And risk losing him."

"—or to tell him all."

"And have him be furious with me and forbid me to have any part of it." More tears came to her eyes. "No, Dory. I have to go on. Somehow I'll make Sebastian understand."

"Aye, m'lady." Dory patted her knee as he used to do when she was a child in need of comfort. "All will be fine. If anyone can win 'em back, ye can."

Chapter Seventeen

As they neared the palace, Roxana heard the gay shouts of greetings. She prayed she would be presentable—that her tears had not stained her face too badly.

Dory helped her out of the carriage, and for a moment she was transported back to the previous May. Was it only six months before that Sebastian had insisted on escorting her in to the queen's birthday ball?

She bit her lip, drawing blood. She must not think of him at the moment. Too much was at stake. Her heart hammered as she realized she still wore the revealing gown. It was one thing to make a fool of herself with good purpose, but now that he was to come to the ball she was loath to make a fool of him, too.

She sighed. It could not be helped. Maybe he would be so tired that he would fall asleep and not come to the ball—and not awake until she returned.

"You are all right, m'lady?"

Roxana returned her attention to her servant. She stared blankly at Dory. "I am fine." She gave him a slight smile as she entered the archway and gave her name and title to the guards, waiting a moment as it was passed down.

Handing her cloak to the footman, she forced herself to smile pleasantly, as if she always dressed this way. As she walked, the black translucent material gave the impression of revealing more than it did, whispering seductively with her every step. She was sure that the dress would help her accomplish her purpose. Berwick was never known to turn down a woman—any woman.

Well, Roxana thought, the dress had been made to create a sensation, and a sensation it was creating. But how would she handle it?

Her heart pounded as she walked down the long gallery covered with paintings. She could hear the loud laughter coming from within the ballroom.

There was a hush about the room as languid faces, powdered and rouged as she was this night, stopped their chatter to stare at her. One gentleman—she thought him to be Lord Hamilton—dropped his monocle, and had to bend quickly to retrieve it.

Lady Conway slid up to her shortly after the crowd's attention had turned to the newest arrival. "Does Sebastian know of this?"

"But of course." Roxana smiled sweetly. "He is coming this night, in fact."

"Is that so?" Lady Conway exclaimed. "I

cannot believe it. I do not know any man if he has allowed his darling, little wife to attire herself in *that*."

"No," Roxana said as calmly as she could, picking up a cup of punch. "It seems you do not know him at all—for Sebastian is not your man. He is mine."

"And who else is yours, my innocent little charmer?" Lady Conway hissed. "I hear that while he has loyally been fighting in the north, you have been amusing yourself here."

"Is that what you hear?" Roxana smiled into her cup as her eyes widened sweetly. "Well, it appears you listen to more gossip than is good for you, m'lady." Setting down her cup, she waved her black fan before her face. Then, shutting it firmly, she turned away.

She had hoped to approach Berwick, but no sooner had she left Lady Conway than the trumpets blared to announce the king. Roxana felt her heart in her mouth as she stepped closer to a pillar.

It was good that the dressmaker had gotten the gossip out so quickly, but she prayed that Sebastian would not hear it—and that James, too, would remain ignorant. If the king suspected she was taking lovers, he undoubtedly would try to force his company on her. Her stomach tightened as she recalled the moment when he had asked her into the gardens. She adored Sebastian and loved his every touch and she did not believe she could tolerate the thought of being close to another man, royal or not.

Her heart thudded as James smiled in her direction and then walked past, signaling for the dancing to begin.

"May I, m'lady?"

Roxana turned to see James Fitzjames, the duke of Berwick, attending her. His red hair was the same flaming color as his father's— his nose, too, the same color as his father's.

Pushing down her disgust, Roxana smiled sweetly up at him. "I would be honored."

"Ah, 'tis nice to hear you speaking my name with your ruby lips. You do look different this night—more attractive than I have yet seen you."

Roxana gave a mysterious smile. "'Tis only that I am with you, I'm certain."

Berwick grinned. "Pray, where is Lord Bristol this night? Steele seldom has let you out of his sight when he can help it, and I have never known you to attend a ball without him."

Roxana shrugged. "I do not know . . . and I do not care," she lied. "I believe he has plans to attend later, but you know how it is. We . . . do not talk much of late."

"Newlywed troubles?"

She accepted his hand and spun at the proper number of steps, knowing that her gown whispered to him, enticing him. "I fear that it is more than that. . . ."

"Oh?"

She glanced down at her feet, not knowing if she could pull off such a lie. "Well, I do not even know how to say this, but. . . ." She glanced up for a moment to be sure she had his attention and looked at him through her thick, dark lashes. Lowering her eyes again, she said, "I did have another love—one to whom I had hoped my uncle would wed me."

"Only he chose Sebastian instead, true?"

"True." She took the necessary steps about him, wishing the dance were over, and yet recognizing that she was making progress.

"Your uncle never did like me." Their eyes met again as his sweaty hands locked over hers. He snorted. "Dare I hope. . . . Pray, Lady Roxana, tell me: who it is that you loved so passionately?"

Roxana swallowed hard, hanging her head and shaking it slightly. "Do not make me say, sir; I cannot. It would not be fair."

"Not be fair? Why would it not be fair?" He glanced up and realized that others were staring at him. Sweating now, his round eyes seemed smaller in his large face.

"I do believe I need a drink," Roxana said deftly, turning to go off the dance floor.

"And I, too." Berwick wiped his brow with his linen, following her closely.

Quickly, he stepped in front of her, pouring out a glass of the punch and handing it to her. In great excitement, he began, "Lady Roxana, I have idolized you ever since you were a child, from the moment I saw you with your mother at Whitehall. I know I was but two and ten and you were but eight, but you had the darkest hair, palest skin and largest, greenest eyes I had ever seen. It was a deep loss to me, indeed, when your mother died and your uncle swept you off to this godforsaken land. How cruel I felt nature to be!" He moved closer to her. "When I found you here, I own I was again ecstatic. Life was again worth living. I could have kissed my royal uncle, His Highness of France, for allowing His Majesty to begin our campaign here—and then, alas, my suit was denied by your uncle.

"Lady Roxana. . . ." He bent his knee slightly, quickly, and wiping the sweat from his brow, he darted a look about to be sure that no one else had seen. "Do me the honor of visiting me in my rooms this night."

"Visiting you in your rooms?" She pretended astonishment. Quickly, she drank the whole of the punch in her cup as she trembled. She had expected she would have to work several days at least to get Berwick to take her into his trust. Now he was falling for her ploy instantaneously. Did he suspect something? No, she was sure that he did not. She could not think of Sebastian now—even though he intruded on her thoughts at nearly every moment.

"My Lady Roxana, I have loved you since as far back as I can remember. I promise you no harm—and no one shall ever know." He poured more punch into her empty cup. "You are so beautiful," he said, bending over as he tried to see past her low-cut gown.

"What—what of my husband?" she asked, bringing up the question that she knew he would expect.

"You have had other loves since your marriage, have you not? What did you do with him then? Can he not occupy himself? I know he has done so before."

Before? She wanted dearly to ask about Sebastian's other occupations, but she could not seem the jealous wife. Glancing up at Berwick's red-rimmed blue eyes, she debated how to approach him. Finally, she said, "I have been unhappy, yes—but other loves? No. You"—she lowered her eyes—"would be the first." Her voice was a whisper now. "I have told you. There is only one man for whom I feel any passion." That much, she thought, was true!

Berwick, understanding only what she wanted him to understand, grinned broadly. "Well, will you come? We can but talk this night—alone, of course—and after, we shall see what will happen."

Roxana did not for one moment believe that Lord Berwick would leave her alone if she went to his rooms, but she smiled sweetly, pretending to be fooled. She forced herself to put her hand in his. "I will find a way to be at your rooms this night."

"Will you? Oh, my wonderful lady." He kissed her hand as he brought it to his lips, slobbering over her. It took all her effort to not pull away.

"We should celebrate. No doubt," he chirruped, grinning, "this will be the first night of many for us, my love."

Roxana said nothing, but merely smiled as he poured yet another drink for himself. She sipped hers while he drank the whole portion of his.

His bleary blue eyes took on a sparkle. "I will bring some of His Majesty's best French brandy, newly arrived from my uncle. That will help us to celebrate more."

Again, Roxana nodded silently, praying that she could get whatever information she needed before she had to put action behind her words. Had she gotten in over her head this time, as Dory feared? No, she would handle it. She could handle anything she had to . . . as long as she knew it was for the men.

Relief flooded her as Berwick walked off. His last instructions were that they should leave at separate times, and he had dropped the key to his rooms in her hand. Using her fan to cool herself, she turned toward the arch.

The fan halted in midair. Her heart seemed to stop as Sebastian's silver gray eyes drilled into her soul. What had he seen? What had he heard? What did he know?

He stepped forward. Displeasure was written all over his face. Anxiety tightened her stomach.

"Where in God's earth did you ever get that gown?" he hissed, taking hold of her arm. "That is not what I expect my wife to be wearing at a king's ball—or at anyone's ball. How many times have you worn it? For whose enjoyment?"

"I have worn it but once . . . only now." Roxana swallowed hard.

"Have you been making a habit of exposing your charms? Have I misjudged you, Roxana?"

She felt the pain that was threatening to

overwhelm her. It wasn't the pain of his hand gripping her forearm; it was the ache that he truly doubted her.

She tried to shake her head, but could not. Liquid pain shimmered in her eyes.

In disgust, he threw down her arm. "You are right, my darling wife. These many months apart, you have changed. I should have come back sooner and seen the Pandora's box I had opened. I had thought that you, of all people, would know how my men were treated and would respect that. If they cannot leave, then neither do I. Like the precious William you so admire," he spat out, "I do not curry favors for my rank. Yet while he gets your devotion, I receive only your scorn."

She tried to open her mouth to speak but no words would come. What could she say? "Sebastian, I—."

"No, my lady." His voice chilled her to the bone. "Two can play the same game. You return and change that dress now—or do not expect to see me in the morning."

Trembling inside, Roxana took a deep breath. It took all the courage within her, all her faith in William, all her love for Sebastian, for her to shake her head. She could not let him ruin her plans, not now.

"It is like that, is it?" His stormy eyes searched her face.

She could barely speak from the heaviness of her heart as she lifted her eyes to his. "It is like that," she whispered.

He stared a moment, as if struck in the face.

Then, crashing his cup to the ground, he spun on his heel. She winced as several people turned. Her heart cried out. She wanted to run to him, to hold him, to comfort him—but how could she?

Roxana recovered as quickly as she could, trying to hide the hurt she felt as Sebastian danced with a smiling Ardella Conway. Her jealous heart wanted to burst, but for this night she would have to ignore it.

Allowing herself to be swept into a second dance with Berwick, she could hear people talking—not only about her gown, but about the way Berwick's eyes had followed her all the night long. She knew it was not good to allow him to dance with her a second time so closely following the first, yet what could she do? No one else had dared offer for her, and she knew that if she sat this one out, watching her husband and that . . . whore, she would go mad with jealousy.

"Bristol does not appear pleased this night," Berwick whispered.

"No," Roxana answered.

"Is it because of us, my favorite darling? Surely, you were not so foolish as to confide to him about us."

Roxana glared at him, hating the sticky touch of his hands. "I have said nary a word to him, though I fear he has a suspicious nature." She glanced up. "May I call you James?"

Grinning, Berwick nodded.

"Well, 'tis obvious, James, that we are"
—she paused—"interested in each other.
Your attentions to me this night have been
quite forward. In fact, I believe that to keep
further talk to a minimum, we should part
ways after this dance. To . . . see each other
later, of course," she added hastily.

His blue eyes, embedded in thick flesh,
looked shrewd. "Aye," Berwick said hoarsely.
"It would not do to have one of His Majesty's
favorites accuse me of cuckolding him."

Roxana blushed and lowered her lashes.
"Pray, do lower your voice, James." She lifted
her eyes, smiling sweetly once more.

Berwick beamed as if nothing were wrong.
As the music slowed, he escorted her back to
the punch bowl. "I do believe I shall have yet
another cup. 'Tis good stuff—but then, His
Majesty gives only the best for his parties."

But not for his men, Roxana thought as she
pleasantly accepted another glass, watching,
sipping, as he drank thirstily and smacked his
lips. The more he drank, the better she believed it would be for her.

"Why do you not ask. . . ." She paused, turning to see Sebastian still in deep conversation
with Lady Ardella Conway. ". . . Lady Conway?" Roxana flushed. "I do hear that she
dances marvelously well."

Berwick turned, seeing Sebastian with his
former mistress. "Faith! I do not like that
woman much. Her tongue is sharp as a razor,
but"—he smiled at Roxana—"for your wish,
sweetings, I will do as you ask."

She waited a moment to see that both Berwick and Sebastian were occupied—Berwick with Lady Conway, and Sebastian, to her relief, with Lord Tyrconnel—before she edged toward the gallery.

How thankful she was that Berwick had already given her the key! She prayed that the information she sought would be readily available. If she could not find it in his townhouse, she would have to wait for him—a prospect that did not thrill her.

She paused a moment more outside to speak with her servant.

"I do not like this, m'lady," Dory complained. "His Lordship is in a foul mood, I hear, and here ye are goin' off to Berwick's. He ain't a man to deal uneven with, if ye know what I mean."

"Aye," Roxana sighed, "but 'tis the only way. Do not question me further, Dory. Gilpatrick said Berwick is the only one with the information, and that this is the best possible way to obtain it from him." She stepped in the carriage, giving him directions to Berwick's townhouse. "Your job will be to see that Sebastian does not leave the ball while I am with Berwick. You will return there once you have left me." Her eyes were like hard emeralds at the thought of possibly having to spend time with the king's son.

"Just be careful, m'lady." The servant paused to closed the door. "I do know what yer going through . . . and I be sorry for what part I had in it."

Roxana patted Dory's hand and sighed.

"Dory, do you think that Sebastian will ever forgive me?"

The old coachman looked into the liquid green of her eyes, and his own welled up with tears. "Aye," he said softly. "He canna help but. We'll go quick like and perhaps ye will get what ye need before Lord Berwick returns."

Nodding, Roxana settled back for the short drive to the lodgings of the royal bastard.

Letting herself in with the key, she wrinkled her nose in disgust. The smell was vile. How could he expect anyone, even someone hopelessly in love with him, to come to a place such as this?

A floorboard creaked. She spun about. A trap? Her heart hammered. She was glad that her hood was still up.

"M'lady." A dwarflike creature appeared and bowed. "The master is not yet home."

"I know that." Roxana muffled her voice through her cloak. "He has told me to wait in his study."

"His study?" The servant seemed confused, but evidently decided to comply. Nodding, he led the way.

Following the little man, Roxana walked up the elaborately carved staircase. In better times, it would have been a showpiece of the house. Now . . . Well, war was war, she thought, following the servant into the dimly lit study.

Bookshelves were all about, but few were in use. It would seem that the duke did not much care for reading. Well, she was not here to examine his tastes in literature. She stood briefly in front of the roaring fire to warm herself, noticing that the servant had left her alone. He was a strange little man, but then so was James Fitzjames.

Taking off her cloak, Roxana laid it on the chair and perused the room in a quick exam. The desk was the most obvious place to hide information, so she started there; but she found nothing save some scrawls of names.

Quickly, she went through the rest of the drawers, determined to leave just as soon as she was able. But she had gone through too much this night already to give up without any information.

Biting her lower lip, she paused and began to walk about the room. Nothing but dust on the shelves. She sneezed, stirring up more dust as her head cleared suddenly.

Dust meant powder. Powder was the form in which most of the medications were shipped. Quickly, she again returned to the desk. Berwick had scribbled some nonsense about putting the powder in the powder magazine. It had not made sense to her before, but now it did. Trinity College had become a barracks to hold "recalcitrants." The chapel had become a powder magazine. What better place than that to hide medical supplies?

Her heart raced with joy. Now, if she could only get there! Then Gilpatrick would certainly be proud of her. She smiled. She would dress in her riding clothes and pretend to have a message from her uncle. It was as simple as that.

Donning her cloak, she realized she would be glad to be out of this miserable dress. She wished she could tell Sebastian; she wished that he would help her. It would be so much more simple—but she knew that she could not. She only prayed that she would be able to make him understand when the time came.

Nearing the door, she stiffened. The muscles of her stomach tightened.

"Roxana, my lady love," Berwick's high-pitched voice squeaked from downstairs.

She closed her eyes in disgust as her throat tightened. She had hoped to avoid this, but it seemed she could not.

Removing her cloak, she took a chair near the fireplace. Her hands went to her head as she tried to think.

"Oh, Roxana, Roxana, you naughty little child. Papa was looking all over for you," Berwick said as he opened the study door. Judging by the red of his nose and his less-than-straight walk, he had obviously kept drinking after she had left.

"I was sure you would realize where I had gone, James." She lowered her eyes. "I could not bear to be in the same room with you and not be near you, not touch you," she said, feeling her stomach tighten more so in disgust.

Berwick weaved over to her chair and put his clammy hands on her shoulders, trying to stroke her neck. It was all Roxana could do to keep still.

"Pray, James," she said, her voice soft

and weak. "I do have such a headache. Perchance you have some powder for such things?"

"Is it truly bad?" He stared at her with his misted eyes.

"Truly," she nodded, making her voice as pained as possible. "I do not think I could bear to have . . . to enjoy the pleasure of your company without it." She stared up at him, her eyes wide.

"Then of course I will fetch a powder immediately, my precious."

He bent to kiss her neck, causing her to shudder as the disgust went through her. She would have Maggie bring her a bath, no matter what time she arrived home!

"I will be but a moment, my sweet. You remain here."

"I could not move—not only for my pain, but for my very great desire for you." She stared up into his rheumy blue eyes.

Berwick smiled and managed to stumble out the door.

Waiting but a moment, Roxana grabbed her cloak. On second thought, she reached also for his ring of keys. He would think he had left it somewhere and these keys would help her this night. Hurrying down the once elegant staircase, she gasped. Standing in the door, pistol drawn, was Sebastian Steele. He had not seen her yet, she was sure. Had he followed her?

There was no time to think on it, for Berwick was returning down the hall with the requested powder.

"Oh, Sebastian! My dearest!" she screamed. She saw Berwick freeze, then disappear quickly. Without another look, she ran down the steps. Sebastian's eyes widened. Not thinking about his obvious anger, she grabbed him by the wrist.

"Come! Quickly!" she hissed, pulling him into the street and toward the carriage, where Dory now waited.

Too stunned to say anything, Sebastian followed her. After they had safely reached the carriage and had climbed inside, Roxana—much to the men's surprise—burst out laughing.

She laughed mainly from relief at having escaped Berwick so easily, but also at the shaken look she had glimpsed on his face before he had chosen to hide like the coward he was.

Finally, holding her side, she managed to calm down.

Aware of the deathly silence from the seat opposite, she righted her position and met the simmering silver eyes of her husband.

"Perhaps now you would be good enough to tell me what this is all about?"

Roxana did her best to hide the smile that was fast creeping back onto her face. How perfect it had gone. "My love, I forget—you do not know, do you?"

"No, my darling wife." His voice was soft, but held a threat. "I do not know. Tell me."

Roxana inhaled, suddenly serious. How to start? How to tell him?

"I would first like to know what you were

doing at Berwick's," he began, seeing that she would not.

She glanced out at the street they were now passing. "I do not wish to talk about it now." She flushed. "It was nothing, Sebastian. Believe me."

"Can I?" His eyes narrowed. She could feel the coldness coming from him, the chill that separated them.

Forcing herself to remain calm, she knocked on the ceiling. The carriage stopped momentarily as she leaned her head out.

"Is everything all right, m'lady?" Dory asked correctly, his expression worried.

Roxana nodded. "Aye, Dory." She sighed. "Let us take a drive to Trinity."

The coachman tipped his hat as she drew the window drapes shut.

"Pray, my dear, why do we pass Trinity College at this time of night? And I will ask again: what were you doing at Berwick's? Why did you act so strangely as we left?"

She glanced at him. Her heart pounded, but she could say nothing. "Roxana, I demand an answer. Now!" He gripped her hand.

"Very well." She took a deep breath and met his eyes. "But you are not going to like it. In fact, I fear you are going to be angry with me."

His eyes were already glowing like coals. "I can be no more angry with you than I am now, Roxana."

She swallowed hard. "I could not keep my promise to you, Sebastian. Not when so many men are dying. Berwick's force made a lucky foray to capture the only boxes of medical supplies to come from Holland this month. Berwick had the information. I needed to know where the medications had been hidden."

"What are you saying, woman? Do you mean to steal them?" His eyes were like flint as his nostrils flared.

She steeled herself for his words. "I mean only to return them to their rightful use—to keep men alive." Her eyes now blazed almost as hot as his.

"So you went to Berwick. Did you sleep with him to get your precious information?"

Abruptly she pulled away, wincing. Her voice was hoarse with emotion. "Would you really care if I did?" Tears came unbidden to her eyes that shimmered now like lakes of green. "When you return, you expect me to be the same untouched loving little wife you left. I cannot be untouched—not when I'm alone for weeks on end, and not when I constantly hear lustful stories of you and Lady Conway!" She swallowed hard. "I care only that the war be soon ended, and that the soldiers I support not die for the duke of Berwick's trickery."

The pain returned and she pushed it down. "If it matters at all, nay, I have not slept with another. It would not enter my mind—though from this night's ball, it would seem that your thoughts are not as pure as mine." Her heart quickened as she stared at him.

Sebastian stared back. She didn't relent.

Finally, he sighed. His voice softened. "Roxana, judging from outward appearances, it would seem that your thoughts are well away from being pure."

Tears stung her eyes. "But they were! I could not even bear that sweaty oaf to touch me!"

A sad smile curved Sebastian's lips. "What makes you think I was not playing to Ardella because I was jealous and hurt?"

She stared at him, angry and suspicious, her eyes wide in the dim light. "You did not plan to spend the night with her? You said you would and I—."

"Roxana, my sweet, would I have hotly followed you to Berwick's if I planned to be with Ardella?"

She swallowed the lump and shook her head. Tears slid down her cheeks.

"In truth, my little imp, I have missed you madly these few months. I thought you understood my need to be with the men. I am not like most of James's commanders, who come home at a whim's drop."

Roxana hung her head. "I do know, and I do not. I am torn between desperately wanting you, and wanting you to do what you believe is best."

"I know." His hand touched her cheek and he moved across the seat to her. "I, too, want the war ended quickly, but I have explained to you: I am devoted to your uncle, and through him to James." He ran his thumb down the line of her jaw, leaning forward to kiss her brow as she smoothed the loose hair from her face. "Come, my precious, let us not argue the politics of the reign. Let us go home and enjoy my brief time here." Again he bent, his lips taking hers.

Even while her senses whirled with desire for him, Roxana kept her hold. She had not come so far this night only to give up. She would not!

Her nimble fingers stroked his back as she returned his kiss with a passion that excited him. Then she pulled back as her hand rested on his pistol, drawing it out.

"I do love you, Sebastian," she said, pointing the gun at him, "but certain priorities come first. This night"—she swallowed hard, seeing the pain in his eyes—"I do what I have planned."

His voice was subdued. "Do you plan to kill me?"

"Kill you?" Her eyes widened. "Nay! Of course not. I plan to have you help me—but I do not know if you would do it willingly. I did not plan to use you, but since you are here, it is best I make use of you."

Sebastian grimaced and stared at the gun. "I do nothing willingly, except make love to one of William's best spies. But, aye, Roxana, I will help you this night—if you put that gun down."

She pressed her lips together thoughtfully. "Can I trust you not to betray me?"

"Have you not trusted me all these months, my dear? One more episode in your sordid career as a spy would not make much more difference."

Roxana gulped. "You realize, of course, they could hang you for knowingly helping me."

His gray eyes were steady on her. "Aye. If the truth be known, however, I would long ago be hanged for what I have already with-held about you."

She placed the gun on the seat beside her. "I do love you." She raised her arms to his neck and kissed him fully, this time without re-straining thought.

As she suspected, the boxes of medication were in the powder magazine at Trinity College Chapel. With Sebastian's help, it was not difficult to obtain entrance. Taking the gun with them, just in case it might be needed, she and Sebastian let the guard think that Lord Bristol had been sent to pick up the supplies because they were needed. Roxana, now dressed as Alexander, was to help him carry the supplies.

"You do not trust me to come with you to drop your supplies?" he asked as the carriage paused by the townhouse.

Roxana lowered her eyes. "It is not my decision. I do promise, Sebastian, that I will be home in a moment."

Sebastian's keen eyes examined her face. "Very well, Roxy. One half-hour I give you. No more. Then I shall come looking for you."

She nodded, climbing into the second seat

beside Dory. Driving off, she turned once and blew him a kiss.

The drop-off went well. Gilpatrick was more than pleased with her. "'Tis said you are one of our most valued men, Alexander."

"Indeed?" She could scarcely believe the compliment. "You are not simply humoring me?"

"Nay! Your information has been of great help. William plans to suitably reward you." He paused. "You are back with us again permanently?"

The question frightened her. She nodded as she thought of Sebastian. He would not be pleased, but she had to continue.

"Good," Gilpatrick said, saluting her.

Roxana was thoughtful as Dory drove back to the townhouse. It had been a half-hour exactly. Should she tell Sebastian she was continuing? Well, if it came up, she would. If not, she would keep her own counsel. She sighed heavily.

She was surprised to see the candles still burning. Sebastian must be waiting up for her. Still, with the shortage, he did not need to use so many.

Letting herself in, she paused in the hall. Another woman's cloak was on the bench. She stopped.

Voices were coming from the sitting room.

Torn at wanting to see who it was and yet not wanting to be seen dressed as she was, Roxana quickly put on her own cape and moved to the sitting-room door, the stranger's cape in her hand.

Sebastian was on the sofa. Next to him, cozy as could be, her head in his lap as they watched the fire and spoke softly, was Lady Ardella Conway!

"Well." Roxana entered the room and strode across the carpet to stand before the fire. "I am glad someone is making use of the fire I ordered."

Ardella Conway sat upright quickly, blushing as she did. Sebastian, too, reddened.

Roxana's heart hammered.

"'Tis rather late for a visit, is it not, m'lady?" Roxana eyed the older woman. "My husband and I wish to retire now."

"You and your husband? What right have you to call him husband when you do not even care about his pleasure or see to his wants? When you neglect him for others?"

Roxana's nostrils flared. Her angry eyes quickly looked at Sebastian and then again at Lady Conway. "I suppose *you* were seeing to his pleasure?" Ardella glanced at Sebastian. Seeing that he was not going to say anything, Lady Conway spoke again. "*Any* time I am with Sebastian, it is good." Her hand went out to him, but he did not take hers. "It is *very* good." She withdrew her hand.

"I suggest you leave now, Ardella," Sebastian said noncommitally. "Roxana and I have some matters to discuss."

Lady Conway shrugged coolly. Taking her cloak from Roxana, she swept it over her shoulders. "I trust your driver will take me home? I did not call mine." She glanced at Sebastian. "I did not expect to need him back before morning."

"I will instruct Dory," Sebastian told Roxana.

She nodded. "He's outside." Sebastian and Ardella left the room together, and Roxana turned to the fire. Tears filled her eyes. Angrily she tore off her cape and threw it to the floor.

Moments later, she heard the door close behind her.

"Roxana?"

"What?" The tears choked her voice. She could not turn to see him.

"Roxana." He came up behind her. His arms went to her shoulders. "Nothing happened, my love."

"I do not want that woman in my house again."

"You are being a jealous shrew."

"Perhaps, but I have so little of you I'll not share what I have."

"Should I, then, be forced to share you with William?"

"That is different," she protested. "That is like me forbidding you to fight for James." She turned.

"Aye," he admitted. "I suppose it is, in truth." He leaned over to kiss her brow. "Nothing did happen. You have asked me to believe in you this night, so you must now believe in me. I am sure Ardella wanted me to make love to her, but I would not."

265

"She did not expect I would be home this night?"

Sebastian grimaced. "Apparently Lord Berwick let it be known that he was planning to see you. Ardella saw an opportunity. Roxana, I detest the idea that people think you have loose morals—but I believe you that nothing happened and nothing will."

"And will nothing happen in the future with you and Ardella?"

He leaned over, grazing her mouth with his. "Nothing, so long as I am assured of your love."

Her arms about him, she returned his passion. Her fingers trailed down his lean hard body, exciting him as he excited her.

"Come," he whispered huskily, lifting her into his arms. "Show me how you will assure me of your love."

"Gladly." She nibbled his ear, leaning her head against him as he carried her to the bed.

Gently, lovingly, he allowed his roaming hands to excite her, undress her, caress her, as she did the same for him.

"You are right!" he laughed, coming down next to her beautiful naked body. "Men's clothes are much easier to do and undo. I shall have to ask you to wear them each time that we make love, and then I shall not have to fumble with your hooks."

She sucked in her breath. "Then you approve of my work?" she asked, hoping against hope.

"Nay, Roxy, I do not approve. I cannot. Indeed, I ask again that you give it up."

She shook her head.

He frowned.

"Do you love me still?" She teased the hairs of his secret place, seeing his desire for her grow.

"Aye," he said, gruffly. "I do." His mouth found hers as his calloused hands magically brought her to wave after wave of ecstasy and pleasure. His tongue licked and kissed over the length of her body, settling on her rosy nipples, sucking, tasting as she arched her hips in desperate desire.

"Oh, Sebastian!" she called out. "Love me, please. Love me!"

Mischievously, he shook his head as his hands stroked her length and began to circle gently up her inner thigh, driving her to the brink of insanity. Gently, he moved his thumbs farther and farther, rolling the motion until she gasped with pleasure, clawing his back with her desire.

In retaliation, she reached for him, but he laughed and moved quickly away. Then, after a moment, he allowed her the pleasure of stroking him. When she heard his ragged breathing, she knew he was ready and raised herself for him, welcoming his hard thrust into her moist satin sheath as she spun into a never-ending vortex. Together they rode the crest of the wave and together they fell.

His breathing was heavy. Sebastian rolled off and kissed her brow. "I do miss you so," he said.

"Then come back more often, like the other men."

"I am not like the others, Roxy. Please, do not ask it of me."

He paused, seeing her sadden. "Very well. I will see what I can do—if you promise to stop your foolishness with William."

She stared at him. "Do you really mean that?"

"Of course." He touched her cheek.

For just a moment, Roxana hesitated. Then tears misted her eyes. "Faith! I cannot. I am needed."

"I, too, need you," he whispered.

She paused, her hand touching him. Were her own needs and his more important than serving William?

Sebastian became angry at her silence. "Very well, Roxana. Have it your way. I will not come home again until you have given up this silly spying—until you have written to me and promised me so. I fear that you use and abuse my trust. Everything you hear from your uncle and from me gets relayed to William."

Tears slid down her cheeks. "I do not . . . abuse your trust."

"Do you not? Even if I were to tell you vital information?" He shook his head. "Nay, Roxana. As long as you work for William, I cannot trust you. The truth remains: you are working against me." He rose and grabbed his clothing from the chair. Quickly, he dressed. "I hope to see a letter from you soon."

She stared after him, after the closed door, not believing that he had gone. Tears flowed freely now. No matter what he said, he would have to understand. She could not stop this part of her. Closing her red-rimmed eyes, she prayed that William would soon win the war and that Sebastian and she would be together again.

Sniffling her tears dry, she fell into a fitful sleep.

Chapter Eighteen

FOR THE NEXT FEW MONTHS THERE REMAINED an uneasy truce between them. She did write, but there was no promise. He wrote to let her know of his health and that of her uncle.

She missed him sorely, but she would not, she could not succumb to demand.

Roxana knew that James, with his superior force, should easily have been able to oust Schomberg, but he could not. Many said that James's presence in Ireland was hurting the man more than helping him. Privately Roxana agreed, especially since the man continually talked of his planned invasion of England, constantly reminding the Irish that they were but a stepping stone to his real desire. Despite the support of Louis XIV, the man was failing miserably.

Roxana's thoughts turned to her uncle. He was a loyal servant to James, yet His Majesty had not rewarded him. Uncle Patrick had been promised the earldom at the beginning of this war, and still he was only the tax collector of the city—and brigadier of the army. The fact that the Irish loved her uncle had no effect on James.

Now that William had landed, she was sure the conflict would soon end. Then Sebastian and she would be able to love without quarreling.

These past few weeks, since William had come, Dublin had been like a city under siege. Food had become scarce, yet Roxana did not mind. Looking in the mirror she realized how gaunt her face had become. Well, if William won, the price would be well worth it.

She hoped that Sebastian was well. She had had no communication from him of late. His last letter was from Castlemont—James's last defensible stronghold. Castlemont had just fallen, and she knew not where Sebastian was or even if he lived.

She paced the room. Was it possible to pray to the same God for two different victories? She prayed for William, but she also prayed for the safety and success of her husband and uncle. Oh, why had she ever fallen in love with one of James's men?

Tears came to her eyes. The knock at the door startled her. "Enter," she called, standing as Dory brought forth the letter she had been hoping for.

"Is it from his Lordship?" Dory asked anxiously.

Pursing her lips, she shook her head. "Nay. It is from my uncle. He says they are both safe in Westmeath, but will soon be joining James on the Boyne below Dundalk, where it appears the next match will be." She glanced up, feeling the heaviness in her heart.

"Is he confident?"

Roxana folded the note slowly and shook her head. "He asks that I pray for them." Tears again came to her eyes. "Oh, Dory, I have waited so long for this moment—and yet if I lose them. . . ." She sank down onto the sofa and sighed. "I suppose there is nothing one can do but wait."

"Aye," the servant replied. "Wait and see— and wait some more."

As June drew to a close, the sultry heat and stink of the city became more and more oppressive. Tempers flared. Roxana wondered how much more she could take. There had to be some word soon or she would go mad—but no word came.

At last she told her servant, "I do not care what Sebastian said. If I have had no word by Wednesday next, I shall go to him myself."

"Will you give him the promise he wants?"

She paused, and then shook her head. "I cannot. Still, I must see him. I must know if he is well." She paced the room, following the well-worn path that she had come to know these past weeks. She had to see him soon or she would die.

On the last night of June, at midnight, she awoke to the shriek of the wind. Pulling her blanket around her, she walked to the window to hear the melancholy howl. Was it the banshee speaking? Was her uncle or Sebastian to die this morrow?

Hastily, she crossed herself as she shivered, and uttered all the prayers she knew to take care of them.

The first of July was hot and bright, as the days before it had been, yet there was a deathly silence that made Roxana know it to be different. Rumors had been rife about the imminent battle. She knew this would be the day.

Quickly she dressed, feeling the sticky heat despite the early hour of the morning. Hurrying to the city gates, she found them already shut and closely guarded. Most Protestants, it seemed, were keeping to their homes, waiting and hoping; but those like herself who had men fighting were in the streets, milling about like sleepers in a lost world.

Each hour brought a fresh report—a different report.

First it was that the French were in Dublin Bay, that William had been killed. Roxana pressed her lips tightly together. She did not think that was possible. She had to find out for sure.

Another—express from Waterford—announced that the Isle of Wight was in French hands.

Then came word that the English on the right wing of the Boyne had been routed completely. Wild cheering rose up among those who waited at the gate. For Sebastian's sake, she was pleased. For her own, she was not.

She watched then as most present returned to their homes, preparing for the parties that would welcome back the conquering King James. Celebrations were sure to follow his victory. Roxana could not leave the gate, however—not until she had some word of her uncle and Sebastian.

The merciless heat continued as Dory begged her to go in. Refusing, she accepted the food he brought, but could eat little.

By early evening the news was different, and Roxana's heart was torn with pain. She saw the Irish stragglers come in on their tired horses. The Irish had had the worst of all beatings. Many had fled the superior Dutch and Danish forces led by Schomberg and William himself.

Roxana could not help but feel pride for the king she supported, and yet her words to all who came were "have you seen Lord Bristol or Mr. Sarsfield?"

The town was now filled with dusty, wounded and weary men. Carriages perpetually came streaming in. Some carried the wounded; some did not.

Over and over, she repeated her questions. Over and over, the answer was negative.

Unsure of what to do, she continued her vigil.

A little after nightfall the heralds announced James's arrival. He came with two hundred horses in disorder, proclaiming that the Irish had played him false—that had it been Englishmen fighting, they would have stayed.

At Castlegate, he was received by a worried Lady Tyrconnel, who kissed the royal hand as she bowed. Roxana found it hard to believe that anyone could still have faith in the man. She wished she could tell him so. Even as he continued to complain about the Irish, she heard one lone peasant woman respond far more boldly than she could have. "Perhaps," the woman called to King James, "the Irish would not play you false, if you yourself were true."

Infuriated, the king rose in his saddle, but the woman had disappeared.

Hard behind the king came the bulk of the Irish cavalry, and with them, the kettle drums.

It was then, despite the darkness, that Roxana saw the unruly mass of red hair she knew to belong to Patrick Sarsfield.

"Uncle Patrick!" she called, running toward him, pushing away people and hearing their curses. "Uncle Patrick!" she yelled again, seeing that he did not stop.

He heard her now, and turned. Defeat, worry and concern were all over his handsome, lined face.

"Oh, Uncle Patrick!" She threw her arms about him, hugging him. "You are alive!"

"Aye." The man's voice was a fraction of his usual boom.

She wiped the tears from her eyes and looked about. All that mattered was that he and Sebastian were safe. "Where is. . . ." She paused, feeling uncertain of their relationship after their last quarrel. "Where is my husband? Where is Sebastian?"

"'Tis not a nursemaid I am, lass," Patrick snapped. "I've had problem enough in preventing harm to His Majesty."

"But where is he? He is not with you?" The desperation in her voice cut through his own irritation and frustration.

"He is probably just behind me, Roxy, lass," he said, somewhat softer. "Be a good girl. Go home now. Sure as the dawn, he'll be home soon."

"You are sure he is well?"

"Would I tell you so if that were not the case?"

Roxana forced herself to smile at him. "I do love you, Uncle." She hugged his dirt-encrusted form to her. "Very well," she said. "I'll do as you say."

"That's my lass," he sighed, "I must hurry now. I must be by James's side. We will see him to the port, no doubt. I do not agree, but others want him safely out of the city. He'll sail to France for new supplies."

She nodded, thinking that there were many who wanted James out of the city permanently. "I will see you at Lucan, no doubt," she said.

"No doubt," Sarsfield responded with a sad smile. Turning from his niece, he hurried to James's side.

"'Tis lost for them?" Dory asked, coming to her.

"It would appear so—unless Berwick, who

is still in the field, can rally them. That I would doubt."

"And his Lordship?"

Roxana bit her lower lip pensively. "Uncle says he is just behind, but I am worried. Dory, I. . . ." She turned to look into the eyes of her servant. "All is not right." Tears came to her eyes. "I do feel that my uncle does not know. Sebastian needs me." She paused. "Will you come with me if I go out of the city?"

The coachman sighed and stared a moment at his mistress. "'Tis not pleasant there. Not only be there soldiers, dead and fleeing, but there be scavengers, too."

"I don't care. 'Tis not pleasant here," she responded. "I cannot wait. If you will not come, I will go alone."

"Very well. I will come with you."

Relieved to have some plan, she returned to the townhouse. Quickly, she dressed in her riding clothes. Food—she would need some food and water. She took what she could from the kitchens, though they were as bare as she had ever seen them. Then she took some linen strips in case bandages were needed. Maybe her uncle was right. Maybe if she just waited, Sebastian would return; but she could not take that chance.

Fire was skittish from the crowd of bedraggled soldiers still streaming in, as well as from the hands of the many who offered her fortunes so that they might have the horse to escape with. With care, she and Dory led Fire from the city.

Not a one could believe that she was headed toward the advancing armies rather than away from them.

"Ye'll be sorry!" one called as Roxana passed through the gates.

"'Tis only the dead behind," another added.

Roxana shrugged, only praying that she would find Sebastian safe.

With Dory walking beside Fire, the going was slower than it might have otherwise been, but the coachman refused to ride with her and refused to allow her off so that he might ride.

Several times her anxiety made her want to push ahead, but she needed Dory and she'd not let him fend for himself against the crowds that still might come, against those desperate to escape. Together, they stood a chance of finding her husband. Alone, she did not.

With the coolness of the night breaking into the colorful dawn, Roxana realized that she had lost track of time. She had not closed her eyes in twenty-four hours—not that she could possibly sleep now! She was thankful that she'd packed the provisions.

Except for an occasional straggler, the meadows were now empty and the road about them silent. They had gone around the long way to avoid the armies, and now she was not sure they had done right. It seemed that all those who had been able to flee had already done so.

"Oh, Dory," she whispered, forcing herself

to sip some of the water, "I am so afraid. What if—?"

"Do not think on that, m'lady," Dory said gruffly. "Maybe he is gone ahead, and we have missed him. Maybe. . . ."

She sighed. Her heart told her that he was yet ahead, among the wounded or dying. She wiped away the tears on her sleeve. If only she could get to him in time! If only she could tell him how she loved him.

For his safety—the thought closed her throat, and she swallowed the painful lump— she would give up William. She would!

She inhaled the misty morning air, seeing the fog as it traveled from the river overland. The day promised to be cooler than yesterday.

"Shall we find him today, Dory?"

Tight-lipped, Dory nodded. "I do believe, as there are bodies just over that hill."

Closing her eyes, praying for God to give her strength, Roxana nodded and directed Fire. "Then, let us continue."

Dory was right. There were bodies, but none of them were men she knew. She forced herself to go from man to man, looking at the grotesque features frozen in death, seeing the missing limbs, missing eyes—and feeling herself grow sicker by the moment. Soon the scavengers would come and there would be nothing left of them.

"Oh, Dory," she sobbed against his shoulder. "I do not think I can take much more of this."

"Shall we go back?" he asked gently.

She shook her head, drawing the fallen hair out of her eyes as she felt the heat beating down on her and the sweat on her brow.

It was in the next field, not far from the river, that tears again came to her. Bending on one knee, she inhaled sharply and crossed herself.

"D'ye know him?"

Roxana nodded as she stared at the white-haired, gaunt figure of the Reverend Walker, hero of Derry. "He did want to be Bishop of London," she whispered hoarsely as tears came to her eyes. There was nothing she could do but close his eyes. She had not even a spare cloth with which to cover him.

"I shall pray for you, Reverend Walker," she whispered as she stood. "I trust you, too"—her voice strained—"will pray for me." She stared a few more moments at the body and turned.

There were not many places left to search. If they did not find him today, she wondered, would they find him at all? Had he been among the group to cross the river?

Sweat beaded her brow. She wiped it away and stared at the sparkling green river, bright and beautiful as if it had never seen the mass slaughter that had taken place.

"Oh, Dory, Dory, *where is he?*"

"Perhaps he is home safe."

She swallowed the sadness and shook her head. "He is not. I would know if he were. I sense him here, somewhere." She stretched her arms out. "Oh, Sebastian," she cried out, feeling the heat as her arms reached to heaven. "Oh, Sebastian, I love you!" Her voice strained as it rose in prayer and supplication.

She closed her eyes, willing for divine assistance. Willing for. . . .

"M'lady! Come! Quick!"

Her eyes opened and she ran to where Dory stood by the trees.

"Is this not part of the shirt you made him last Christmas?"

The shirt! The shirt! He had been wearing her shirt! She touched the material reverently.

"Yes!" Her green eyes lit as bright as the river. Hope glowed from her. "Yes, it is. On, Dory!" She hugged her servant. "Come, we will follow the river. He has gone upstream. He has been hurt and he has gone upstream, but he will be fine! You'll see."

Nodding, Dory followed her.

Ten minutes later, they broke into the clearing and found him, lying on the ground, his face white with pain and loss of blood.

"Oh, Sebastian! Sebastian!" she screamed, running to him.

He opened his eyes. "I dream," he whispered. "I am in heaven."

"Nay, foolish man!" She forced herself to laugh as her salty tears touched his parched face, and she lifted his head gently onto her lap. "You are not in heaven, and I hardly think myself to be an angel. You are here with me and I shall take care of you. Oh, Sebastian," she sobbed again.

Sniffling, she realized that it was his leg

that needed attention. The stain on the ground indicated he had lost much blood, and would probably lose more from the still-seeping wound.

Thankful she had brought some bandages, she quickly padded the gaping hole where his leg had been shattered and tied a tourniquet above the wound on his muscular thigh. He was again unconscious, and as much as she wanted to be with him, she would not wake him.

With Dory's help, she built a crude shelter, protecting them in some small way. "You are sure you will be all right here?" Dory asked for the sixth time.

"I will be fine. Now, go. Bring back help," she ordered. "Sebastian needs care that I alone cannot give him. I would go with you, but I do not wish to leave him again."

The servant nodded. "I will be back. That I do promise."

Dory left her alone in the clearing, and she shuddered with the chill of the coming night air. The presence of scavengers made it a poor idea to build a fire. She had covered Sebastian with her cloak. Gently, she lay down next to him. Even if he did not wake, it was enough just to be with him. If only she did not feel so helpless. If only there were something she could do!

His arm went about her. An automatic gesture?

"Sebastian?"

"Um."

"Are you in pain? I did think to bring some powder, but there is precious little water."

He grunted.

Raising herself, she prepared what she had in a spoon and fed it to him.

His eyes were bright silver from fever as he stared at her. "Why have you come?"

"Because I was worried about you. Because I missed you . . . and I love you."

He grunted again. "Do you not know what might have happened to you out here?" He spoke with effort. "You are lucky you are not hurt." He sighed. "'Tis because of you that my hair does turn gray before its time."

She gazed at him lovingly. "Is that so bad? I rather like gray hair. It will match your eyes."

"Aye," he whispered. "But to worry about you—that will make me old before my time."

"At least you will live to be an old man. Had I not come, you might not have done that."

His head gave a slight nod. "As usual, my imp, you have an answer." His smile was obviously forced. "Come. Stay with me as you were a moment ago. I should like to feel your sweet body next to mine."

Obligingly, she lay down next to him. Her arms went about his neck. "I do love you so, Sebastian Steele. If only you get well, I will do all that you ask of me."

He grunted in return, closing his eyes. She wondered if he had heard her. Seeing his faint smile, she rather thought so.

Chapter Nineteen

As he'd promised, Dory had returned, and had brought his two sons. It was only after they had safely gotten Sebastian back to Lucan that Roxana learned that James had indeed fled the country. Supposedly, as her uncle told her, he went for more supplies; yet Roxana knew it was truly just to lick his wounds. Well, at least he had left. Moreover, before doing so he had at last given her uncle the well-deserved earldom he had been promised. She sighed. Now that her uncle was an earl, he was more determined than ever that James would be king. He and Lord Tryconnel were now at Limerick, and planned to continue their fight.

She stared at the river again, thinking how glad she was that she was working for William—else she would not have use of his private physician to heal her ailing husband. Did he appreciate that? She doubted it.

Well, if he did not, she certainly did. She did not know what she would have done if Sebastian had died. She hoped, now that William was in Dublin, that Sebastian would give up his obsession with James and they would be able to have a normal life.

The Dubliners approved of William—or at least made a show of it. Special services had been held at St. Patrick's to welcome the new king, and the Catholics of the city had good reason to be thankful to the Protestants who prevented plunder of the homes and artifacts.

She paced up and down the river path. Everything would be perfect if her uncle would just acknowledge defeat, and if Sebastian would give in.

She glanced up and saw her husband standing by the rose trellis. Pleading, she turned to him. "Can you not talk some sense into my uncle?" With tears in her eyes she approached him, putting her arms about him. It had been two weeks since his wounds, and but for a slight limp you could not tell that he had even been injured. "Must you return to him—to Limerick?"

"I must." Sebastian's face was stony in his determination. "However, I shall do what I can. Stubborn pride does seem to run in this family. He'll not give up James any more than you will release William."

"But William has won. 'Tis a fact now."

"Not to your uncle, nor to Tyrconnel, nor to the Hamiltons."

Roxana was becoming frustrated. "William has offered all of them amnesty if they will just pledge to him. Do you not understand what that means? He is being more than fair. Certainly it is not something James would have done." Her arms went about him again as she pleaded with her liquid green eyes.

"You are right in that—it is not something that James would have done." He leaned forward to kiss her gently on the mouth. "If I can persuade your uncle to change sides, my sweet, I shall. Otherwise, I will stay with him." His tongue traced the outer line of her lips, parting her mouth. Pressing herself closer, she opened herself to him, welcoming him. Her desire rose as his hands roamed her.

"Do not leave me this night," she whispered huskily. "Stay. Just one more night." She looked up into the silver eyes she loved so well.

"Nay, darling, I shall not—and neither shall you."

"What?" She stepped back, pleased. "I may go with you? Finally?"

Sebastian ruefully smiled and shook his head. "Nay, my love, you misunderstand. You are to France."

"What?" Her brows knitted together. "To *France*? Why? Do you go there, too?"

He shook his head again. "'Tis not safe here for anyone of James's following—despite what you say of William's amnesty."

"But William would not harm me! I have no fear. I have supported him all the while."

"Few know that. I will not have you here, nor have me worried for your health and safety. James apparently planned his escape ahead of time and had two boats sent—one for himself and one for his immediate court. Since your uncle refuses to leave and I do not go with him, it is only fitting that you take your uncle's place."

"Well, if you can say you do not go without my uncle, I am saying that I do not go without you." She made a face.

"Roxana." His patience was wearing thin. "Despite your antics, I do believe I love you." He came and took her into his arms again. "Please. I do not want you hurt. Go, for me."

Tears sparkled in her eyes. She could not speak.

He pressed her closer. "I do not believe your employer, William, will be pleased at your refusing such an excellent chance to spy at James's court in France."

She buried her face in his chest for a moment. "Perhaps he would like that, but I cannot—I *will* not—leave you."

His lips devoured hers again, weakening her. "You must. I insist."

The boats at Waterford were few, and already many noble Catholics had claimed space in them. Among them Roxana noted Lady Ardella Conway.

"Do you not come, Sebastian?" Ardella put her arm through Sebastian's, not heeding Roxana at his side. "Versailles is *merveilleux* —and will be even more marvelous with you there."

Roxana stood silently by her husband, watching the woman play. She did not like the way Sebastian smiled at Lady Conway. In fact, she liked nothing at all of this idea.

Finally, when they were again alone in the corner, she hugged him once more. She was still determined not to be sent away, yet she could find no hope for it.

"Will you not even wait for the boat to depart?" Tears streamed from her eyes.

He touched her cheek gently. "'Tis not possible. Your uncle awaits me." His lips grazed hers. "Before I leave, tell me that you love me, Roxy."

"Why?" She narrowed her eyes, wanting to hurt him for sending her away. "The truth is . . . I do not," she lied. "I have been pretending all this time. Had you not backed me into a corner, I would not have dreamed of wedding you. It was only for William's sake that I married you."

"Is that a fact?" His eyes glinted silver as he searched her face. Yes, the hurt was there. She could see it.

"It. . . ." She felt the tears come down her cheeks. "Nay," she said weakly, "it is not true." She pressed her head to his shoulder, her tears wetting his clothes. "Oh, Sebastian, do not make me leave. I fear I shall never see you again, never hear you scold me, never—."

"Hush, my precious imp." His mouth silenced her. "You will see me—and soon. All will be well, I promise. This farce cannot go on much longer. Sooner or later, your uncle will come to his senses. I do believe you can take care of yourself far better than he."

"Aye," she admitted, hanging her head. "My

uncle has no sense of timing, though I do love him so. Will you tell him that I pray for him?"

Sebastian nodded. With a last hug and kiss, he mounted his horse and was gone.

Roxana stared after him, her heart heavy. She could not leave him. She could not go off to France—not even if it might benefit William. She knew now that the time had come to make a choice.

Turning toward the boat, she saw the crowd of people pressing forward at the gates, begging to be allowed to take the boat.

At random, Roxana pulled aside a young girl approximately her own age and size. "Do you wish to leave?"

"Aye, miss." The girl nodded fervently. "That I do. My father did fight for James and I do fear William."

Roxana wanted to tell this girl that there would be nothing to fear from William, but she could not be certain of that. Besides, she needed her to go. "Come then." She pulled the girl to the side. "Let us change clothes. I shall give you my papers." She glanced quickly about, making sure that Lady Conway was not in hearing.

The girl's mouth hung open. "Yer staying, miss?" Her disbelief was clear.

Roxana nodded. "My husband continues the fight. I will not leave without him."

The girl's surprise slackened a bit as she nodded in understanding. Quickly, she did as Roxana requested—before Roxana could change her mind.

Once in the peasant dress, Roxana wasted no time in leaving the area.

Her first plan had been to follow Sebastian directly, but she realized that this would be hopeless without a horse. Instead, she made her way to Lucan. Once she had changed to her own riding clothes, once she had Fire back, she could ride first to William's camp. She would make her final resignation to Gilpatrick and then go to find her darling Sebastian. He would be pleased that she had finally resigned—and she would prove her love to him.

It took Roxana longer than she had planned to reach Lucan. For just a moment, she debated letting Dory know she was back—but no, he was still in Dublin. And she must not tell Dory her plans. Though she intended to be with Sebastian soon, Dory was likely to tell him a lot sooner. Dory, it seemed, had a habit of siding with Sebastian. If he informed his Lordship of her presence before the boats sailed, Sebastian would force her to leave— and she would not leave Ireland without Sebastian.

Changing into her men's clothes and taking what she needed from the house, she mounted Fire. It was good to be on her own horse again.

"First stop is William's camp," she told the animal. "Then we find Sebastian."

Fire snorted, as if understanding. Shaking his mane, disagreeing with her, he started off toward the west, toward Limerick. "No!" She pulled in the reins. "We do not go to Sebastian yet. Has he won you over, too, Fire?" It seemed as if everyone was under her husband's spell.

The horse neighed again, once more shaking his mane.

"Oh, very well," she sighed. "Have it your way. We will go west." What would be, would be.

Shaking his head again, Fire began his free and easy gallop toward Limerick.

Less than two hours later they came to what appeared to be another camp. As they approached, Roxana realized that William had obviously moved his headquarters to be nearer Limerick. Well, Fire had been right— The first person to greet her was Gilpatrick.

"Were you searching for me, Alexander, lad? Is there more news? Faith, I did not think ye knew I had come this way."

Roxana shrugged. She would let him think that she had known. She would also, she decided, not tell him of the boats, nor of the fact that her husband had joined Tyrconnel and her uncle behind the Limerick wall. She was sure that others would tell him soon enough, and she would not endanger her loved ones any sooner than necessary.

"There is no news that you do not know," she responded. "Yet I do fear my usefulness is at an end."

"Do you leave us?" Gilpatrick had a saddened expression.

"Aye," Roxana nodded.

"Well, lad," he said helping her off her horse, "for me own part, I be sorry to see ye go, though sure I am that we'll meet again. 'Tis to England I assume ye've been summoned, eh, Alex?"

She stared at him, then gave a quick nod. Did he assume that she had heard from William through a source other than himself? Well, she supposed it was possible. She also supposed that sooner or later her support for the Dutch king would indeed cause her to return to London. She smiled slightly. Would he be surprised to learn who she truly was?

"Come, then. Have a last drink with us, and say good-bye to Rory Donaldson. 'Tis he who made all your assignments."

Roxana nodded again. Indeed, she wanted to meet the man who first ordered her to befriend Sebastian. What would he say to her having married him?

"Aye, I will come, but not for long. I go to Dublin soon," she lied, following Gilpatrick's lead through the rows of tents, pausing as she saw men who looked familiar to her. It seemed that a goodly portion of James's men now belonged to William.

She thought of her uncle. How many loyal men did he have now? How could he expect to fight against such a superior force?

Her heart pounded with pain. In his own way, Patrick was as much a dreamer as she. With her, it had been "Alexander." With him, James.

She paused, hearing her uncle's name mentioned. A chill went through her spine as she stood, paralyzed with fear, listening. She glanced toward Gilpatrick a few feet ahead of her. He had not heard. She wanted to follow him, but could not. Her feet would not move.

She swallowed hard, realizing that the men within the tent were talking about the earl and Lord Bristol. As they were two of Ireland's heros—two of the most popular of James's men—the men felt that if they could kidnap them, the rest of the country would fall to William without problem. In truth, Roxana thought, they were probably right— yet what did they plan once they had captured the two?

Goose bumps rose up and down her spine. It was true. The war needed to end. The deaths had to stop—but there had to be another way than kidnapping her uncle and Sebastian! Her heart went to her mouth. Neither man would allow himself to be captured alive. She would have to warn Sebastian. She would have to warn them both—even if it meant telling her uncle what she had been doing these past months.

Gilpatrick returned to her side. "Alex, yer white as a ghost! Is something amiss? Are ye ill?"

Roxana shook her head, turning to him as she tried to think. "Nay," she said hoarsely, "I am not ill, but there is yet one thing I must do before speaking with Rory."

"And what is that?" Gilpatrick's eyes narrowed.

"I must get the final count and placement of Lord Bristol's forces—and those of the new

Earl of Lucan as well. 'Tis the least I can do. They know my face, and . . . and do not suspect me."

"Aye," Gilpatrick nodded. "That would be of help. But why the sudden change of heart?"

Roxana shrugged. She knew not what to say. "Call it my final gesture before I leave for London."

"You will return here then?"

She nodded, feeling the lump in her throat. "I will return."

Not even her ride to Derry had been as fast or as furious. Even so, it was already dark when she arrived at Limerick. She had assumed they would be inside the walls, but they were not. Tents had been spread out before the city gates in a confident manner, almost as if her uncle lived a dream. Did they not understand the dangers? Were they so blind? James would no longer come to their aid.

It was impossible to tell which tent was Sebastian's. How would she find out which was his and which her uncle's? She had to warn them both, but it was Sebastian she must warn first. He would be the easiest to tell—or would he?

Sucking in her lower lip, she arbitrarily chose one and slipped inside silently.

It took a moment for her eyes to accustom themselves to the blackness, to realize that yes, there was a man lying on the cot and that it was indeed Sebastian. Was that a cut on his arm?

Immediately alert, he sat up, pistol in hand.

"What the—." He stared as he lit the candle by his bed. "Damn it, Roxy, it is you! What are you doing here? You should be on the boat! Besides, I nearly blew your head off just now! Take off that foolish cap and come here."

Doing as he asked, she hung her head and approached.

He grasped her wrist. "Will you never listen to me?" He pulled her down onto the cot next to him. "Why have you come, Roxana? Answer me. Why did you not go on that boat?"

Her voice was a whisper. "I could not. Oh, Sebastian." She put her arms about his neck but he shrugged her off. "I did miss you so dreadfully. I could not stand being without you."

"Missed me? I have been apart from you but two days."

"If I went to France . . . oh, Sebastian." Her arms again went about his neck. "Do not send me away! Do not make me leave you."

Her searching mouth found his as she pressed herself to him, inciting his desire, opening his mouth with her tongue as their kiss became passionate. He responded to her, his hands about her back.

After a moment, he pulled away. "Oh, Roxana, my little imp. What will I do with you?" He paused. "Nay, I shall not hit you. I do not believe in physical punishment—even for errant wives who act like children."

She laid her head against his shoulder and looked up at him longingly. "Shall I tell you what to do with me?"

He grinned. "I know you want to stay. I do not know why."

"There is only one reason why." Her hand slipped under the neckline of his open shirt, feeling the fine hairs of his chest. She let her fingers massage the muscles there, softly, gently. "You could make love to me." She grinned up at him mischievously. "If you make love enough to me, if you satisfy me completely, I might be content to be away from you for a few days."

"A few days," he groaned. "Is that all the respite I shall get? I do not even know if I can satisfy you for that long, little nymph that you have become." His hand reached under her shirt, teasing her nipples taut. Roxana gasped.

"Well, my lord. . . ." She started to stand. "If you do not think you can adequately satisfy me—."

"Come back here," he growled, pulling her down on him, then laughing so that they both broke into merriment. "Kiss me, my imp." He pulled her to him, his lips grazing her brow and then sending butterfly kisses all over her face. "My darling, I do know that you've had moments of doubt because of my position with your uncle and because of my former reputation, but I do swear Roxy, since I have known you, there has been no one else."

A warm glow suffused her. She touched his cheek with her hand. "There never was one for me but you." Her hand trailed downward, and she heard him groan. "And there never shall be."

"Never?" He lifted her shirt to tease and suck her rosy hardness, licking her breasts until she squirmed and cried out. He was forced to place a hand over her mouth.

Laughing softly, he said, "You must calm yourself, my sweet. It would not do for the men to know I have a visitor—especially one dressed in male clothing."

"Aye." Her eyes twinkled with the candlelight. "That would not be good for your reputation." Her hands sought him and stroked him until he was strong. She bent her mouth to receive him for a moment.

"It is like that, is it?" he growled goodnaturedly. His thumb and forefinger found her delicate center, stroking her to a passion, holding her squirming body so that she could only strain against him, savoring the heights to which he brought her until she begged him to take her.

Plunging his fingers forward, he grinned and shook his head. His mouth devoured the rest of her now naked body. Desperately she pulled and tugged at his breeches, but he resisted. "There is no knowing how long it will be before I can take this pleasure with you again, my sweet. I shall make the most of this. You,"—his mouth sought her moist center again, so that she wanted to scream in agonized ecstasy—"shall remember this night all your life."

Roxana gasped again as he renewed his attack on her vital parts. Moving and straining, she playfully tried to escape the invading force, her legs locked about him. Her hands gripped his hair until she touched his nipples, sucking at them as he did her, stroking his hard member.

"I will consummate this, my love, only if you tell me that you love me madly."

Roxana nodded. "I. . . ." She could barely think to talk. "I . . . love you . . . madly." She gasped, feeling relief as he parted her legs and thrust himself into her very core, to the center of her being, heating her flames with his rhythmic gestures, stoking the fire so that it would burn, it seemed, for centuries to come —hotter and hotter, brighter and brighter.

Just when it seemed as if she would die, she strained against him and reached the blessed top as he released his passion within her and brought her over the edge into heavenly bliss.

Silently, they lay there together for the moment, each basking in the other's glow.

It was the distant voices that startled Roxana, alerting her that all was not well outside the tent, and her hand went to her mouth in horror and shame.

In the excitement of seeing him, in her worry, in her desire, she had forgotten to warn him. She had not told him of the plot! What would happen now?

"Quick!" she hissed. "Get up!"

Giving her a strange look, he rolled off her. Roxana grabbed for her shirt. Her dark abundant hair streamed loosely over her shoulders. There was no time to put it up now.

"Get something on!" she cried desperately, wanting to make him understand and realizing that the power was failing her. She was helpless in the face of her own love for him.

Staring at her silently, his silver eyes like daggers, Sebastian slipped into his breeches. Realizing that she was about to run somewhere, not giving her a chance to speak, he grabbed her arm.

"Not so fast, Roxana. You will tell me what this is about—now!"

"There is no time to speak. Come with me! You must—."

"I must do nothing at this moment but hear what mischief you have been up to this time."

"Sebastian, *please*," she begged, glancing toward the tent flap. The voices were closer now. "'Tis not of my doing. I only came—."

"Yes?"

Her answer was lost as the flap opened and she darted behind his dressing screen.

Surprised by the gun in his face, Sebastian could say little. Finally, he found his voice. "What is the meaning of this?"

"You are coming with us, *Lord Bristol*," the man sneered, emphasizing the title from James.

"I go nowhere without my men!" Sebastian folded his arms, resisting them.

"Then we shall be forced to resort to other measures."

From behind the screen, Roxana knew she could not allow them to hurt him. It was all her fault—her desire for him had kept him so long here.

She stepped from behind the screen. Grabbing the pistol from his night table, where he had left it during their lovemaking, she cocked the gun and aimed it.

"You are taking him nowhere!" She pointed the pistol evenly at the heart of the first man, brushing the long hair from her eyes with her free hand.

Both men turned, and Sebastian, too, stared at her.

Sebastian's voice was quiet, but to her, deadly. "You have turned me in, Roxana."

Roxana's mouth dropped open as she recognized the man she was prepared to shoot. "Gilpatrick! 'Tis you involved with this scheme!"

Gilpatrick gave a low whistle. "I should have known you were no lad, Alexander. Too pretty a boy ye made!" He burst out laughing. Quieting, he became stern. "Did you truly plan to stop us? But why?"

Roxana glanced nervously at Sebastian. His obvious rage was enough to make her shiver.

"Yes, my dear wife, what means this?" His voice was soft. "Perhaps you thought to gain yet more information from me for your precious William—and to detain me until his men arrived. You are a consummate actress, madame. It would have suited you better to be on stage. I did for a short time believe that you loved me. Perhaps your precious William will get you a place in Drury Lane—though I hear he does not much like the theater. Of course, you might simply perform for him as you did just now for me."

"'Tis not what you think, Sebastian." Tears streamed from her eyes as she turned toward him, pleading. It was a fatal error. She cried out as Gilpatrick grabbed her pistol.

Covering her eyes, she sank onto the cot. "'Tis not what you think," she cried once more.

Sebastian glanced toward the men still holding their guns on him. "It would seem that you have at last accomplished what you always wanted—to have me out of your life."

"No! That is not what I want!" She tried to rise but Gilpatrick stopped her.

"I was a fool over you, my sweet imp." Sebastian continued bitterly. "I thought my love for you might change things. I should have known it would not. I should have turned you in when I first suspected you—on the night you had mud on your hem."

Her eyes went wide. He had known then? Numb with hurt, fear, anger and frustration, she knew not what to think. She stared at him with tears in her large, green eyes as she silently pleaded for his love.

"*My sweet wife,* despite your *obvious* pleasure at being with me, these men do have a prior claim on my attention." He glanced at Gilpatrick. "Alexander, eh?" He looked back to Roxana, and his daggerlike gaze seared her heart. "Just one last question, m'lady. Was he one of your lovers, too?" He jerked a thumb toward Gilpatrick. Numbly, she shook her head.

"Of course, there is no point in my asking you. You say whatever suits your purposes. I doubt every professed bit of love you have claimed for me. *Adieu*, Roxana Steele." He turned his back on her, ready to leave with his captors.

"No!" She stood, finding her voice again. "Sebastian," she cried, running up to him, "you must believe me! I love you, I do!" Her sobs couldn't be controlled now. "Truly—I—do. You must. . . ." The tears streamed down her cheeks as she shook.

His scathing, unbelieving silver stare of anger seared her soul. "Good-bye, Lady Bristol." He saluted her.

The tent flap opened, and then he was gone. Only Gilpatrick remained behind. "I would have never known, Alexander."

Roxana stiffened. "Do not call me that, please." She turned toward him, feeling her throat tighten, feeling the tears again pouring down her cheeks. "I have . . . just resigned."

Gilpatrick's hand went to her shoulder, but there was no comfort there.

Chapter Twenty

THE FLOWERS WERE AGAIN IN BLOOM, AS THEY had bloomed last year and the year before. The royal gardens were her favorite place. But despite the beauty of the spring, despite the safety and luxury that being a member of William's court had afforded her these past three and a half years, the heaviness of her heart had not left her.

Numbly, she sank into the garden seat near the pond. Every time she came here she thought of Lucan, of those days in the garden when Sebastian had courted her, when he had loved her. This was the only place she could sit and think of Sebastian. Oh, how she loved him still—but alas, he would never know.

She closed her eyes a moment, feeling the summer sun warm her face. Gilpatrick had become her friend, and had helped her over those roughest first months. He had personally brought her to the king. William, of course, had not been surprised by her sex; he had known all along. But he was deeply saddened by her loss. He'd given her the best apartments in the palace at Whitehall, and the best of attendants when she learned that her last night with Sebastian had brought forth a fruit of their love—but this comfort could not make up for Sebastian's hatred and scorn of her. He had said she would recall that night for the rest of her life. She sighed. Indeed she would.

What was he doing now? Where was he now? With her uncle still?

Roxana had learned that Sebastian had escaped the guards that night shortly after his capture and had rejoined her uncle, this time within the walls of Limerick. Both had fought to the ignoble end, when there had been no choice but to surrender.

Roxana clenched her fist. For all of her own pleading, William's men had not dealt kindly with her uncle. His life had been spared, but at the expense of his pride and at the price of his hard-earned title. All had been stripped from him—even me, she thought, even me.

She had cried for her uncle. She had wanted him here in England with her. She had even written to him, begging him to come—but he would not. If only he would acknowledge William as king, she knew she could get him a pardon. If only. . . .

She pressed her lips tightly together, wondering if her uncle now knew of her deception. She prayed not. He had suffered enough hurt. Yet, she supposed that in his bitterness Sebastian had informed him.

She picked up a rose, plucking the petals from it, feeling the velvety softness and the dew. Somehow it reminded her of Sebastian— but then everything reminded her of him.

Was he on the Spanish front, fighting again with the French, or was he at Versailles with Lady Conway, dallying with other women of his choice?

Tears misted her eyes.

"Mama! Mama! Why do you cry so?" The little boy clad in a blue velvet coat ran up to her. "I demand that you stop crying! My papa will come back. I know he will." The boy reached up to her and she took him onto her lap.

"Do you know that for a fact?" She smiled at his confidence while the tears continued to spill from her eyes. How like his father he was. Nearly three, he had the same dark curls, the same light gray eyes. "You're quite sure, my darling Alexander?"

Roxana hugged him to her as she swallowed hard. Kissing his brow, she smoothed away his damp hair. Even his smile was like Sebastian's.

"Aye," the boy said solemnly, leaning his head against her breast. "I do. He loves you as I do."

She smiled and forced herself to laugh. He was a charmer, just like his father.

"Oh, Alex," she sighed, hugging him again.

"I do hope you are right." She looked up at her son's nurse. "But meanwhile, 'tis time for your nap, young sir."

"Will Papa be proud of me if I do it?"

"Aye," came a rough voice from behind them. "Your papa will be very proud."

Roxana turned, scarcely believing her ears. Her heart had nearly stopped; tears shimmered in her green eyes. It was Sebastian! She stared at him as he stood by the rose trellis.

He moved a step closer.

Alexander broke the silence. Climbing down from his mother's lap, he ran over and caught the legs of the stranger. "Are you my papa?"

Sebastian bent to lift the boy to him. Roxana felt her heartbeat slow with fear as he examined the boy, studying the dark hair, the dark skin tones, the silver eyes. "Yes, child, I do believe I am." He glanced at Roxana as Alex put his small arms about Sebastian's neck.

"I am glad you are here. So is mama. She cries every day for you."

"Alex!" Roxana was horrified.

Sebastian glanced at his wife. "Does she now?" He cocked his head, studying her. "Then we must see that she does not cry any more, eh?" He tousled his son's dark hair and handed him over to the nurse as he moved closer to Roxana.

"How are you, Roxy?" His voice was subdued.

She swallowed hard and gave a slight nod.

Her senses were full of him now—his smell, his look, his touch. He bent to kiss her gently on the lips and she tasted him. It was as she remembered. It was better.

"I—I am fine, as you see." She spread her hands about her, motioning to the gardens. "I have . . ." She swallowed again. "I have all that I could ask for, and soon"—the tears stung her—"I shall have Lucan again. 'Tis William's gift to me."

"That would be fitting," he said softly. "Your uncle would be happy with that."

She pressed her lips tighter as the tears came up again. "And how is he?"

Sebastian touched her hand gently. "He died a hero's death, brave until the end—and" —he gave a quick laugh—"stubborn, just like his niece."

She glanced up quickly at him. "Did he know? I mean, before I wrote and offered him William's pardon?"

The look in his gray eyes told her. "It was not something I could hide from him, and I was mortally hurt. I did truly believe for many months that you had come to betray me, that you had wed me just for information—until your friend Gilpatrick put me right. Had I not been so impatient for you that night, so in love with you, had I but given you time to speak, I believe you would have warned me."

"Aye." The word was a whisper. "That was what I had planned." She swallowed hard. "Oh, Sebastian, I did truly love you, despite our differences. I could not bear to see you or Uncle captured. Nor could I bear to be without you. These many months I did not think I could survive."

"*Did* love me?" he repeated, caught on her words. "Have you any of that love left?" His hand touched her cheek, turning her face toward him. Through the glistening tears that veiled her vision she saw that there were wet drops sparkling in his silver eyes. "My little imp. You are not someone who is easy to forget."

"Nor are you," she whispered hoarsely, her hand reaching up to him, touching his roughened cheek, touching him with the longing she had felt all these months. God, how she had missed him.

Sebastian drew her toward him. His kiss grazed her brow, tasted the salt of her tears and parted her mouth in a tender reunion. At last he spoke.

"William has given me pardon, on the condition that I can lift you from your poor spirits. Do you think I can do that?"

"Aye." Her arms went about him as her heart lifted, and she smiled. "Aye, my lord." She rested her hand on his cheek. "I pray that you do not mind I have named our son Alexander."

He grinned. "I do not mind so long as you do not fill his head with tales. Even if I did mind, I do not think it would have made much difference—for I doubt you would listen to me."

"'Tis not so! I will listen to you in all matters from now on. Truly." Her lips touched his. "I will be an obedient wife."

Sebastian laughed out loud. The lines about his eyes crinkled. He stood back for a moment, then swept her into his arms. "Well, I do expect you to be obedient to me for the next few hours—but my darling Roxy, had I wanted an obedient wife, I would never have wed you."

Her arms went about his neck, hugging him close to her as he carried her through the gardens. She kissed him once more. "That is a relief," she laughed. "Then you do not mind if our next son is named Patrick?"

His fingers touched her lips; his eyes touched her heart. "Nay, my imp, I do not mind."

Enjoy your own special time with Silhouette Romances

Take 4 books FREE!

Silhouette Romance novels take you into a special world of thrilling drama, tender passion, and romantic love. These are enthralling stories from your favorite romance authors—tales of fascinating men and women, set in exotic locations.

We think you'll want to receive Silhouette Romance regularly. We'll send you six new romances every month to look over for 15 days. If not delighted, return them and owe nothing. There's never a charge for postage or handling, and no obligation to buy anything at any time. **Start with your free books.** Mail the coupon today.

Silhouette Romance